PRAISE F

"Chiavaroli delights with .... to Louisa May Alcott's *Little Women*, featuring a time-slip narrative of two women connected across centuries."

PUBLISHERS WEEKLY on *The Orchard House*

"As a longtime fan of Louisa May Alcott's *Little Women*, I was eager to read *The Orchard House*.... [It] invited me in, served me tea, and held me enthralled with its compelling tale."

LORI BENTON, Christy Award-winning author of *The King's Mercy*

"Captivating from the first page....Steeped in timeless truths and served with skill, *The Tea Chest* is sure to be savored by all who read it."

JOCELYN GREEN, Christy Award-winning author of *Between Two Shores*

"*The Hidden Side* is a beautiful tale that captures the timeless struggles of the human heart."

JULIE CANTRELL, *New York Times* Bestselling author of *Perennials*

"First novelist Chiavaroli's historical tapestry will provide a satisfying summer read for fans of Kristy Cambron and Lisa Wingate."

LIBRARY JOURNAL on *Freedom's Ring*

"*The Edge of Mercy* is most definitely one for the keeper shelf. "

LINDSAY HARREL, author of *The Secrets of Paper and Ink*

WHERE LOVE GROWS

HEIDI CHIAVAROLI

Hope Creek Publishers

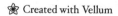

To Dad,
Because I love you
(and because there's a guitar on the cover)

PROLOGUE

Twenty Months Earlier

A sher Hill opened the email, adrenaline rushing to his limbs in the same way it did when he was heli-skiing or bungee jumping or placing first in a triathlon. His eyes skimmed the numbers in the report, landing on the bold one at the bottom of the page.

He jumped out of his chair with a hearty, primal shout of victory and pumped the air with his fist. The door of his office burst open. His best friend and president of Paramount Sports stood at the threshold. "Sales numbers that good, eh boss?"

"Yeah, buddy. Man, it feels good to be on top."

"We'll be saying the same thing at the top of El Cap by the end of the weekend." Lucas pocketed his phone. "Checked with the tech team, and they're all set to film. I'm heading out. See you tomorrow, bright and early."

"Sure thing."

"Don't work too late—the missus won't be happy." Lucas chuckled at his joke and closed the office door.

Alone, Asher leaned back in his chair and smiled. Hiring the new director of marketing had been a good choice, after all. Another few months like this and Asher would hand out hefty bonuses to his team.

He closed his eyes, and imagined climbing over the last ledge of the Dawn Wall in Yosemite. The rush. The scent of pure, fresh air. The feeling that nothing was impossible.

Though he'd never free-climbed the mountain, victory rushed through his blood already. Those sales numbers were just a fore-taste of the success to come this weekend.

Asher's phone rang, her name lighting up the screen. The fact that those five letters didn't make him apprehensive or urge him to run away was both foreign and strange.

He picked up. "*Mon cheri*," he said, low and seductive, already anticipating their time together that night—the scent of her long blond hair and the softness of her honey skin. How her laughter reminded him of a bubbling brook, or the sound of the first bite into a crisp apple.

"Asher Hill, I don't care if you are one of *Forbes 30 Under 30*. I don't care if you are the hottest guy I've ever dated…Asher, you do not stand a girl up—you do not stand *me* up—for dinner."

He looked at the display clock on his laptop and cursed. "El, I'm on my way right now. Just tying some things up at the office."

"You're always tying things up at the office."

He sensed what she doesn't say heavy beneath her words. *When are you going to tie things up with us?*

He shivered at the thought of marriage. "Give me twenty minutes."

"Tonight was supposed to be about us. What if you fall off the top of that horrid mountain and I never see you again?"

"Free climbing, Elise. It doesn't mean we don't use protective gear, we just don't use special gear to help us ascend. I'm not stupid. I'll be home safe and sound and into your waiting arms by Sunday night."

"Okay, but hurry over now. I want every last minute I can with you." Her voice turned husky. It stirred desire within him. "I promise I'll make it worth your while, especially if you leave your phone at the door."

"Oh, really?" He played into the game. "And how would that be? The hottest guy you ever dated deserves some details, don't you think?"

She giggled, and he thought of that bubbling brook again. Could this be the woman he was meant to be with forever?

"I'll see you soon, Mr. Forbes."

Asher hung up the phone while loosening his tie. He slid his laptop in his briefcase and walked out the door of his office. He passed down a long hallway, each room now empty, and into the reception area where a large professional picture of him hang gliding was suspended above the desk. *Asher Hill Takes on the World*, the *Sports Illustrated* headline read. The magazine had interviewed him about his hobby-turned-multi-million-dollar business.

On a normal night, he would stay a few minutes and enjoy the quiet heartbeat of the company he built, but Elise's words propelled him out the glass double doors.

He pushed the button to the elevator. It opened to reveal a grungy-looking fellow closing a guitar case. There was a music agency on the floor above Paramount run by a family friend of his parents.

Asher whistled long and low after getting a glimpse of the guitar. "That a Gibson?"

"Sure is, and it just got me an agent."

"Sweet. Congrats, man."

Asher's gaze dwelt on the guitar case. Someday soon he'd pick up his guitar. When things settled down, when he could be sure the company he'd worked to build could survive without his constant supervision.

He said goodbye to the guitar man as his phone rang out from his pocket.

His lawyer. Asher groaned. The man didn't call to make small talk.

"Ted, what's up?" He pushed open the door and entered the busy city streets of Los Angeles, vibrant and hopeful. As full of opportunity as it was of culture and diversity, greasy food and nightclubs.

He passed a man in ragged clothing with a cardboard sign asking for handouts and Asher dug into his wallet for one of the coffee shop gift cards he kept for such a purpose. He may have grown up privileged, but he always gave to the less fortunate. Life handed out hard turns, and he often wondered if he'd be where he was today if he wasn't raised in the home of his childhood. If he hadn't had the privilege of going to the best schools and getting a lesson on any sport he'd taken to at the moment. If his parents hadn't been so obsessively encouraging.

Thinking of his family reminded him of the deep-sea fishing trip he promised his younger brother Ricky the month before. Asher made a mental note to scour the internet tonight for a boat to take them out on the water. Tonight, after his time with Elise.

Ted's voice brought him back to reality. "Nothing good, sorry to tell you. You remember that lawsuit I told you about?"

Asher searched for a cab. The sky spat rain. The air smelled of wet pavement. "The guy with the prosthetic who claimed we fired him because he was handicapped when, in fact, he was smoking pot on our time?"

"That's the one. Well, I hate to say it, but it sounds like he actually has a leg to stand on. No pun intended."

Seeing a vendor selling flowers, he decided to get Elise a bunch to make up for his tardiness. He craned his neck to peer around the slight turn in the road. It was clear. "We spoke to the manager. Seemed straightforward to me. What's the issue?"

He pressed his phone to his ear and began to jog lightly across the street as the sky opened up.

Not until he was halfway across did he realize his mistake.

Elise hated flowers. She was allergic and would much rather have something tiny and sparkly, something that adorned the third finger of her left hand. She'd told him so last week.

He hesitated for a split second, thinking to turn around, hearing Ted's voice drone in his ear about a disability act and the guy with the prosthetic. He heard a horn and turned. Too late, he saw a car glossier than that Gibson guitar careening toward him. He tried to move, but for once, his body failed him. All he could see was the hood of the car, the Mustang logo in between the sting of raindrops. A scream overpowered the murky air, foreign and so filled with primal fear it couldn't belong to him.

And then, everything went black.

Present Day

It wasn't the glossy black truck that first caught my attention. Nor was it the incredibly handsome face or the muscled arm that grabbed the coffee from the donut shop's drive-thru window. It wasn't even the fact that he may very well pay for my coffee again.

No, it was the gentle curve of the guitar case sitting in the back of the cab that attracted my notice. The window was clean, free of any stickers or adornments, and I could make out the cased neck of the instrument. I imagined those strong fingers on wood and strings, wondered what kind of music the mystery man played, if he leaned more toward rock or jazz, contemporary or country.

The girl at the drive-thru window handed the mystery man some napkins.

Seven Fridays in a row I had found myself behind the man with the guitar at exactly 7:48 a.m. in the donut shop drive-thru. The third week, I noted he wore no ring on the left hand that grabbed the coffee. By the fifth week, I had conjured up all sorts of exciting careers and hobbies for him—was he a park ranger somewhere in the White Mountains? Did he hike for fun, like I did? Perhaps he played in a band on the weekends. Perhaps he did charity work on the side—he was certainly generous paying for my coffee every week.

The rational part of me believed he must pay for the coffee of whoever was behind him each and every day. The irrational part thought that perhaps—despite the odds—this was *him*. The guy meant for me.

Not that it mattered, for I would never get up the nerve to talk to him. My younger sister Amie had been in the drive-thru line with me last week, had apparently seen "love" written all over my face, and promptly urged me to jot my phone number on a piece of paper so she could run up and hand it to him.

I'd been mortified.

"Come on, Lizzie. If he doesn't call you, it's not like you have to see him again. There are other coffee shops around town, you know." She scribbled my number on a torn corner of notebook paper.

"Amie, no." I said the words low, but with as much ferocity as I had ever mustered. Only because I'd come close to tears had she given up on the idea. But days later she continued to ask me about what she dubbed "Mission Mr. Coffee."

"The man of your dreams could be five steps away, and you're doing nothing about it!"

I now contemplated my dramatic sister's advice.

Five steps.

Not so far away, unless you're in a drive-thru line. I snuggled into the beat-up seat of my Honda Accord, the comfortable boundaries of metal and glass between me and Mr. Coffee. Surely it was illegal to get out of one's car in a drive-thru line, anyway? And if he wanted to introduce himself, wouldn't he have given *his* number to the girl at the window to pass on to me?

Not to mention that I would never consider pulling an audacious move like my sister suggested.

I studied the man in his side-mirror. Beard neatly trimmed and skin tanned, I could picture him hiking the White Mountains or Camden Hills State Park. Maybe even with me by his side.

He smiled at the girl in the drive-thru window, and I shrunk farther into my seat. My face heated as I pulled up to the window, the scent of coffee wafting from the building into my car.

"Woohee, he's a cutie, isn't he?" the girl at the window said, staring after the truck.

"Um, yeah." My hands shook as I fumbled for my cash. "How much do I owe you again?"

"It's paid for."

I couldn't hide my smile as I thanked the girl, took my coffee, and drove away, thinking what a beautiful, promising Friday it would most certainly be. I would go make music with my students. Tomorrow, I'd get in a good hike and spend plenty of time in the garden. And I'd do it all while savoring the possibility that maybe one day, Mr. Coffee would indeed pass his number back to me in the drive-thru line.

❧

If there was a time to be like my sisters, it was now.

I opened my mouth, pushed forth words that jumbled on my tongue. "But Mr. Snizek, I don't understand. I thought my working as a volunteer this past spring would help the music program survive at least another year. After our New Year's Eve fundraiser..."

The older man with a slight paunch looked around the small music room where I had taught for the last year. I followed his gaze, took in the piano where I'd instructed students. The guitars standing at attention along the wall. The cases cradling brass. The drum set, which attracted many a preteen boy.

"I'm afraid it's not my decision. It's the board's. Apparently, keeping the program is too much money, even with you volunteering your time. They want to give the kids a good start in learning a language, or perhaps begin a career and computer class."

"But the kids...they need music."

"I'm sorry, Lizzie. Maybe we can plan an after-school music program in the fall for students who'd want to participate. We could charge a small fee to make it work, and that way, you'd actually get paid."

I swallowed down more protests. If I were Josie, I might argue with the principal. If I were Maggie, I might plan another fundraiser on the spot. But I was not like either of my smart, outspoken older sisters.

In truth, working for free wasn't working. I had school loans to pay. I had dreams to achieve. Dreams that required money.

But the kids...my family...they'd worked so hard on the fundraiser. I hadn't summoned the courage to tell them we didn't raise enough money for both the music and art programs, or that I volunteered my part-time hours to finish out the second semester, living off the small amount I earned from the family bed and breakfast.

Now, though, it seemed my career hinged on the hazy potential of an after-school music program. It could be a blessing to a few kids who loved music and whose parents would lay down the money, but not a way to make a living.

"I understand," I whispered, even though I really didn't.

<hr/>

"IT'S OKAY, LIZZIE. YOU'LL FIND SOMETHING." MY BROTHER Bronson shoveled a heaping fork full of blueberry pancakes bathed in maple syrup into his mouth.

"You could apply to other schools." Amie sipped her coffee.

Her blond hair piled neat on her head, makeup done to perfection, despite the fact it was Saturday morning.

"I looked. No one's hiring a music teacher within seventy-five miles."

Josie dribbled syrup on her pancakes. Nine-month-old Amos sat on one knee, eyeing the pooling syrup with interest. "Would another fundraiser help?"

I blew out a long breath. "The music program can't live off fundraisers."

Across the open floor plan and from the nearby kitchen, Mom carefully arranged two pancakes on a plate and sifted confectioner's sugar on top. She placed two sprigs of lavender on the side, did the same with another plate, walked over, and handed both to me. "For the Neilsons."

I breathed deep, preparing to greet our guests. The first few months after the bed and breakfast opened, Mom served the food. I'd been so scared of dropping a plate of culinary perfection or speaking to so many strangers at once. Only seeing Mom completely overwhelmed in the kitchen one morning had prompted me to offer to serve the food.

Our method saved Mom's sanity, and so I continued. I took one table at a time, focusing on a singular task before planning my next move. Whatever it took to get through the breakfast rush.

I licked my lips and walked through the butler's pantry that separated the kitchen and our living quarters from the main living area of Aunt Pris's Victorian home. We'd turned the old house into Mom's dream—The Orchard House Bed and Breakfast, complete with author-themed guest rooms and a five-course breakfast. Pride filled me at the thought of all we'd done, and all we continued to do.

Two plates in hand, I pushed open the door of the pantry with my shoulder, finding the middle-aged couple at a table-for-two near the fireplace. I forced a grin. "How was the coffee cake?"

Mr. Neilson patted his stomach. "I dare say you've managed to ruin every breakfast for the rest of my life. We sure are spoiled here."

I placed the two plates on the laced paper placemats and cleared away the fruit dishes and coffee cake plates. "We're glad you're enjoying your stay."

"Pardon, dear? I couldn't hear you." Mrs. Neilson leaned closer to me.

I forced my shoulders back, pretended I was outspoken Josie or graceful Maggie or endearing Amie. Any of my three, outgoing sisters. I projected my voice. "We're glad you're enjoying your stay. Can I get you anything else?"

"Perhaps more coffee?"

"Absolutely."

I scurried back to the kitchen, making brief eye contact with the other couples at the tables out of my peripheral vision and giving them a slight nod of acknowledgement.

"The Marsdens just sat down," I told Mom upon entering the kitchen.

Mom glanced at the orders our guests had indicated the previous day, tacked neatly to the refrigerator. "They both want the Eggs Benedict."

I checked the bacon crisping in the oven. "Almost done."

Mom whisked melted butter and egg yolks together for her Hollandaise sauce. "Hey, Lizzie...we can talk about this after breakfast, but with spring upon us, not to mention solid bookings, I could pay you a bit more. Perhaps we can do some flowers along the landscaping to spruce up the place? If you wanted, that is."

My heart near burst at her words. "Really? I would love to help with that. But I don't want you to pay me more. This place is still new. Let's let it sail for a year before you start giving raises."

"Not a raise so much as more hours. If you're doing more work around here, it's only right you're paid for it."

I kissed my mom on the cheek, grateful for her efforts. "That sounds great. Let's talk later, okay?"

"I'm out." Bronson rinsed his dishes in the sink before loading them in the dishwasher. "Wish me luck with the kid I'm tutoring this morning. He's a doozy."

Josie knocked the brim of Bronson's hat with a flick of her finger. "You weren't a star student yourself, if I remember. You'll relate to him just fine."

I tickled Amos's belly. "Need me to watch the bookshop today?"

"Can you stop by around lunch so I can feed this guy?"

"Sure thing."

My older sister studied me. "You feeling okay? You look a little pale."

"Never better," I brushed Josie off, hating the extra attention that an eight-year-old illness still managed to muster in my family.

I escaped to refill Mrs. Neilson's coffee. As much as serving strangers intimidated me, it was better than succumbing to the over-zealous concern of my family.

❧ 2 ❧

I'm still me.

Asher Hill ground his teeth against the sentiment as he used his arms to propel himself out from under the hood of his truck.

I'm still me.

It was something his doctors reminded him about a lot. So did his therapists—all of them. Physical therapists, occupational therapists, recreational therapists, psychotherapists, even his family who *thought* they were therapists.

But he had trouble believing those people. All of them.

Because he wasn't really still the Asher Hill who had walked out of the offices of Paramount Sports the night of September 22nd, twenty months earlier. He was another version altogether. A version who couldn't bungee jump or run marathons or climb the Dawn Wall. Heck, he couldn't even go to the bathroom like he used to. If he was any type of version of Asher Hill anymore, it was a very different version. A flawed and broken version.

He pushed himself to a sitting position on his creeper seat and craned his neck towards his workbench, searching out the headlamp he'd forgotten to bring beneath the truck. He spotted it, right beside the radio that played *Don't Stop Believing.*

Yeah, right. Believe in what? Believe in who? Certainly not himself anymore.

No doubt about it. He'd taken his legs for granted. What used to be a quick jump up and walk over to a workbench to grab a forgotten tool was now a project and practice in patience. He backed himself up to his chair, locked the wheels of his creeper seat, placed his hands on the handles of his wheelchair and used his arms and abs to lift himself up and backward. His skinny legs dragged behind, and he raised them one by one onto the footrests.

Elise had tried to stick around. She'd made it three months after the accident. In the end, she blamed leaving on his poor attitude. She said *he* was the one who had pushed *her* away. Though he couldn't deny it, it didn't make the wedding invitation sitting on his low, custom-built kitchen counter any easier to bear.

Elise and Lucas.

Ouch.

Some best friend. Good thing Asher didn't have to see his face at the office anymore, day-in, day-out. Weekly virtual conference calls were so much easier than Monday through Friday in-person meetings.

After grabbing his headlamp and lowering himself back on the creeper seat with his tools on his chest, he shimmied beneath the engine. He placed a container beneath the oil pan before using his ratchet wrench to unscrew the drain plug. Oil streamed out.

He positioned his wrench to unscrew the filter but struggled to loosen it. Readjusting his grip, he thrust his muscle behind the tool. His oily hands slipped off the wrench. His knuckles smashed against the truck frame.

He cursed good and loud, shaking out his hand.

He could have simply gone to his mechanic, but he liked accomplishing what he could himself. He thought he did, anyway.

Especially when it came to his truck—one of the only places where no one could see the brokenness of his body. He could smile at the kids making faces at him from the back of a school bus, sit at a crosswalk to allow an elderly lady to pass by, or buy a coffee for the car behind him. No one had to know.

Asher Hill takes on the world. Ha, what a joke.

He was far away from it all now, both in physical distance and physical ability. Far away from the family and the friends he'd grown up with. Far away from Elise and his corporate office.

He could still hear his mother's voice from their latest conversation.

Come home, honey. We'll give you your space. We promise.

But it wasn't so much about space. It was about navigating this new life away from pitying eyes. It was about finding his way. Alone.

Piano Man ended on the radio and the morning show DJ came on, announcing it was time for their *Connections* hour.

The DJ's voice rang through his garage, loud and clear. "We have Lizzie from Camden on the phone. Let's see if we can help her find her drive-thru dreamboat today. And if so, will it be a connection or a misconnection? Lizzie, why don't you go ahead and tell us about the man you're trying to find. Perhaps he's listening right now."

Asher positioned his wrench again, placed as much pressure against the tool as possible. Still, it didn't budge.

"Hey, Melanie. Thanks for giving me this chance. So, I've been going to the donut shop on the corner of Elm and Norwood Street for the last several Fridays and I happen to be behind this man in a truck. And every time he pays for my coffee."

Asher lowered his wrench, interested. He did go to that shop every morning, as it was right down the street from his house.

"Oooh, so we have a chivalrous hero providing a much-needed morning dose of caffeine. Consistently, too."

The woman on the phone laughed. "I'm sure he must do it for

whoever is behind him, but I'd love to find him and thank him in person. Especially since I've been the one behind him for the last seven Fridays."

The DJ's sultry voice came out over the airwaves. "Coincidence? I hope not for your sake, Lizzie. Could you give us a description of the truck, or of this man so, if he's listening right now, he'll know we want to find him?"

"Well, he's in a black Chevy Silverado. He's pretty cute. I think he has a short beard." The woman on the phone giggled, and Asher rolled his eyes. If she only knew.

He wiped his oily hands on his shirt, raised his wrench again, twisted hard.

"Oh, and he has a guitar in the back cab of his truck. That really caught my eye because I play guitar, too. I like to write songs."

Again, his hand slipped and he banged the same knuckle, cursing up a blue streak as he pushed himself out from beneath the truck.

On the radio, the DJ put out a call for the handsome coffee shop man in the Chevy Silverado with a guitar in the back of his truck.

Asher wiped his hands on a rag, noted his bleeding knuckle. He thought of the woman on the radio, searching for him. She sounded nice enough. Maybe in his former life they could have dated. Maybe it would have turned into something. Or maybe not. What kind of a girl was desperate enough to call into a radio station about a man who bought coffee for her in a donut shop drive-thru?

He thought of the wedding invitation with Elise and Lucas's names in elegant script at the top. His knuckles burned. He looked with scorn at the dead weight of his useless legs.

He dug in the pocket of his wheelchair for his cell phone.

Better to set things straight for this girl now before he passed her at the coffee shop again.

૭૪૭

AFTER I FINISHED THE BREAKFAST RUSH WITH MOM, I ESCAPED to the gardens to weed. Later, after I cleaned the guest rooms, I'd head out for a hike. Maiden Cliff, probably. There was nothing like a dirt trail beneath my feet and a canopy of trees to inspire a song in my head. I grabbed up late-spring weeds by their roots and shook off the dirt, quietly singing the song I'd started writing last week.

My deepest song to date, I was trying to tap into some of my own insecurities and fears, to travel to places I hadn't yet taken my music. Perhaps the music would heal some of those old fears inside myself.

My hand found the scar at my neck, the spot where they'd taken out my thyroid when I was fifteen. In my head, I knew the cancer could come back at any time, to any part of my body, but in my heart I knew I'd been healed. That God had given me victory over the illness.

While I wanted to sink into that, my family—by means of their sweet attention—had rendered me weak. Everyone looked out for me, and while I loved them for it, I couldn't help but wish they'd throw their extra attentions around Amie or Bronson. Hover over someone else for once. I was strong. I felt it. If only what I knew inside showed on the outside.

It was one of the reasons I loved hiking. Alone in the woods, conquering mountain upon mountain, I proved myself tough, resilient. There, victory and healing sank deep in my bones. While my family sometimes inadvertently confirmed my weakness, the mountain trails confirmed my strength.

I chastised myself for the ungrateful thoughts, turning my attention back to my song. If there was any fear left within me— and I knew there was—the music always drowned it out, made me forget. Like the voice of a sweet friend, it called and assured.

I sank into the song, singing the first verse over and over to myself, hearing the melody and the tune playing on my guitar, trusting the next line to enter my mind in time.

"Lizzie!" The scream snapped me from my song and my work. I jumped up from where I'd knelt beside the raised herb beds, the scent of thyme and basil fresh in my nostrils.

Amie ran toward me, phone in hand.

"What's the matter? Is it Isaac?"

Maggie, my oldest sister, had a son who'd been diagnosed with type one diabetes last fall. He'd been doing well, but I still remembered the rough start, the hospital trips, the fickleness of the disease.

Amie shook her head, eyes wide. She smothered the phone in her sweater. "Don't be mad, okay?"

"What?"

"I—I called the radio station. You know how the morning show has a *Connections* hour?" The corners of her mouth inched up into a smile she tried hard to contain.

My breaths came fast and hard, my knees weakened. "Amie, no. What did you do?"

"It's only because I love you and I want to see you happy." She studied me, air in her cheeks. She let it out in one whoosh. "I pretended to be you. I told them about Mr. Coffee. Lizzie, he called in! He's on the phone right now and wants to speak with you."

"Amie, no. How could you?" If I was the type of person to see red, the brightest scarlet would have flashed before my eyes. Instead, I knew only betrayal. Horrible betrayal. And fear. I was no stranger to fear, but this...this was paralyzing. Tears pricked the back of my eyelids. I shook my head, wanting to deny the last thirty seconds. "No. I am not talking to him."

"Lizzie, he called in. If he wasn't interested, he could have ignored you. This could be your chance. The chance to meet the guy of your dreams! Take a risk for once."

Take a risk for once.

"I can't. You already pretended to be me. Why don't you keep it up? Maybe he's *your* dream guy."

She shook her head, held out the phone. "He's waiting, Lizzie."

I looked at the phone, the seconds ticking off, the red circle bright and inviting at the bottom. I should reach out and tap the button to end the call. Sever this nightmare and any chance I had with the handsome guy in the pickup.

A pickup with the potential for off-roading adventures and cozy camping trips. A guitar with the potential to play romantic love songs. Unbidden, an image of a crackling campfire and the handsome stranger strumming a guitar came to mind, effectively weakening my resolve.

I stared at the phone, my heart knocking hard against my ribcage.

Take a risk for once.

If I didn't take this call, would I forever wonder? I'd just been thinking how I was stronger and braver than others saw me. When the chance came, would I prove it, or would I slink away with my tail between my legs?

3

I made the decision quick, without deliberating—my last thought being Amie's words echoing in my head.

Take a risk for once.

My hands trembled as I took the phone from my sister and raised it to my ear, remembering too late that I didn't much like shaking things up. I wasn't Josie or Amie—ready to take on the world. I was only me—plain Lizzie, the peacekeeper. The one who tried to get by without being noticed.

"H-hello?"

A peppy voice came on the line. "Lizzie from Camden, we're putting this coffee shop man on the line. For those of you tuning in, we have a woman looking for a handsome man in a pickup truck that habitually pays for her coffee in the drive-thru. And he's just called in. Will it be a connection or a misconnection?"

My knees wobbled and I lowered myself to the lip of the raised herb bed. Spots danced before my eyes. I leaned into Amie.

"Hello?" A deep baritone voice came through on the line.

I shook my head, pushing the phone back at Amie. She refused it, shoving it toward my ear.

"Hello to you!" the DJ said, completely unaware of my discomfort. "Could you tell us your name?"

A clearing of the throat. "My name's Asher."

Asher.

I couldn't deny the wonder of knowing Mr. Coffee's name, despite my state of distress.

"We're so glad you called in, Asher! Now, could you confirm the vehicle you drive and which coffee shop you occupy on any given morning?"

The man did, the details checking perfectly. This was really him.

"And what kind of instrument do you play that happens to be in the back of your truck?"

Asher sighed, and something like warning bells went off in my head. Was he reluctant to play into this game? Well, that made two of us.

"I play guitar."

"Lizzie—Lizzie are you still there?"

I swallowed, my throat dry. "Yes," I croaked.

"It seems we've found the man who pays for your coffee! Do you have anything you'd like to say to Asher?"

A breath trembled up my throat. "Thank you...for the coffee."

"No problem. I usually buy for whoever's behind me."

I wanted to shrivel up into Mom's garden bed and become the tiniest of insects, hidden beneath the shade of basil and mint leaves. Of course, Mr. Coffee—Asher—didn't only pay for *my* coffee. He was simply a Good Samaritan going about his day. I was the freak who had to go and fantasize ridiculous daydreams and then share them with my nosy sister.

"Well, that's awful generous of you," the DJ said. "So, we're wondering, Asher, if you have anyone special in your life? A girl-friend, a wife, a partner?"

A slight pause. I held my breath. Not that his response

mattered at this point. It was going horribly wrong regardless of his answer.

"No."

The DJ's pushy voice cut in, quick and eager. "No, as in you're a single man?"

Another clearing of his throat. "Yes, I'm single."

"And would you have any interest in taking a young woman who shares an interest in music on a date?"

I squeezed my eyes shut, heat consuming my insides until a thin sheen of sweat crept over my skin. My armpits, my upper lip, my back, the middle of my chest.

"I actually don't know if that's a good idea."

I cringed. From the sound of it, the DJ did too. "Oh. Is there a reason you'd care to give her? An excuse? Give the poor girl something, Asher."

Poor girl...

I opened my mouth to tell her not to bother. It was okay. He probably saw me in the drive-thru line looking dull and plain. Who could blame him? But before I could push words from my mouth, he spoke.

"Well, I just don't think this girl wants to date someone in a wheelchair."

I blinked, frozen. Mr. Coffee was in a wheelchair. All my silly fantasies came crashing down upon me. There would be no hiking. He wasn't a park ranger. He didn't climb the White Mountains. Maybe he didn't even enjoy the outdoors.

I hated that him being in a wheelchair changed my view of him. I didn't think of myself as a shallow person. It was character that counted. The inside, not the outside. How many times had I wished a nice guy would take a look past my plain exterior to see the real me? And yet, who was the real me?

I was twenty-three years old, and I didn't have a clue who I was. Until Mr. Snizek fired me yesterday, I figured I'd teach forever at the school and help Mom with the B&B. Perhaps someday a guy would come along and I'd be blessed enough to have a family. But the real me? It was nothing captivating—nothing that would attract an average person off the street.

Truthfully, it wasn't the wheelchair that bothered me so much as the crumbling of my ridiculous daydreams. Finding a man who could share in the things I enjoyed. Who saw the divine in nature and wanted to experience it as much as I did. Was that possible in a wheelchair?

"Lizzie, are you still with us?" The DJ's peppy voice morphed into a more serious one.

"Y—yes, I'm here."

"What do you say about going on a date with Asher? Does him being in a wheelchair change things for you?"

"Look." Asher's voice cut in. "I didn't call looking for a date from a desperate girl. I called to set things straight. I'm going to keep buying coffee for the cars behind me in the drive-thru line because that's what I do. I am not looking for pity dates."

I found my voice. Barely. "I—I am *not* desperate. And I'm not sure if I am interested—but not because of your wheelchair. Because of your attitude."

Beside me, Amie bounced on her feet, cheering me on. I could strangle her for getting me into this mess.

The man laughed. "Say whatever you like, Miss Lizzie. I've done what I called to do."

I held back a grunt of frustration. He didn't believe me. He thought I was making up an excuse not to go out with him.

The DJ cut in. "Well, I wish this had gone better, but at least you two had a chance to talk. I guess we'll have to call this a misconnection. Better—"

"No," I broke in.

"What was that, Lizzie?" the DJ asked.

"I want to go out with him if he wants to." There. Put the ball in his court. No way was he blaming me for ditching him because of his wheelchair. Especially on live radio.

The bold move flipped a switch within me. It felt good to make a decision. To speak up. To control my life.

"Well, this is a turn. What do you say, Asher? You still up for a date? Apparently, the wheelchair isn't a deciding factor for Lizzie."

He laughed again, and I couldn't make out what was behind it. "Yeah, okay. Let's have a date." Was that scorn? Bitterness?

"Okay! Our producers will connect you two to chat and, hey, maybe we can plan to talk to you both in a couple weeks and see how it went. Perhaps we have a connection, after all."

⚜

ASHER PRESSED HIS LIPS TOGETHER AS THE DJ, MELANIE, SAID goodbye and the producers took his information. Then he was left alone with the woman named Lizzie. After the buzz of the radio and being on air, the hum of silence overtook the line, unnerving him.

"You still there?" He gentled his voice, admitting to himself that he'd been a bit of a jerk on the phone. He stretched his fingers where he'd smashed his knuckles beneath his truck.

"Yes." Her quiet tone sounded so unlike the bubbly version on the radio—the one he'd heard when he first called the station. No doubt the news of him being in a wheelchair squelched her enthusiasm. Rough luck.

"Listen, you don't have to do this. We don't have to do this. They never have to know we didn't go out." There. He was giving her a way to bow out gracefully.

"S-so you don't want to?"

He shrugged, stared at his bony legs, useless beneath his jeans. "I don't think it'd be fair to you, actually. I don't want to waste your time."

It was the most truthful thing he'd said since dialing the station.

"I'd like to, actually. Really. Unless you don't want to..."

"Let's keep it light, agreed? I need to eat dinner every night anyway. You free Friday night?"

"Um...yeah. You want to meet somewhere, or..."

Picking her up might be awkward. He'd either have to wait in his truck and beep the horn like a no-manners loser or roll up to her walkway and throw rocks at her house door from the bottom of her steps. "Yeah. The Waterfront at six?"

"Yeah. See you then." She cleared her throat. "You're not going to stand me up, are you?"

Her vulnerability surprised him. Maybe he'd pegged her wrong. "Actually, I don't do *any* standing up these days."

Her breath hitched.

"You're not going to stand *me* up, are you?" he asked.

"No." Was that a smile in her voice? He tried not to read too much into it, tried not to care, but for the first time, he wondered about this woman.

She said she played guitar. He wondered what else she liked. What she did for a job, what she looked like. If she truly didn't mind dating a guy in a wheelchair.

4

I truly believed families were the most beautiful thing in the world. Mine was everything to me. I lived and breathed for the precious people that made up the Martin family.

If only those I lived and breathed for didn't try to suffocate the living daylights out of me.

"I don't like this, Lizzie. I heard the guy. He doesn't sound stable. More like a jerk, if you ask me." Bronson stood at the door of my bedroom, a basketball tucked under one arm.

"She *didn't* ask you." Amie pulled the curling iron from my hair, leaving a soft ringlet at my shoulder.

I smiled at her through my vanity mirror. We'd never been close. Never friends, exactly. I'd always been nearer to Josie, my confidante. Amie had always chased after Maggie.

Of course, Amie and I loved one another—we were sisters. But we were complete opposites—Amie, the pretty, outgoing one always straining against rules and expectations; me, the homely, good one, eager to please and keep the peace in exchange for being loved.

It meant a lot that the one time I defied expectation in accepting the date with Mr. Coffee, she stuck up for me.

Of course, it was the least she could do after her little imper-sonation on live radio.

"I don't want you getting hurt." Worry lines creased the hand-some edges of my brother's face. Poor Bron. The only boy, the one nearest to me in age. He'd always felt responsible for us girls, but since Dad died two years ago, it seemed his burden quadrupled.

"It's just a date, Bron," I said quietly. I wondered if he'd react this way if it were Amie. Probably not. Amie could take care of herself. As could Josie and Maggie. Though I was the middle child, sandwiched between two siblings on either side, everyone treated me like the baby. The vulnerable, sensitive child.

And perhaps I was.

"What did you say?" Josie appeared at the threshold, Amos on her hip. He grabbed at the loose strands of his mother's hair falling out of her low ponytail. "Is our Lizzie going on an actual date?"

I bit back a groan. "*Please* don't make a big deal about this."

Josie ducked into the room. "It *is* a big deal. Why didn't you tell me?"

Was that hurt in her voice? The last thing I wanted was to cause any of my siblings pain—but especially Josie, who'd always been my champion.

"It was...unexpected," I managed.

"Because Amie couldn't keep her nose out of Lizzie's busi-ness," Bronson cut in.

Amie gestured wildly with the curling iron. I stooped out of the way. "If it were up to her, she never would have talked to the guy! I was trying to do Lizzie a favor. At least if he really is a jerk, she'll know and won't waste any more time daydreaming about him."

My cheeks burned.

Bronson pulled himself up to his full six feet. "What you did was low, and you know it, Amie. The way you put her on the spot on live radio—"

"Wait. What?" Josie shifted Amos to her other hip. "The radio?"

"Yeah." Bronson flung his arm in disgust. "You know that cheesy *Connections* hour on the morning show? Amie called and pretended to be Lizzie looking for this guy who buys her coffee in the morning."

Amie slapped Bronson's basketball from his hand. "If it's so cheesy, then why were you listening, huh?"

"Hey, they play good music when they're not trying to play matchmaker."

Josie shook her head. "So Lizzie's going on a date with a guy the station set her up with?"

"A guy that sounds like the backside of a donkey," Bronson said.

"Well, if she wants to give it a try, I don't see the harm—"

"Thank you, Josie! Finally, someone's on my side." Amie brushed the left side of my head a little too hard.

"Please stop," I begged. I hated arguing. Especially when I landed at the center. I absorbed the negative emotions and words like one of Mom's dish sponges soaking up water. I didn't deal with stress well—I knew that about myself. My family knew it, too—if they really cared about me, wouldn't they stop arguing over my life as if I wasn't here?

"Did I mention he's in a wheelchair?" Bronson flung out the words with enough force to knock me backwards.

"And what do you have against people with disabilities?" Amie asked.

"Nothing at all. But you know how soft-hearted Lizzie is. Even if he *is* a jerk, she'll pity him. Give him more credit than he deserves. Guys who can't walk can be dangerous, too."

"Lizzie's a big girl," Josie said, her chin firm. "I say we give this a—"

"Stop," I shouted.

It did the trick. Three pairs of eyes—four, if you counted Amos's inquisitive ones—peered at me. I dragged in a breath. "I appreciate everyone's concern, but I'm almost twenty-four years old. And I'm going on a date. That's final."

Josie's eyes shone with something like pride. Amie stuck her tongue out at Bronson, who retrieved his ball from the hallway before squeezing my shoulder.

"Okay, Liz. But you call me if you need anything. Deal?" he said.

I nodded. "Deal. Thanks, Bron."

He gave me a small smile before leaving the room.

"Good for you, Lizzie." Amie twirled a piece of my mousy brown hair around the curling iron. "He has no right to tell you what to do."

I raised an eyebrow at her. "And I suppose you'd never do that?"

Amie swallowed, growing serious. "I sure hope I didn't screw this up for you. You do realize you don't owe this guy anything, don't you? A wheelchair doesn't give anyone an excuse to be an idiot."

"I know." I glanced off to the side of my bed where my old doll, Johanna, sat alongside my throw pillows. How many times had I tenderly sewn on an arm or patched her dress or combed her hair when I was young? Always trying to help and heal the broken parts.

No wonder Bronson was worried.

"I do feel sorry for him. He was so sure I would turn him down because he can't walk."

Josie plopped on my bed. She bounced Amos on one knee. "I think a lot of girls would."

"Would you have?" I asked.

Josie pressed her lips together. "I suppose I can't say without being in the situation. Luckily, I'm a happily married woman. What about you, Amie?"

Amie shrugged. "I think it might be a hurdle to get past. If I thought about it hard enough...well, part of what makes a man attractive to me is his ability to walk. Is that shallow?"

"It's honest, anyway," Josie said. "But lots of people are in fulfilling relationships with people who have disabilities."

Amie released a last ringlet before running her fingers through my hair, creating a wave that I didn't naturally possess. "I guess... well, what about long term? What about babies and...sex?"

"Amie!" My face heated again. "It's a *date*."

"Well, let's say you two hit it off and it becomes serious. Let's say he proposes one day. Can you pretend that wouldn't be a factor?"

I swallowed. "I suppose if you really loved someone and shared the same values..."

"Paralyzed people can have babies. And most of the time, sex. It's just...different. I did a psych research paper in college," Josie explained.

I shook my head. "Can we please stop this? It's one date. We probably won't hit it off at all. I'm nervous enough as it is without talking about proposals and babies and—"

"Sex." Josie finished for me.

"Yes." I avoided their gazes by tapping my phone on the vanity before me. "I have to go, anyway. Wish me luck."

Amie kissed my cheek. "I'll wait up for you."

Josie yawned. "I'd say the same, but this guy kept me up last night. Early bedtime for me. But I'll be over first thing in the morning to hear the details."

"You guys are putting my stomach in knots."

Amie gave one last tussle to my hair. "It's dinner. That's all. Dinner."

I nodded, wished for her easy confidence. I should be mad at her for getting me into this mess.

But all I could manage was gratitude that my sisters were here to see me through it.

5

A sher took the key from his ignition.

Five forty-five.

Good. He'd counted on being early. No sense having the woman's first impression of him be wrangling his wheelchair out of the back cab of his truck.

He tried not to care what she might think of him, but old habits died hard. His entire life had been spent trying to earn the approval of everyone around him—first, his parents by excelling in whatever sports lessons they signed him up for, then his friends, then the world. He didn't discount himself from that equation, either. Up until two years ago, he'd been more than comfortable in his own skin.

He opened the driver's side door of the truck, then the smaller back door of the cab. Keeping himself belted in, he lifted his legs onto the step bar and slid the frame of his wheelchair to the side. Holding it with his left hand, he reached around for a wheel and screwed it in place. Then the other, adjusting his seatbelt as he went so he could better work without the risk of falling out of the truck.

Once he had the frame settled, he placed it on the pavement

and shimmied the wheelchair pads in place. Only then did he unbuckle himself. Using the steering wheel as a grip and moving his legs down from the step bar, he carefully guided his body into the chair with his left hand. His right leg fell, his foot hitting the ground. He lifted his legs onto the footrests of the wheelchair, straightening his pants leg when he saw it had slid up to reveal a pale, skinny ankle.

There. He shut the doors of his truck and searched for his keys.

A feminine voice came from behind. "Um...excuse me. Are you Asher?"

Great. So much for his date not witnessing his transfer excursion. He whirled around, trying to hold his tongue.

He stopped.

Asher wasn't sure what he expected from this radio date woman. When he'd first heard her on the station, he sensed her easy confidence. He wondered if she were shallow, flighty. Probably beautiful. Probably not used to guys telling her no.

The last thing he expected was this little mouse of a thing in front of him. Wavy brown hair, rosy face. Pleasant looking, absolutely, but rather ordinary. No one he would stop twice to notice when walking—ahem, wheeling—down the street. She wore a pale blue dress with small flowers on it, and something about the way she crossed her arms over herself made him throw assumptions of easy confidence out the window.

He wondered if she'd witness the dead weight of his leg fall from the truck. If she'd seen the pale scrawniness of his calf when his pants had ridden up his leg.

He sighed. Too late now. "Yes, I'm Asher. You're Lizzie?"

She nodded.

He held out his hand and she took it, the delicate bones of her fingers in his reminding him of a fragile bird.

"Thanks," she said, releasing his hand.

"For what?"

"You know...for not standing me up."

He pressed his lips together. "Suppose I should say the same. Hungry?"

She adjusted the strap of her bag over her shoulder, nodded again. She sure was more talkative on the radio.

He gestured for them to cross the street and after looking both ways, they did. He went into a wheelie as he crossed—a habit that made the act of rolling a wheelchair a little less...well, pathetic. Some guys had a swagger when they walked, he had a wheelie when he rolled.

She eyed him but didn't say anything.

"I made reservations."

He told the hostess his name and she led them to a table for two by the water. The hostess moved a chair out of the way and he breathed in the salty sea air. He couldn't get enough of the ocean, especially when the temperatures started to warm and he could explore the open sea in his kayak. It was one of the reasons he'd moved to the coast of Maine.

Maine was wild and beautiful, tempered and majestic. Something about it spoke of independence and tenacity. That it was three-thousand miles away from his overzealous family was only the icing on the cake.

The waitress came and they ordered drinks—a Heineken 0.0 for him and a sparkling water for her. They looked over the menu in silence and he wondered if this could get any more awkward. He'd banked on her keeping the conversation going.

"You regretting this yet?" he asked after the waitress took their orders.

She looked like a deer in the headlights. "What? No. Are—are you?"

"You were a lot chattier on the radio."

She cleared her throat, and he noticed a pale, long horizontal scar at the base of her neck.

"So...did you grow up in Camden?" she asked.

"Nope. Moved here six months ago from California."

"Wow. That's a long way away from your family. I could never imagine…unless your family's not there. I mean, if you have family." She babbled, her nervousness apparent. Was she anxious about eating dinner with a guy in a wheelchair or nervous about dates in general? She certainly didn't *look* as if she got out on the town much.

"I do have family. But it was time to move on."

"Moving across the country would accomplish that."

He nodded. "What about you?"

"Camden. All my life. I can't imagine living anywhere else. The mountains behind me, the view of the ocean in front of me. Nothing better."

For a moment, something sparked and came to life inside of her, something that reminded him of the enthusiasm he used to have for life. For his sports, for his business. But before that spark started to flame, it vanished.

He thought about Lucas running the bulk of things at Paramount Sports back in L.A. Of planning a wedding to Elise. Of living the life Asher was supposed to live.

He shook his head, chastising himself for the negative thoughts. He'd been getting more involved again with Paramount since moving to Camden. Baby steps. It was still his business. He knew it best. No matter if he couldn't climb El Cap or skydive or heli-ski or win triathlons. The chain in Camden opening next month proved it. He was still useful. Still had something going for him. He hoped.

The waitress brought their food and he didn't miss his date's slight pause, her eyes closed as if in prayer. A church girl? Great. He gulped down his beer and dug into his fish tacos.

Even if there was a woman out there for him who didn't mind his wheelchair, he very much doubted it was this quiet, reverent one who no doubt had been desperate enough to call the radio station.

THIS WAS *NOT* GOING WELL.

I raised a bite of chicken stir fry to my mouth, trying to savor the flavors of orange ginger sauce, scallions, and rice noodles. But all I could think about was escaping to the restroom and calling Josie or Amie—asking them how in the world I could survive the rest of this night.

When I'd first met the man named Asher and he took my hand, I couldn't deny that the flutter of attraction I'd first sensed in the drive-thru line was still there. No matter the wheelchair, the guy's clean-cut beard which hid a striking face and strong profile—not to mention the very pronounced muscles rippling along his forearms—definitely caused a pull of something pleasant in my gut.

But as we sat at the table, face-to-face, and I honestly forgot about the wheelchair altogether, everything stalled. It wasn't so much what he said, but a feeling—a feeling I was most definitely not what he expected. Or probably, wanted.

I'd opened up about my love of the mountains and ocean and he'd shaken his head at me, as if in disgust. Had I said something wrong? How could I try to enjoy his company if I had to walk on pins and needles, trying not to say something that might inconvenience or offend?

I chewed carefully. Amie had pretended to be me on the radio. Maybe I needed to pretend to be Amie now, channel some confidence into myself. If for no other reason than to get through the rest of this date.

"So, you play guitar?"

He wiped his hands on a napkin, then carefully wiped his mouth, his manners impeccable. "Some."

I allowed a small smile. "Me too."

"That's right. You write songs."

I cringed. How much had Amie said on the radio before I'd picked up the phone?

"No, nothing..." I stopped. My family told me I always put myself down, that I should be proud of my songs and my music. But even if I thought my music held an inkling of potential, I couldn't bring myself to admit it—not to Josie, but most definitely not to this stranger. "I teach music," I blurted out, grasping for something solid in the dark tunnel I buried myself.

He stopped mid-bite, nodded his head toward me. "Where?"

"At a small, private school in the next town over. Actually, they've been struggling with funding. My family helped me put together a fundraiser at our bed and breakfast last year, but it wasn't enough. So, right now I'm out of a job." I sounded like such a downer. "But it's okay. I'll find something. And I don't mind working at the bed and breakfast. I don't mind being home." I stopped to catch my breath, surprised at the words I'd allowed to fill the air. In my large family, I was so used to everyone filling the silence. But here, with this man that seemed as hesitant to talk as I did, it appeared I'd stepped it up.

"A bed and breakfast, huh?"

Was he bored, or was I paranoid? More than likely he felt as awkward as I did. A girl could hope, anyway.

"The Orchard House Bed and Breakfast. There's never a dull moment," I said.

"I don't know if I could manage having strangers under my roof."

"Aunt Pris's home is huge, so we have lots of privacy. Overall, we're really enjoying it."

"But is it what you want to do forever?" For the first time, he seemed to study me. My stomach trembled beneath the intensity of his gaze. Bronson had been afraid I'd pity this guy. But the man was all hard edges. There was nothing soft within him *to* pity.

"I'd like to teach music again, I suppose."

"No, you wouldn't."

I blinked, scrunched the cloth napkin in my hand. "Excuse me?"

"If you wanted to teach music, you'd be doing whatever it took to do it."

My bottom lip quivered.

Some date this turned out to be. I glanced at my half-eaten plate, wished I could gobble it down and be on my way home for the night. Amie would commiserate with me over how sad my date with Mr. Coffee turned out, I would vow to find a different morning coffee stop, and I might very well lock myself inside Orchard House for the rest of my life. Become a spinster, do crossword puzzles beside widowed Aunt Pris.

"I don't know about that," I whispered. "What do you do?" Anything to get the subject off me. Besides, this guy obviously thought he had every answer. I couldn't wait to hear *his* big accomplishments.

"I started Paramount Sports five years ago."

I slumped in my seat, feeling suddenly small. "Wow. I've heard of them. They're huge. I ordered a hiking backpack from them last year. Hey, aren't they building a new store right in town?"

His deep brown eyes lit up, and for a moment, if I could forget his off-putting nature and focus on the strictly physical, I could honestly say he was the most handsome man I'd ever seen.

"Yup. Scheduled to open next month. A lot of focus on water sports. Indoor rock climbing as well as guided rock climbs in the state park. All the gear. It should take off."

I wondered if he became paralyzed while doing one of these extreme sports. How long ago had it happened?

"Sounds impressive." I opened my mouth to tell him I liked the backpack I bought from his store, but the thought of him bullying me into something more extreme than a simple hike in the woods caused me to clamp it shut.

"I'm just saying, if you want something, go after it, you know?"

"What are you, some motivational coach on the side?"

Did I really say that? Channeling my inner Amie really *had* worked.

He grew quiet. "Only trying to help."

I thought of my music, of the songs in my head, swirling like a whirlwind, picking up thoughts and feelings with each revolution until finally, verses erupted up like a geyser from a place deep inside.

But would anyone else see value in them? Anyone besides my supporting family?

Asher insisted on paying for dinner, so I didn't argue. We left the restaurant and headed toward the street. My stomach quivered.

"So, we tell the radio station we gave it a shot, right?" A small smile tugged at his mouth. Hard to believe such a breathtaking smile could hide such harshness.

"Yeah. I guess so." Then, because I wanted him to know, I said, "and it's not because of the wheelchair."

"Right. Sure."

"You don't believe me?"

"If I did, it wouldn't be saying much about me."

"I'm sure it's hard dating when...I mean, I find it hard dating... I mean..." I groaned inwardly, then studied his broad, muscled torso, his arms a distinct contrast to his skinny bottom half.

"We didn't really click, did we?" he offered.

I gave him a small smile.

"Well, it was good meeting you. I'll see you around at the coffee shop."

"Okay," I said softly.

He rolled away toward his truck, and I sank into the comfort of my car, turning the key and driving straight out of the parking lot, taking the long way home so I could avoid seeing him one last time.

❧ 6 ❧

The power of finding beauty in the humblest things makes home happy and life lovely.

I straightened the wall hanging as I read Louisa May Alcott's words, encouraged by their truthful simplicity. I looked around the largest guest room of The Orchard House Bed and Breakfast—the Alcott Room—and breathed a sigh of contentment.

While Amie scoffed at the idea of cleaning up after our guests, I found humble satisfaction in putting things to order. In taking the unorganized and making it welcoming and beautiful.

I stripped the bed and replaced it with fresh sheets, smoothing the top quilt with care until not a wrinkle dared bump the sea of covers. I ensured the blinds rested at identical heights, halfway down the window, and replaced tired, wax-melted candles with cheerful ones. I cleared empty water bottles and dirtied wine goblets and replaced them with new. I added two chocolate mints beneath a fancy glass-covered dish and dusted the furniture. I straightened the binder of laminated information on all things local and placed it back on the half-moon desk, inspired by Louisa's own at Orchard House in Concord, Massachusetts.

As I grabbed up old towels off the bathroom floor and scrubbed the faucets and sinks and mirror and floors until they shone, I sang the song I'd been working on quietly under my breath.

"The way the sun covers the trees
the way the ocean swallows the beach.
The way the moon absorbs the dark,
is the way you grabbed my heart.
It's the way you...consume me."

I didn't have much more. What I'd thought would be my deepest song was turning into a love song. And yet how could I sing about romantic love—something I knew so little about?

I sighed, hung fresh white towels and filled the toiletry basket with a new facecloth to remove makeup as well as small shampoos, bath bubbles, and conditioners from local Camden shops. I checked the tissue box and ensured the toilet paper end was at a point. Mom had taught me that details mattered and she'd shared what she'd learned from her time as a chambermaid at the Bar Harbor Inn when she was a teen. Details made our guests feel loved and our home happy.

Before wrangling the dirty laundry to the wash downstairs, I allowed my gaze to wander over the room one last time. Pictures of the Alcotts hung on the wall and I walked toward the one of Elizabeth, carefully running my hand alongside the frame. I studied her young face, the severe part of her hair above her pleasant eyes and a mouth that seemed to hide secrets. She was in her early twenties at the time of the photo, only a few years younger than me. I wondered if she sensed she would soon die, much like Beth March did in *Little Women*.

I traced the thin line of the familiar scar at my neck.

It was no secret I wasn't a fan of being named after the March sister whose life had been cut short at such a young age. Both Elizabeth March and Elizabeth Alcott had suffered terrible illness before succumbing to death. While outsiders thought our parents naming us after the characters in *Little Women* was cute, I couldn't deny the way it sometimes haunted. I was the most timid Martin sister. I did love home more than the rest. I was content with a simple life. And I had been the one to fight a scary disease at fifteen. Would it come back to take me one day, too?

But those were old fears. Weren't they? I was healed. End of story. I needed to think of my namesake as a reminder that life was precious, rather than a harbinger of things to come. Life was short. Too short to waste on not going after my music. Too short to lament drive-thru coffee men who turned out to be nothing as I expected. Was it too much to want a simple, nice man who looked at me the way Tripp looked at Josie, the way Josh looked at Maggie? Whom I could share my music and life, the blessings of my faith?

Apparently it was. I thought of Aunt Pris, content at Orchard House. That could be me. I loved this home—truly didn't want anything else. I could surround myself in the beauty around me— the climbing hills and rolling ocean, the creativity that fed life within me. Who needed a man? Who needed someone always there, to share every detail and blessing and challenge that life brought?

I closed my eyes, prayed that God would give me wisdom to focus on what He wanted me to focus on. His love, my family, blessing and serving our guests, and blessing others with music.

I scooped up the laundry basket I'd kept in the hall along with the dirty dishes. I passed the large window seat and stained glass on the landing and trotted the rest of the way down the stairs.

"Maggie! Didn't hear you come in."

"Oh, hey." My oldest sister stood up from the desk to give me a brief hug, her rounded middle making it a small challenge. She pointed at her laptop. "Would you believe we're booked solid until September? We have a stray night open here and there, but I came in this morning to five more reservations. I keep thinking we have beginner's luck, but no, we really have something here."

I grinned. "I think we do."

"Hey, how was your date?"

I groaned. "Word gets around fast in this family."

Maggie tapped her pencil against glossed lips. "Not fast enough for me to know it didn't go too well from the sound of it?"

"Let me put it this way—next time Amie tries to set me up, I'm going to hog tie her to the veranda and make her watch endless episodes of *My Big Redneck Wedding*." Josie'd found the show one night while flipping through the channels and found it extremely entertaining. Amie was so grossly offended, she promised to move out if we ever made her watch it again.

"That bad, huh?"

I shook my head. "I'd rather forget the awkward humiliation. How are you feeling? How're the boys?"

"I feel good. Big, but good. Oh, did I tell you our final inspections are next week? We'll be moving in soon, Lord willing."

"That's great, Mags." They'd sold the house Josh had bought with his first wife and moved into Josh's parents' house for the last few months. While Maggie appreciated her in-laws' generosity, I knew she looked forward to having her own space, especially with the baby coming in a few months. "And how's Isaac?"

"Great, actually. Of course the moment I say that is the moment his blood sugar will decide to throw another wrench in our plans, but for right now, things are good. Thanks for asking, Sis."

"I miss them. Someone in this big old family has to have a birthday or something coming up soon, don't they?"

Maggie laughed. "Memorial Day's next week. Mom mentioned a cookout after the town parade."

I adjusted the laundry basket on my hip. "I knew there'd be some reason to get together." I pushed open the door of the butler's pantry, which connected the guest dining and living area with the kitchen and our private living quarters.

Mom washed dishes at the sink, and I placed the basket down

on the tile and arranged the wine goblets I'd brought from the bedrooms upstairs in the dishwasher.

"Still at it, huh?" I asked.

"I told you you'd be doing dishes all day with that five-course breakfast, didn't I, Hannah?" Aunt Pris piped up from the adjacent breakfast nook where she played a martyr to her crossword puzzle, the top of her coiffed curls shimmering a pretty gray in the sunlight coming through the window. Behind her, the orchard had traded brilliant white apple blossoms for full, vibrant leaves.

"I don't mind, Aunt Pris," Mom said in that practiced, patient way of hers.

I grinned, walked over and kissed Aunt Pris's paper-thin cheek. "You're not complaining about the five-course breakfast, are you now, Aunt Pris?" It was no secret that the prospect of eating Mom's food was a factor in Aunt Pris allowing us to turn her old Victorian into a bed and breakfast.

Aunt Pris pressed her lips into a narrow line, gave me a half-serious glare, then returned to her crossword puzzle. "Never mind that, girl. What's the capital of Norway?"

I took out my phone. "I could look it up."

"No, no, no. That's cheating!"

Mom laughed. "Oh, Lizzie—I almost forgot. The Dickinson Room is free next Tuesday night. Does that work for you?"

"You bet."

Mom liked to stay in each of the rooms at least once a year to get the perspective of our guests. I usually joined her for the sleepover and another point-of-view. Last month, we'd decided to move the bed in the Hawthorne room after realizing that guests could see both the television, and the view, better from another angle. We'd decided to go with a different brand of towels after staying in the Alcott room, recognizing that although they were soft as goose feathers, they didn't absorb a lick of water.

"It's a date." She slid her hands out of her dish gloves and gave me a second look. "Everything okay? You look a little tired."

I hated this. Hated it but had learned to keep the peace by succumbing to it. "I think the chicken I had last night didn't agree with me."

"That's right! Your date. How did it—"

"Morning!" Josie barged into the back door with Amos and tucked him into the high chair perched at the end of the table.

"Morning?" Aunt Pris kept her pencil poised above her cross-word. "It's nearly noon, girl. What's the capital of Norway?"

"Oslo."

"Oslo! I always knew you were my favorite."

Josie stretched, then moved to the cabinet to grab a box of Cheerios. She poured some on the tray in front of Amos and he fisted them up, dropping one on the floor.

"I went to bed so early last night, I woke up at 1AM and had a burst of inspiration. I've been writing all night. The little guy went down for an early nap, so we've been sleeping the morning away, taking advantage of Rose's help in the bookshop." Josie leaned against the kitchen bar and wriggled her eyebrows at me. "So. How'd it go? You look exhausted, so either it went really well or really horribly."

"Gee, thanks." I scooped up the empty water bottles and opened the pantry closet to throw them in the recycling bin.

"Well? Spill it, Lizzie. How'd it go?"

"Horribly."

She groaned. "What happened?"

"I really don't feel like talking about it." Why relive the embarrassment?

If you wanted to teach music, you'd be doing whatever it took to do it.

Ugh. What kind of guy talked like that on a first date? Worst of all, he was probably right.

Mom gave me a kiss on the cheek. "Then we respect your privacy."

"Wait. What? No, we don't." Josie straightened. "Inquiring minds want to know!"

"Inquiring minds should leave well enough alone." I grinned.

Josie wagged a finger at me and grabbed a bottle of apple juice from the refrigerator. "So was Bron right? Was the guy a jerk?"

I hesitated. Was Asher Hill a jerk? When I got home the night before, after answering Amie's badgering questions, I'd given in to curiosity and Googled Paramount Sports and the history behind its creation—and creator.

That's how I found Asher's last name. I'd scrolled through hundreds of photos of a vibrant, active man who tackled any challenging sport he went after. I had to admit, his story was inspiring. He started his company from nothing, his vision was impressive, and part of the proceeds from Paramount sales went directly to helping inner-city youth get involved in organized sports.

Maybe he wasn't a jerk, exactly. Maybe it was his A-type go-get-'em personality I found off-putting. Maybe he realized life was precious and didn't beat around the bush. Problem was, my sensitive nature couldn't deal with such intensity. I absorbed things, people. I picked up on feelings and conversations around me and I sucked them into my spirit. All I could feel from Asher Hill was a furious fire brewing within, chasing after something intangible. I didn't want to be anywhere nearby when it blew up.

"We didn't click, that's all. We both agreed we gave it a shot and that's that." We were cut from far too different bolts of cloth. Now I knew and could stop daydreaming about Mr. Coffee.

Josie shrugged, seeming to let it go at that. I hadn't been so lucky last night with Amie.

"It wasn't meant to be." Mom started the dishwasher and brushed her hands together. "I'm heading to the market. You girls need anything?"

"We're good." Josie said. "Tripp and I have an appointment in an hour to go look at some land. Finn's going to watch Amos."

Amos's birth father, Finn, lived in the apartment above Tripp's grandfather's garage. He'd been in a skydiving accident last fall but was on his way to recovery and had secured an apartment and a job at the community college in Augusta for September. Though he could have gone back to teaching psychology at NYU, he'd chosen something closer to be near his son.

"I can't wait to see what type of house Tripp will build for you." My sister and her husband had put an offer down on a house at the end of last year, but it had fallen through. After more thought, they had decided to build a home in Camden.

"Don't expect one of his monstrosities. I want homey and simple." Josie screwed a lid onto a sippy cup of milk and handed it to Amos, who banged it noisily on his highchair, giggling when milk splattered on his face. "I know real happiness can be had in a plain little house, and that's all I need."

"Whatever it is, it will be beautiful."

Mom gathered her market bag, brushing aside her slightly graying hair that looked more like blonde highlights. "Tripp knows you better than anyone, Josie. He'll build the perfect home, I know it." She turned to me. "Let's talk landscaping later, okay? I'm thinking more hydrangeas. And some begonias in the front for the growing season. We'll swap notes."

"Sure thing. I was thinking an arbor could be pretty at the entrance to the orchard. We could plant a clematis on each side?"

"Love that idea. Beautiful. Okay, we'll talk soon."

Mom left and Aunt Pris went to her room, leaving me alone with Josie. Her gaze grew more intense.

"You sure you're okay?"

I hated the way she studied me, as if she half expected me to keel over right in front of her.

"Don't tell me I look tired again. I feel great. I was up late last night is all."

She tapped her short fingernails on the countertop. "Right. Because of your date. Your date that went horribly."

No. Because by the time I answered Amie's one-hundred

questions and online-stalked the man who had given me a horrible date, it was past midnight. What was wrong with me?

"I'm fine, Josie. Really. How's the writing coming anyway?"

She leaned toward me in a conspiratorial way. "Promise not to tell anyone?"

I nodded.

"I don't want to make a big deal out of it, because it might be nothing, but I had an agent ask for the full manuscript of *Where Grace Appears* two days ago. She emailed me again yesterday and wants to set up a call."

"Josie! That is amazing!" I grabbed her hands, squeezing tight.

"I'm trying to keep my cool. It might not mean anything, but it's the most I've gotten so far."

"It certainly sounds promising. I am beyond excited for you."

Amos fussed in his chair and Josie grabbed a banana from the fruit basket and began peeling and mashing it with a fork in a small plastic bowl.

"I'm excited, too. She's an A-list agent. Represents tons of bestselling authors. Our secret though, right?"

"No worries. This is your news to tell. Will you let me know as soon as you talk to her?"

"Sure thing." Josie continued smashing the banana and then stirred them in the bowl until they were nice and mushy. She grabbed a small spoon from the utensil drawer and brought it to Amos, who kicked his legs excitedly at the prospect. I ruffled his dark hair, so like Finn's.

Josie fed a spoonful to her son, scraping the sides of his wet lips with the spoon and then putting it back into his eager little mouth. "So, what about you? How's the song coming?"

I sighed, hoped she wouldn't be disappointed in me. "It's not."

Josie gave me a pensive look before she spoke. "When I first submitted my manuscript to an agent, I felt so...naked. Exposed. Like a piece of my heart was out there for anyone to step on and tear up and criticize."

It was my turn to study my sister. The mass of wild chestnut hair was pulled back into a ponytail, and wisps escaped the sides. Her freckled cheeks and fresh face were void of any makeup. It was hard to believe that anything could phase Josie. My bold, brave hero.

She continued. "But I think some risks are worth it. Lizzie, you have such talent. It's not meant to be bottled up. I think it's time for you to get serious and put yourself out there."

"I'm not like you, Josie. Who's to say that creativity and music can't be solely appreciated by the ones we love? I've never had big plans for myself. When I start to think about putting my music out there, part of me gets so hopeful and excited and part of me is so terribly horrified that I don't know which direction I should go."

If I finished my song, there'd be nothing holding me back from singing it for others. Safer to stay on this side of unfinished.

"You need to book a recording studio. Take yourself seriously. Give yourself a deadline. Send your work out to people. You have what it takes, Lizzie. I want the world to see how amazing my sister is."

Tears pricked my eyelids. Josie had always been the one to see me the way I wanted to see myself. "I'll work on the song. I promise." And I would. And that promise would buy me time, if nothing else.

But finishing the song meant next steps. And a recording studio cost money. Money my family thought I had. But without a job for the last five months, my meager bank account had dwindled faster than Amos's sippy cup of milk.

Besides, a studio meant performing in front of a stranger on the other side of the glass. Recording my music was so much more official than singing in front of my classroom or putting on a show for a fundraiser. It was putting myself out there—a first, active step in pursuing long-held dreams.

How could I sing with the depths of my being with a judging

stranger behind the glass? The thought was enough to make my knees buckle.

Josie squeezed my shoulder and went back to feeding Amos. I lugged the basket of dirty sheets and towels to the laundry room and started the washer. I turned the center knob, swishing the water and soap into a whirlwind of bubbly chaos. Much the way the insecurities of my heart stirred inside my soul.

≈ 7 ≈

A sher pushed one paddle through the water, then the other, thrusting his kayak forward. It sliced through the surface, smooth and clean. He loved the resistance of the water, the control he held when he pressed against the force of it, the speed of the boat gliding over the sea.

The repetitive movements lulled him, and he worked that way for another half hour before pulling off to a wooded cove. Only then did he rest the paddle and take a swig from his water bottle.

His thoughts turned to the night before. He ran a frustrated hand over his eyes. What a nightmare. If he could push the girl out of his head and forget about her, it wouldn't be half bad. But she'd haunted his thoughts the whole night.

The problem was his wheelchair, of course. Women used to flock to him—sure, he wasn't bad looking, but they'd liked more than his appearance, hadn't they? His confidence, his personality. But this Lizzie hinted that his wheelchair wasn't the problem. Did he believe her?

He sure as Hades didn't want to, because if his inability to walk *wasn't* the problem, that meant the problem was something else altogether—him.

He thought of Elise's accusations, her pouty tone when she'd walked out that final day.

You don't even want me to try *to help you. Asher, you get offended when I ask if I can get you a cup of water. I'm tired of walking on eggshells. This accident is not my fault, and it's not yours. But you go around acting like we're both to blame for it.*

He shook off the thought. Maybe he *had* pushed Elise away. But she'd been all too willing to go. To turn her attentions to able-bodied Lucas.

No, the problem hadn't been him. Not with Elise, and not last night with Lizzie. More than likely, it was as he thought—him and Lizzie just didn't click.

He couldn't say he would've hated spending more time with her. True, she wasn't his usual type, but there was something about her...something almost wounded that made him want to dig deep and learn more. Something he wanted to fix.

Huh. The guy in the wheelchair wanted to fix *her?*

Perhaps he did have some problems.

That didn't sit well with him, though. Better if she turned him down because of his disability rather than some character flaw.

In the ways that really matter, disability does not change you.

The piece of advice from some book he'd read in the early days of his recovery popped into his mind.

At the time, the thought had been a comfort. But the thing was, him not being able to walk threatened the very concept of who he believed himself to be. And that was an unsettling fact.

More so, was the new idea that whoever Lizzie had seen last night *was* the real him—wheelchair aside. And it hadn't attracted her; it had repelled her.

He tapped his fingers on the side of the kayak, inhaling the briny air, aching for a swim. But the water was still too cold this time of year—he didn't need to risk pneumonia or a slew of other potential hazards. While his body seemed to regulate his internal temperature fairly well, he'd heard horror stories from others with spinal cord injuries. He wouldn't risk a dip in the open waters until mid-July. This was Maine, after all.

Asher's phone rang out from the waterproof pouch hanging from his side. He scooped it up, half expecting it to be the landscaper working on the Camden Paramount building, or his marketing director. Most of the Paramount team had gotten in the habit of going to Lucas while Asher recovered, but he'd made it clear in a company email last month that he wanted that to change. For the love of all that was good, this was his business. It was time to take back the reins of control.

He turned his phone over and suppressed a groan. Not anything to do with the business, after all.

He sighed, slid the button to answer the call. "Hey, Mom."

"Hey, honey. Am I interrupting anything?"

"I'm out doing some rowing."

"Oh, Ash..." She appeared to be holding her tongue. As much as she could, anyway.

"It's perfectly safe. Plenty of others around." If you counted the bunnies and birds nestled in the wooded forests of the cove.

"Well, that's a relief."

His mom had been his champion during those first days and months of dealing with his disability. She'd been the one to break the horrible news to him when he'd woken up. She'd been the one urging him through rehab, coaching him to put his will and might into those precious early weeks when the hope of possible recovery—however slight—was still high.

She'd also been the one he wanted to get away from most.

"I was thinking about Lucas's wedding," she began.

He remained quiet, pictured her wriggling in her seat at her posh Malibu home.

She continued. "Well, Glenna told me they sent you an invitation. I was hoping you might come? You could stay at the house if you wanted. It'd be great to catch up. I—I feel like we left things on a bad note."

The understatement of the year. His mother threatened to cut him out of the will if he left to go out on his own. As if he needed their rotten money. As if he'd capitulate to her demands after such a low-blow blackmail.

Did she know him at all?

"We did, Mom."

"Asher, I'm not proud of how I acted, what I said. You're a grown man. I suppose after taking care of you in the months after the accident...I worry about you is all, honey. What if you got sick or something happened to your chair? Maine is such a back country sort of place. What if you couldn't get the help you need?"

"I'm doing fine. It's not all horse and buggy here, you know. They even have pretty good cell phone service most of the time."

"Oh, don't tease me." Her voice turned light, and his heart softened.

He'd been a grown man on his own when one bad twist of fate put him at the mercy of his mother. He could still remember her running down the hall at the hospital, demanding that someone come in to shave him. He'd wanted to tackle her, stop her from humiliating him further. But he could only sit there, helpless, wishing with his entire being for a miracle or, in his worse moments, death.

If anything pushed him to learn how to live life in a wheelchair, it was his desire for some semblance of independence. After living with his parents again, he could hardly wait to be on his own. And when living half an hour away hadn't allowed him to escape his mother's overbearing protection, when it became obvious that Elise was not going to stick around, he'd planned something drastic—a move to the other side of the country.

His mother's soft voice sounded in his ear. "Won't you at least consider it? Lucas is your best friend. I can still remember you two running around as Batman and Robin for Halloween."

Asher snorted. That's right. He'd always been Batman—the

main attraction, the one who spearheaded projects and ideas, tethered problems, and got things done. Lucas had always been the sidekick. Man, things had changed.

"And Ricky misses you."

The mention of his younger brother poked a hole in his heart. They'd always been close, but the accident stole the relationship they'd had—one that had been waning the last several years as Paramount grew. How could Asher be the strong one now? The one Ricky always looked up to, when he now sat three feet below him in a wheelchair?

"I don't know, Mom." Easier to stay away, to not face his old world.

She paused for a minute. "You're being selfish. None of us would have chosen this path for you—for us." She gentled her tone. "I want to rebuild our family, Asher. I respect your decision to be in Maine, but...we still want you in our lives, Maine or not. Please, I'm begging you. Won't you come home, at least for a visit? Or we could visit you—"

"No, no. I'm not ready for visitors." Maybe after the store opened. After he had tangible proof of the successful life he was building on the east coast.

"Will you at least think about the wedding? I know it will be hard, but—"

"I'll think about it."

She breathed out, long and slow. "Thank you."

After he hung up, he dropped his phone back into the pouch and closed his eyes, breathed deep. He couldn't go back home. Not now, possibly not ever. Telling his mom he'd think about it was a way of buying some time until the inevitable.

You're being selfish.

Without warning, Lizzie's words from the night before echoed alongside my mother's.

It's not because of the wheelchair.

I'm sure it's hard dating when...

When what? When he was in a wheelchair? But that's not really the feeling he got from her.

An uncomfortable notion clawed at his conscience, and before he could erect a wall against it, it took root, uninvited, and tunneled through him.

Though she hadn't said it in so many words, he sensed that Lizzie judged him. The horrible suspicion that he was found lacking—and not because of his wheelchair—pulled at the edges of his frayed ego.

One of his psychologists used to tell him that a disability didn't alter who you were—that it only peeled back the layers of what was already there.

Disturbing, to say the least.

Had Lizzie seen through those layers?

You're being selfish.

He groaned. He didn't think of himself as selfish. He was generous, always buying coffees for the cars behind him, always trying to encourage and help others...

When it was convenient for him.

He picked up his paddles and began rowing back toward shore. He did the best he could—what did everyone expect of him? Running a huge company. Trying to expand it while convincing himself his life had worth.

He pulled hard on the oars, thinking of the new chain in Camden, of the tasks to accomplish. His thoughts turned to Lizzie and back came that niggling, unsettling feeling that lodged itself deep in the pit of his stomach.

Perspiration beaded beneath his beard and on his forehead from the exertion of paddling. An idea came to him.

If he had the guts to pull it off, it might take care of the entire notion that he was indeed selfish.

8

Pine trees embraced the winding path before me. I tackled the steep incline with my hiking boots, feeling strong with each step. Strong. Free.

Across a rocky riverbed and exposed tree roots and up again. Birch and maple and pine trees tucked me in on the eight-hundred-foot incline.

The trail was quiet this afternoon.

I thought of the landscaping plans I'd discussed with Mom. The Orchard House gardens were steeped in history. Heirloom irises, daylilies, and peonies lined rows, but Mom and I wanted something a bit less organized, a bit more wild. Something that would honor the history of the gardens but bring them to life in a new way.

I'd suggested digging up some of the old plants and creating new beds for them around the gardens. Bordering the path along the herb gardens with lady's mantle and peonies, planting hydrangeas and dwarf lilacs around the vegetable garden. We could scatter additional seeds to keep the cost down—foxgloves and bellflowers and poppies. Each seed and plant with its own story to tell—whether new or old.

It would be beautiful. I'd start on it the next day.

I allowed my mind to return to the new song I'd started, singing it softly as I soaked up the quiet of the forest. I savored the warm, comforting feel of my backpack on my shoulders, the dirt below my feet, the canopy of trees above me.

"Some people press and search for the crowds,
The buzz, the noise, all that's loud.
But I've learned there's a certain comfort in being on the outside.
When I'm feeling small and weak,
When I don't trust the world to hold onto me,
Is when I seek the outside.
At the edge of longing is where I found you waiting..."

I hummed the tune, imagining the next notes and chords that would come for the chorus, trusting they would.

"Shadows stalk,
Lighting talks.
Courage dries,
My heart cries.
Will I ever be free?
Free to love,
Free to be?
I found you when I was on the outside."

I sighed, releasing the song to the wind as I neared the top of Maiden Cliff. A large white cross stood at the top, reining over Megunticook Lake and the hills beyond. I breathed it in, wondered for the hundredth time about the young girl for which the cliff was named.

Her name was Elenora French, and she'd been eleven years old. According to the story, she'd climbed the cliff with her older sister and friends on May 7, 1864. I could imagine her chasing after her companions, the way I used to chase after Josie and Maggie and Tripp. Always pressing to find that elusive bravery they seemed to possess. Always wanting to be a part of things but always staying at the outskirts of belonging.

When a gust of wind had blown little Elenora's hat off, she'd successfully caught it, but crept too close to the edge and, while putting it back on, fell the three-hundred feet down the rocky hillside. Her friends had climbed down to get her—surprised not to find a single broken bone. But the next day, Elenora died, the internal injuries too much for her little body to take.

I swallowed, ran my finger along the scar at my neck. The cancer had been growing for months inside of me before I noticed the lump. The surgery had removed it all. I hadn't needed chemo or radiation. I was blessed.

I remembered Mom and Josie's comments that I looked tired. Surely they didn't see something I didn't feel? Was there something lurking inside me, hidden internally like there had been with young Elenora?

I shook my head, casting off the idea. I was done with these old fears. My latest checkup showed nothing but health. I needed to focus on the strength I knew, not the doubts my family's worries planted inside of me.

I found an out-of-the-way rock and eased my bag from my shoulders as I sat, guzzling large gulps of water. After, I closed my eyes, listening to the songs of the birds, the wind in the trees, the slight hum of a distant boat on the lake. Josie's words from that morning came to mind, and I slid my phone from my bag, Googled recording studios near me. I clicked on the first one that looked professional and scrolled down to the pricing. Not unmanageable, but more than I had in the bank. And yet was it money that made me hesitate, or the fact that in taking this step, I was finally asking to be taken seriously? There would be no turning back.

My phone dinged, signaling a text, and my stomach lurched when Asher's name popped up. What in the world...?

I swallowed and tapped into it. My hands shook. Why was I letting this guy get to me?

Hi, Lizzie. I'm looking for some help in the new Camden store. I figured since you mentioned you're out of work, you might be interested in making a little extra money. Let me know. Asher

My mind spun. Questions illuminated my thoughts like a meteor shower. Why would Asher want me to work in his store? Retail was the farthest thing suited to me. No doubt this was some sort of pity call. He felt badly for the way last night went, or he didn't want me calling the radio and spilling the truth about how unchivalrous Mr. Coffee turned out.

I thought of the price tag on the recording studio. How much could I make working a few hours a week at the Paramount store? Enough for an hour or two at the studio? Enough for the sound engineering to go with it?

But no. I refused to take a pity job or pity money.

I don't think that's a great idea, but thanks for thinking of me.

I pushed send.

Waited for a reply. Nothing. I slid my phone back in my bag and stood. I didn't need a response. For whatever reason Asher wanted me to work for him, I had a sneaking suspicion that if I took the job, I would most definitely regret it in the end.

WHAT WAS HE DOING?

Going crazy, apparently.

He glimpsed the sign of The Orchard House Bed and Breakfast well before the driveway to the inn. He turned right and pressed the gas button harder up the hill. He should have known Lizzie would turn his proposition down, should have expected she'd want nothing to do with him after last night. Why had he bothered?

He wasn't the type to beg, but he could not get this woman out of his head. He was trying to be the good guy—couldn't she see that? And yet, what did he have to gain by getting into this mouse of a girl's good graces?

The iced coffee he'd bought her from the coffee shop sloshed slightly as he drove up the hill. A neat-as-a-pin Victorian with a generous veranda, massive flowering hangers, and a sprawling backyard orchard came into view. He whistled long and low.

The way Lizzie talked, he'd been expecting something a bit more...humble. Something a bit more like her. Though historical and quaint, it pulled off an elegance and grandeur that surprised him.

He pulled into the back, where a sign on a barn read *Bookshop* above large windows he could see through. Inside, rows of books lined walls and a spiral staircase led to a loft that showcased more. He put his truck in park.

No stairs to the bookshop.

Before he could swing open his door to get his chair, though, he spotted two figures in the far backyard. One, a pretty, middle-aged woman and one, Lizzie.

He studied her as she pointed toward the corner of the house, then talked animatedly with her hands, gesturing to another place in the yard. She seemed to have a sudden thought, for she grasped the older woman's arm and spun toward the bookshop, pointing excitedly.

Her demeanor shrank when she spotted his truck. No, *shrank* was the wrong word. *Shriveled* was more like it. Wow. Was he really that bad? Sure, he hadn't exactly been Prince Charming on their date, but considering it was the first one he'd been on since his accident, he thought it had gone decent enough.

He waved, vacillating between sitting there like a slug on a log or wrestling out his wheelchair in front of an audience. The two women approached him. Lizzie wore shorts and a light blue t-shirt.

He pushed open his door, slid one leg out but didn't unbuckle. "Hey."

Her gaze was wary. "Hey."

He gave the older woman one of his smiles and stuck his hand out through the open window. "Hello, ma'am. I'm Asher. Lizzie's friend."

He hoped she'd forgive him for the stretch of truth. *Lizzie's mystery coffee guy*, didn't seem quite appropriate considering the circumstances.

The older woman smiled. "It's nice to meet you, Asher. We can catch up later, Lizzie?"

"You don't have to leave, Mom." Was she begging her mother to stay?

Her mother squeezed her arm, glanced one more time at him. "I actually have to switch out a load of laundry. If you'd like to come in for a drink and a slice of banana cake, please do, Asher. It's nice to meet you."

"Nice to meet you, Mrs...."

"Hannah," she finished before walking toward a raised bed of herbs and slipping into the back door of the Victorian.

He grabbed the coffee from the console. "I brought you something." He thrust the sweating coffee out to her.

She hesitated a moment before taking it. "Thanks. I think."

"I realized I missed you at the coffee shop yesterday."

She squinted up at him. Nice that he hadn't made a move to get out of his truck, that he could speak to her at this height.

"Is this about me not taking your job offer?"

"Yes...and no. Can we talk?"

"Um, sure." She gestured to two white chairs in the shade where she and her mother had been standing. "You want to get out or...?"

"Yeah, sure." He swung open the door of the cab and wrangled down the wheelchair frame.

"Can I do anything to help?"

"Nope. I got it."

She sipped her coffee, the creamy drink traveling up the straw to her delicate lips. He blinked the vision away and focused on assembling his chair, conscious of her gaze but trying not to let it bother him.

"It's a lot of work, huh?"

"Yeah, but I'm getting used to it."

"How long ago..."

"Almost two years." He unbuckled and slid himself down into the chair.

He expected the next, obvious question, but thankfully, it didn't come. *What happened?*

He shut the doors of his truck and started slowly wheeling toward the backyard. Lilies peppered the yard. A row of strawberry plants lined a vegetable garden. Very neat and trim.

"I don't feel like I put my best foot forward last night." He cleared his throat. "Well, I guess I technically didn't put any foot forward."

Realization dawned on her face and she brought a hand to her cheek, hiding a smile. "You're horrible!"

He grinned, more relaxed than he'd been last night. "Joking helps, you know? People are too serious about my not being able to walk sometimes." He was too serious sometimes. Bad enough he still had trouble labeling himself *disabled*.

"I think I can understand that."

"Anyway, I really do need help at the new store. You talked about hiking the mountains, and I could tell you get what makes people want to be a part of the outdoors. You need a job. Why not give Paramount a chance?"

"I—I didn't say anything about hiking..."

"Sure you did. You said you bought a hiking backpack from Paramount."

Her mouth parted into the shape of an *O*. She swallowed. "You don't take 'no' for an answer very well, do you?"

"It's how I got to the top."

"Are you sure it wasn't your humility?"

He chuckled. Being open might be a better way to wear her

down. "I was nervous last night. I haven't been on a date since... you know. I'm sorry."

She paused a moment and he thought she might blow him off. Instead, she met his gaze. "You're forgiven." She lifted the coffee. "But consider us even. I don't need you to offer me a job."

"I really could use your help. I haven't hired a team lead for our hiking and camping department yet. I could use someone who knows the trails and can recommend the best gear for our customers. I bet you know some great spots to take pictures. We could do some group hikes. I'd need someone to lead them."

He didn't miss the way her eyes lit up at that last part. Good. She really did like to hike. It'd been a gamble. Anyone could order a hiking backpack off a website. But if the sparkle in her expression was any indication, she had a passion for it. They stopped at the chairs and she sat down so they were eye level.

"I don't know...I've never done retail. I don't see how I could be much help."

"You could be a huge help. I'm tying up a lot of loose ends right now. The crew's coming in next week, but my assistant manager is having emergency heart surgery. I have a feeling we're cutting it close. Any extra hands would be a help. It'd be a bonus to have someone in the store who knows the trails when we open."

"I'm not really a salesperson..."

"We don't push anything at Paramount. We offer quality products that serve our customers and merchandise to enhance their adventures. That's it. You're not selling anything."

She stared at the ground, the ice coffee on her bare leg, its condensation making a ring on her smooth, pale skin. He swallowed.

"And this would be strictly professional?" she asked.

He brought his gaze from her leg to her face. Busted. "Yes. We tried the romantic route and it was a fail. No doubt we'll have better luck with a working relationship."

"Is this so I don't badmouth you to the radio station? Because if so, you don't have to worry. I never want to go on air again."

"If I cared what people thought of me, don't you think I would have been a little more charming when I first called the station?"

"Good point." She tapped her booted foot on the ground, her mouth set in a thin line. "I *did* work at Hannaford when I was sixteen."

"So you do have retail experience."

"If you want to call bagging canned goods retail..."

"I do. What do you say? Help me out for a little? If it doesn't work, no hard feelings."

She studied the ground at her feet and pulled in a breath as if it hurt to make a decision. "I suppose I could use the money..." She nodded, met his gaze. "Okay. We try it."

"Great. I'll have a job offer drawn up for you. Can you swing by the store Tuesday morning?"

"Yes. That would work."

"Great. It's a deal, then." He thrust his hand in her direction.

Slowly, she inched her hand into his and squeezed. His stomach lurched in a foreign but pleasant way.

Before meeting Lizzie last night, when was the last time he'd had physical human contact? He'd been so busy pushing everyone away the last couple of years. For the tiniest of moments, he regretted that they'd closed off the possibility of another date so quickly.

"Now if it's not too forward of me, I think we should seal it with some banana cake."

9

"So now you're going to work for this pinhead?" Amie looked between me and Josie from where we sat on the picnic bench behind the B&B. Bronson and Josh had set up a volleyball net and corn hole, and as soon as we finished eating, the Memorial Day competition would begin.

"I'm just going to help him with the hiking department. Point customers toward some good trails. Earn a little bit of money. What else do I have to do with my time?" I avoided my sister's eyes—instead concentrated on Amos crawling toward Davey and Isaac, who ate hot dogs and potato chips off paper plates several feet away.

"You told me you never wanted to see the guy again. I spent a good hour consoling you after your date the other night."

I let my hand fall on the table, directed my words to Josie. "You really should have given her better parts in our plays when we were little. She has a gift for drama."

Josie laughed, scooping Amos up before he could snatch one of the twins' chips.

Amie rolled her eyes. Her healthy blond hair shone in the sun. I studied her immaculate makeup, the macramé jewelry she made herself. She had so much style. No matter my attempts to imitate it, I always failed.

"What brought this on, is all I'm asking. What's his motivation?"

I pressed my lips together. She didn't think Asher could want my help because he genuinely needed it. She didn't think I was capable enough to launch a hiking department. And could I blame her? I'd thought the same thing. But something about the way he asked spoke of authenticity. I didn't want to doubt it and had spent half the last two nights dreaming up a pamphlet that would point customers to some great hikes in the area. I could put my name at the bottom and organize some of those group hikes.

Somewhere along the way, I was getting excited about the job. Excited about feeling useful.

"I...I think he genuinely wants help. I don't know...he seemed like a different guy when he came by the other day. Taking dating off the table made him relax. I know it did me."

Amie threw up her hands. "Now you're defending him? Okay, I give up. You know I'm behind you. But don't come crying to me when it goes south."

"Don't worry—I'm her favorite sister, anyway," Josie quipped. "You can come to me, Lizzie."

I smiled, hiding the hurt that they both seemed to have so little confidence that this could go well.

"What's this business, anyway?" Amie took a bite out of her hamburger. An avocado slice slid out of the bun and she caught it with her finger.

I cleared my throat. "It's a sports company."

"What's it called? What kind of sports?"

"Extreme sports, not that hiking—."

"You mean Paramount Sports?" Josie gawked at me. "As in the big Los Angeles chain store that's opening up soon?"

"That's it," I squeaked out. I stuck my fork in my potato salad, scraped a little mayo onto the side of my plate.

"And Mr. Coffee's managing this store?"

I cleared my throat. "He owns it, actually," I mumbled.

"What?" Amie craned her neck so her face was practically in my potato salad.

I let my fork fall to my plate. "He's the CEO of Paramount, okay? He started the company."

Amie slapped the picnic bench with her hand. "You have *got* to be kidding me! Well, this changes everything."

I stood. "It changes nothing."

Josie popped a corn chip into her mouth. "I'm with Liz. Why should power and money change anything when it comes to love?"

"It doesn't. But if a guy swimming in *moola* should happen to fall in love with our Lizzie, I could think of worse things to happen." Amie pulled me back down to sit beside her on the bench. "You said yourself he was different when you talked to him. Different how? Was he flirting?"

I put my hands against my ears. "No—I don't know. I don't think so. Please, Amie, I refuse to think of Asher any differently because of who he is or how much money he has. His bank account is sort of like a wheelchair to me—in the end, it's not what matters."

Amie sighed dreamily. "It sure doesn't hurt things, though."

"Don't listen to her, Lizzie. Take the job if you want. But your music is your passion. That's where you should be putting your focus."

I jiggled my right foot. "You guys are freaking me out. I'm just helping out a friend and making a little extra cash. That's it. I don't want to devote the rest of my life to retail. I don't want a boyfriend right now. I only want to help mom with the B&B and play in the garden and go on hikes and write my music. Is that too much to ask?"

They all wanted big things for me. But was it so bad to be

content in the here and now? I thought about the recording studio idea, the reason I'd accepted Asher's proposition in the end. I wondered if recording songs, if putting them out for the world to hear, was really what I wanted. Or was it more my family's expectations than what I sensed God asking of me?

A gentle hand rested on my forearm. Josie. Then an arm around my shoulders—Amie.

"You're right, honey. I'm sorry. It's not too much to ask. I get carried away is all. You know me. Forgive me?" Amie squeezed me in a hug.

"Of course."

"Me too?" Josie asked. "We only want the best for you. It's tough for us to admit you might know what that is better than us."

I clasped both their hands. "Thank you. What do you say we go start a game of corn hole?"

Josie stood, Amos on her hip. "First, I need to find my husband."

I pointed to the bookshop, where Tripp hung a ladder horizontally between a window and the door of the shop. Mom was at his feet, pointing.

"What's he doing?"

"I saw it in a magazine. We're planting wisteria. Amethyst Falls. It's gorgeous. It will climb along the ladder and give the shop a lovely wild, vintage look."

Josie grinned at me. "You do have talent, Lizzie."

"I didn't invent it—we're copying the idea."

"But no one told you where to put it," Amie added. "You have taste. That can't be reproduced. I bet you'll be loads of help to Mr. Coffee."

My heart softened toward my sisters. They really did have my best interest at heart.

"Uh-oh. Looks like Aunt Pris is going to have her say about

the ladder business. Watch out." Josie tossed Amos into the air, eliciting a gurgle of infant giggles.

"You think we should go rescue Mom and Tripp?" I asked.

"Oh, I don't know. It might be more amusing to watch." Amie slung one arm around me and the other around Josie. I squeezed her tight.

"Where's Maggie? She's got to get in on this sister love," Amie said.

"Right here!" My older sister ran over to us, practically waddling with the weight of her belly.

She wiggled an arm around Amie. "What's this for?"

"Amie needed emotional support," Josie teased.

I laughed. "I'm so glad I have you guys," I said. "I'm not sure I could love anyone as much as I love my sisters."

※ 10 ※

On Tuesday morning, I pulled up to the address Asher had given me. I parked in between two newly painted lines of the massive parking lot alongside Asher's empty truck. I stared up at the boxy building with gigantic windows along the front. My stomach gurgled and I dragged a breath in through my nose, ordering myself to relax.

My gaze raked over the tasteful landscaping on either side of a paved path that led to the door. A tiered wall of cobbles adorned one side, each step holding vintage hydrangeas, cheery New Guinea impatiens, and elegant dahlias. A bubbling fountain with ornamental grass decorated the other.

I pushed open the door of my car. The scent of freshly laid asphalt assaulted my senses. I closed my eyes, tried to convince myself that I belonged here. Helping. In retail.

Grabbing two coffees from my console, I shut my car door with my backside and approached the building, pausing in the front to gather my courage.

I approached the large double door, and it slid open. I stepped into the foyer to glimpse the huge store beyond. Most of the shelves yawned with emptiness, but various kinds of bikes lined one part of the wall, a slew of surfboards and water skis and kayaks, snowboards and wetsuits and scuba gear scattered another. An entire rock-climbing wall took up one large corner, as well as helmets and harnesses and other gear. Rollerblades and sneakers and camping equipment and every kind of sport gear or clothing imaginable filled the rest of the store in chaotic fashion.

"What do you think?"

I startled at the voice to my left and turned to see Asher rolling toward me. He looked small in this massive store, and yet bigger all at once. For he was the brains behind it. Behind this and hundreds of other stores like it around the country.

"It's...big."

He laughed, eyed the coffee in my hands. "Is one of those for me or are you expecting to need extra caffeine this morning?"

"Oh, yes." I stepped forward, handing him the regular iced coffee. He looked almost boyish in a backwards Dodgers baseball hat. A lock of light brown hair wriggled out of the cap on his forehead, bringing attention to his handsome face, that bold nose above the freshly-trimmed beard. "I didn't know what you usually order, so I went with classic."

He stirred the drink around with his straw, dissolving some of the sugar on the bottom. "Good choice. I'm a classic kind of guy."

I turned my attention back to the store. "This is huge. When did you say you were opening?"

"Three weeks."

Three weeks to fill this store with merchandise. The more I stood here, the more I began to think this a bad idea.

"And when is the crew starting?"

"Friday."

I pressed my lips together.

"How about a tour of the store to start off?" he asked.

"Uh, sure. Yeah." Though I was already hopelessly out of place. Extreme sports—or sports in general—weren't my thing. I'd been getting excited about the hiking aspect, but it seemed a leisurely stroll in the woods was swallowed by the myriad of intense sports this store would offer.

He must have sensed my hesitation. "Come on, nothing in here draws your interest?"

I allowed my gaze to glide over the boogie boards and then onto the water skis. Each section awaiting more product to fill its space. "The kind of hiking I do isn't exactly extreme."

"We have something for everyone. Come on. I'll show you where our hiking section will be."

He led me toward the right of the climbing wall. I wondered how much not being able to participate in these sports bothered him. I wondered what kind of accommodations were occurring in the world of disability for that to change.

I took in a large unpacked box of backpacking tents, another box with a picture of rechargeable headlamps. A pile of hiking poles lay on the ground.

"As you can see, we still have a lot of organizing to do." He pointed to another aisle. "Backpacks will go there, water filtration systems and other gear in that section."

I swallowed. "How do you know where everything is supposed to go?"

He looked around, his gaze landing on a small pile of papers on top of a box labeled YETI. He scooped it up. "Here. Did you ever build LEGOs when you were a kid?"

"I helped Bronson build a ton of kits."

"And there was a map, right? Well, this is the map—the model, or mod—for what this section should look like. The good thing about a chain is that my marketing team back in Los Angeles already figured out the best layout for the store and our products. We just have to follow the map."

"I should warn you that I always encouraged Bronson to think outside the map—to make his own creations."

He raised an eyebrow. "I'm not opposed to some change here

and there. But do me a favor and stick with the map for now, Martin. If you have any ideas, run them by me first."

I nodded, stepped closer to peer at the mod for the hiking section. The first page showed a diagramed overview. Asher flipped the paper to show a more detailed section of the backpack aisle. He pointed. "See, North Face Borealis backpack there, Camelbak Velocity on the other side. Like a puzzle."

He went over the section a few more minutes with me, pointing out how hooks and end caps should be set up.

"You mind if I take those papers home with me?"

He grinned. "It's not a test. You'll be fine."

"I'd feel better..."

He shrugged, handed the papers over. "Where do you like to hike? What's the tallest mountain you've climbed?"

I hated to tell him I hadn't ever climbed anything taller than Mount Battie. Would he think me unqualified for the job?

It wasn't that I didn't want to hike more, but venturing far away from home by myself didn't interest me. Josie would rather run than hike, Amie hated anything that involved sweating, and Maggie preferred the indoors. Mom was too busy with the bed and breakfast. Bronson was the only one who might be persuaded to take a trip to the White Mountains, but I wasn't about to ask. What twenty-two-year-old guy wanted to spend a couple days with his sister out in the boonies?

"I mostly stick around Camden. Mount Battie and Megunti-cook and such."

"Are you kidding? How about Washington?"

I shook my head, hated the way he made me shrink into myself again.

"Well, you should. I hear it's beautiful."

I sucked in a breath, along with my courage. "You know, some people don't feel the need to climb the highest mountain or compete in the craziest sports. Some people are okay with a simple hike in the woods, a simple hill to climb."

Not to mention the absence of my thyroid sometimes made hard exercise a trial.

He studied me as if I were some sort of anomaly. "Yeah...yeah, I suppose you're right. I've always had trouble understanding people like you, but I've known you were out there."

I snorted. "Thanks."

"Well, would this interest you? It's our most popular product in the store for women."

He stuck his hand into an already opened box and pulled out a pair of lightweight pants and handed them to me. I read the label. My face heated.

Empower Pants.

Then below, attached to a zipper that opened from the front waistband: *Go Pee Without Feeling Vulnerable!*

I hastily hung it back on the rack. "That's...interesting."

"It solves a real problem, doesn't it?"

Sweat broke out at the base of my chest and along my bra line. This guy really didn't know his audience, did he?

I cleared my throat. "I suppose it does." I couldn't deny it was a great invention—one I might order online. I just didn't feel the need to discuss *feeling vulnerable* with this particular man.

"Like I said. One of our bestsellers." He took the pants from me and tucked them back in the box. "The paperwork's in my office. Come on."

I followed him back toward the front entrance. "Have you always wanted to run a business?"

For a moment, there was nothing but the soft whizz of his wheels against the new linoleum. We passed a small station with posters of skateboards featuring a slew of options for customers to build their own board.

"I've always wanted to excel. For as long as I can remember, I loved sports—the more extreme, the better. I lived off rock climbing and skiing, backpacked through the Rocky Mountains with my dad. Competed in marathons and triathlons. Won more than my fair share. I wanted to help more people experience what I did. I ended up in business classes in college, mostly because I figured running my own business would be better than working for someone else. I came up with the idea for Paramount my sophomore year. By senior year, my best friend was on board with me. I never graduated, started the first store instead. Our growth the first three years was almost unmanageable, but I sought good people to be on our team and we spread through California and eastward. This will be our farthest store east when we open in three weeks."

"You love it," I said.

"Yeah, I do."

"Is your best friend still in on it, with you?"

"Lucas. Yeah. He's manning headquarters while I'm away."

"While you're away...so you just came east to set up the store?" The thought caused something heavy to lodge in my stomach.

He shrugged. "Not sure yet. I've thought about heading south to Philly or the Carolinas to set up the next store, but I like it here. I could see myself staying. Who knows?"

"I can't imagine moving so much. I've never known anything besides Camden."

"And you don't have any desire to go out, to see the world?"

I smiled. "You sound like my sister, Josie. She used to want to travel the world. Until she realized that everyone she loved most was right in one place. Here."

Asher cleared his throat. "Yeah, well...good for her."

Did I imagine the bitterness in his tone?

The sun splashed bright through large windows as I followed him toward the cash registers. He took a right and led me down a carpeted hall to his office on the left.

A large window occupied one side while a neat-as-a-pin desk sat beside it.

"So what do you think, Martin? Are you up for the challenge? Helping set up the hiking and camping department, organizing a few group hikes on behalf of the store? It'll be a great way to introduce us to the community and I need a good pair of legs to accomplish it."

I looked down at the papers clutched in my hand. It didn't seem like rocket science. And I couldn't deny the spark of excitement at leading others on my favorite trails, sharing the beauty of nature with people longing for a milder extreme experience. No use denying the extra income would be a huge help as well.

"I teach Tuesday and Friday afternoons for another couple of weeks before summer break."

"No problem."

"And if it doesn't work out, no hard feelings?"

"None whatsoever."

My neck grew hot. "And you realize I've never done anything like this before."

"You sure like to beat a dead horse, don't you?"

I smiled. "Consider this your full disclosure."

"I'm disclosed. When can you start?"

"Tomorrow?"

"Great." He handed me a few papers. "If you can fill these out and bring them back tomorrow, that'd be great."

"What time?"

"You mentioned helping your mom with breakfast. I'd hate to steal you from her too early. I don't think I'd die a happy man if I never tasted her banana cake again."

My stomach did a pleasant jump at the warmth in his tone. "I could manage nine-thirty."

"That works."

I followed him out of the office and toward the front, where the automatic doors slid open to abundant sunshine.

"See you tomorrow, then?"

I nodded.

"Thanks, Lizzie."

Was that the first time he'd spoken my name? I couldn't

remember, but something about it tickled my spine. We said goodbye and I chastised myself for being drawn back in by him. That is *not* why I was here. I was here for the money. That was it.

I watched the back of him as he wheeled inside, those muscled, tanned arms seeming to push himself with little effort. I shook my head and grabbed my phone from my pocket, making hasty notes by memory about what Asher explained about the mods.

I stood in the front path, the gentle sounds of the fountain bringing an inexplicable peace in the midst of the monstrous building. I sighed, actually looking forward to the next day. Though whether it was the work I looked forward to, or seeing Asher, I couldn't quite discern.

Asher stared at the trifold pamphlet on his desk at Paramount. The picture on the front showed a beautiful photograph of Camden Harbor, taken from Mount Battie. Below, it read *Camden Hills State Park Trails*. Across from him, Lizzie fidgeted in her chair, feet tapping, a bundle of nervous energy.

"I mentioned the idea to my sister Maggie—she does the marketing for the B&B—and she kind of flew away with it. I thought it might be nice for your customers to have something physical to point them in the right direction." Her voice shook, and something in him softened.

"This is great." He flipped it over to a small map on the back which showed how to get to the park from the center of town. "We should definitely use this."

He couldn't help but enjoy her stunned look.

"Really?"

"Definitely. It's brilliant. In fact, it might be a good idea to coordinate with my team back home to get more of these out in the individual stores. You know, a local hiking guide. It'd be a great service to individual communities." He angled the pamphlet in her direction, and she scooted her chair forward, closer to him. She smelled like milk and honey and pine and sea. He wondered if she'd gone for a hike that morning.

He pointed at the back of the pamphlet, below the map. "Let's come up with a tentative schedule for some group hikes and print it here. Why don't you take a look at your calendar and tell me a few days that work for you? Your favorite hikes that you want to share with our customers. We can advertise them in newspapers and during our opening celebration."

"I—I could do that. Mount Battie is a favorite, but there's some lesser-known hikes with some great views. I can think about it and get back to you by tomorrow."

He gave her a sideways glance, her lips parted, her breaths coming fast. He sensed her timidity. He wondered if he made her nervous. He hoped not. "Good job, Martin. You're off to a great start. What'd I tell you—this job is perfect for you."

"I'm glad you like it." She avoided his gaze, pointed toward the door. "I'm not so certain I'll know what I'm doing out in the store, but I've been studying the mod all night."

He couldn't stop the grin spreading across his face. "You're amazing."

The compliment seemed to snap the life from her, thrust her back to her timid self.

"I should get to it, then."

But she didn't leave. He followed the direction of her gaze to the smattering of pictures set up on the corner of his desk. He'd placed them there when setting up his office. Pictures he'd packed when leaving his L.A. office. Pictures that sometimes made him remember his old self—the days when he walked, when he had a normal life. A photo of him and Ricky the day of his brother's high school graduation. A picture of him hanging off a ledge in Red River Gorge. Him and his parents at the opening of the first store. Him and Elise jet skiing on a brilliant, sunny day. He remembered that day as though it had happened that morning.

They'd pulled up alongside his parents' boat on the double jet ski, and his mom had snapped the picture. Elise in a hot pink bikini, tan arms around his bare waist, her blonde hair slightly damp and frizzy, long against that honey skin. His legs, tan and muscled and strong and whole. Elise had leaned over to give him a kiss on the cheek, just as his mom took the picture.

Suddenly angry, Asher knocked the picture facedown. He didn't want to look at it anymore. He didn't want Lizzie looking at it, either.

Lizzie jumped. "I—I'm sorry."

"You did nothing."

"Who—who is she?"

He ground his teeth. There was no need to be angry at Lizzie. She had nothing to do with his red emotions. He should have never displayed the pictures to begin with.

She's my best friend's fiancé.

"She's nobody."

He opened his desk drawer, took out a pen to sign the papers Lizzie'd brought in that morning. "Pay period is every two weeks, on a Thursday. So your first check will be landing in your bank account the middle of the month." He wrote down a generous hourly wage and showed it to her. "Sound good?"

Her eyes grew wide. "This is an awful lot—"

"And you've already put in an awful lot of work. Take it, Martin. Paramount treats their employees well because they're the backbone of the company."

She held his gaze for a moment and those doe-like brown eyes melded into him. "Thank you."

It'd been a long time since someone had looked at him that way—as if they genuinely appreciated him, as if he were admirable, even.

As Lizzie walked out of his office, he watched her leave. So small, unassuming. She didn't walk with any sort of self-satisfied stride. He looked down at the pamphlet.

He hadn't been overly generous when he'd given her his opinion on the pamphlet. It was the perfect touch to the store. Who would have thought?

He picked up the framed picture of him and Elise. He studied his old girlfriend's face, tried to tap into the betrayal and hurt he'd known during those early days. But he couldn't quite reach it.

The only thing that tugged at him was regret. Regret that he was no longer the whole man in the picture. For so long, Elise had represented his old life—what it meant for him to be complete. But he was beginning to separate her from that. She was moving on, marrying Lucas. He'd never wanted to marry her before the accident. Studying the picture now, he wondered if he'd really ever loved her.

More likely, he'd loved the way she'd made him feel. A nice addition to his shiny life.

Perhaps she'd been right to leave him, after all.

❧ 12 ❧

The shadows came often, stalking when I'd least expect. Sowing doubt. When they were at their worst, I'd stay close to home—wouldn't even venture to hike my beloved mountains.

They'd dissipate over time, like a bad dream, as I sought pockets of hope and light, clinging to God's promises and choosing to lean into a strength not my own.

The music would help, too. It would flow through me, almost like liquid, weaving in and out of my dark places, coaxing light into the shadows.

It did that now, as I sat in my room with my guitar on my lap, strumming chords and notes from the song I'd told Josie I'd finish. The worn wooden neck of the guitar curved in my left hand, like an old friend who would always hold my hand without asking questions. I strummed with a pick, relishing the synchronization of the notes with my words.

If only the next line would come.

Two days now. Two days since Asher had written that number on my job offer paper. A week of work would be more than enough for a half day at a recording studio. I had no excuses.

And yet it seemed to freeze my creativity. Finishing the song meant there would be nothing left to stop me from taking that next step.

A knock sounded at my bedroom door.

"Come in."

Josie peered around the door, a smile wreathing her face. "Sounds great. I was listening at the door."

I placed my guitar beside me on the bed. Josie sat in my desk chair.

"I haven't written much more. Writer's block, I guess."

"I can understand that." She couldn't seem to keep a silly grin from her face.

A sudden knowing leapt in my throat. "You talked to that agent, didn't you?"

"Yes..." Her smile grew more lopsided.

I leapt off my bed, grabbed her arm. "And?"

"She wants to represent me. She loved my book."

I squealed. "This is amazing! Huge."

"Monstrous."

"Ginormous."

"Astronomical!"

We collapsed into giggles.

"Did you tell Mom?"

Josie shook her head. "I told Tripp after I got off the phone, then I ran over here to tell you. It's not a publishing contract or anything, but...Lizzie, I couldn't have done this without you."

Wetness gathered at the corners of my eyelids. "Yes, of course you could have."

"No—I mean it. Not only did you read my stories when we were young, but you helped me make this one so much stronger. You've always been my biggest fan."

I couldn't hold back the tears any longer. I threw my arms around my sister. "I feel the same way."

"She wants me to make a few tweaks to the manuscript before

she sends it to publishers, but as soon as I do, we're going to sit down and nail this song. Okay? I'll help you. Writer's block will be no match for the two of us."

My heart melted. Josie had always been my champion. And she was right—writer's block would be no match for us. But then what?

I glanced at my sister, glowing from her news. I was happy for her. *So* happy for her. She'd always expected grand, noteworthy things from herself. But did she also expect me to walk a similar path? For my songs to make it big like she hoped her book would?

I thought of Mom and Dad, always pointing to smart Josie and responsible Maggie as my examples. Amie's, too. Sometimes, it'd been hard to tell who *I* was. Then I'd gotten sick. And my identity became clear. I was the frail one, the weak one, the sensitive one. The one that needed care.

And wasn't that what Josie thought she was doing now? What would it be like for us to finish my song together? My writing had always been a private thing—the one area of my life that was mine alone. Would I be able to let her in on it? Did I want her in on it?

I pushed the ungrateful thoughts aside. "Can we go find everyone and tell them?"

"Girls!" My mom's voice, normally singsong and calm, called up the stairs, harried and frantic. Josie and I looked at one another and started down without hesitation. We found her in the laundry room grabbing up old towels.

"What's wrong, Mom?" Josie asked.

"Mrs. Hinesman in the Frost Room fell asleep with the bathtub running. Maggie noticed the ceiling of the sitting room dripping and when we went up to check, there was water in the upstairs hall. The bathroom floor is flooded."

I scrambled to grab more towels. "Oh no!"

Josie punched numbers on her phone. "I'll see if Tripp can get here with a wet vac."

"Ask him if he has a dehumidifier, too." She groaned. "There'll be no getting around the damage."

We rushed up the stairs, our arms loaded with towels. Josie spoke to Tripp on the phone, her words coming out a mile a minute as she explained our predicament. I tried to calm Mom by reminding her of the good insurance policy we'd purchased.

We reached the top of the stairs, where Mrs. Hinesman, a widowed woman in her seventies, flapped around her room, a damp towel in hand. "Oh, I can't believe I fell asleep! I am so, so sorry. I will take care of the damages, please know that. I simply can't believe I fell asleep!"

I cringed at the water encroaching at the edge of the hardwood floor of the room. Josie and I attacked the offensive mess with towels, pushing it away from the guest room and back toward the bathroom. Mom spoke to Mrs. Hinesman in soothing tones, suggesting she grab one of the brownies she'd made for an afternoon snack and sit on the veranda while we tried to get the flood under control.

I gave her credit. From the looks of things, the Frost room might be out of service for at least a few weeks. After we cleaned up here, we'd have to check the Hawthorne room to see if any damage had leaked over. Ugh. We were going to lose a ton of money.

Ten minutes later, the towels and our feet were thoroughly soaked. Tripp and his brother August, who had recently returned home for the summer from college, took over with the wet vac. After they'd cleaned up the mess and inspected the Hawthorne room, we met in the downstairs sitting room where Tripp looked up at the wet ceiling, now slowed to a dribble.

Tall and sympathetic, he watched a single drop splash into a bucket Maggie had positioned there when she'd first noticed the problem. "We set up the dehumidifier, so hopefully that will suck up most of it. I suppose it's fortunate we laid down tile for the bathroom last year, but this ceiling has permanent damage. I won't be able to tell until I replace it if we'll need to replace the bathroom floor as well."

"I'll call the insurance company. How long will we be out of commission?" Mom placed her hands on her hips, worry lines creasing her pretty face.

"A few days at most. Just the Frost room. Although a construction crew at the height of the tourist season might not be the ideal environment for your guests."

Mom bit her bottom lip. "I suppose it can't be helped. Perhaps we'll offer a small discount for guests staying during that time?" She looked at Maggie, who nodded agreement.

A small knock came at the front door, which led to the veranda. Mrs. Hinesman stood outside, knocking timidly.

"Mrs. Hinesman!" Mom rushed to the woman. "You didn't have to stay out there this entire time!"

"Oh dear, I feel simply terrible. Terrible, I tell you. If I could curl up and disappear, I think I would."

My heart went out to her. "We're drying it up now."

"The only thing is, you have quite a loud dehumidifier in your room," Mom said.

"Oh, I don't mind. Now, I want you to send me the bill as soon as it's complete, you hear? I won't be able to stand it if you won't let me pay for the damages."

Mom smiled. "We'll work something out, Mrs. Hinesman. But these things are bound to happen every now and then. It's why we have insurance."

The older woman chattered on, saying nothing like this had ever happened to her, and how badly she felt, and she wondered if losing her husband last year had caused her to lose some of her wits as well.

My phone buzzed in my pocket. I glanced at it, seeing Asher's name light up the screen.

I excused myself and slid out the front door onto the empty veranda. A gust of fresh sea air met my nostrils and I breathed it in, preparing myself for Asher's call. Had I completely messed up the mod I'd set up the day before? I thought I'd done everything right, counting peg holes for the hooks and placing the proper product upon them. Backpacking food, compasses, GPS navigation systems, rechargeable battery packs. What had I missed?

"Hello?"

"Lizzie." His voice sounded strained, edgy. I wondered if he'd changed his mind about offering me the job.

But then a slight intake of breath sounded in my ear. My heart seized.

"Is everything okay?"

"Yeah. Yeah, it is. But I'm wondering if you might be willing to do me a huge favor?"

"Uh...sure. I can try."

"Thanks." It seemed he struggled to speak. What was up with him? "I have a guy coming by the shop for a job interview in half an hour. But I'm tied up right now. Is there any way you can meet him over there and run the interview? It shouldn't take more than fifteen minutes."

Run an interview? Did he realize how nervous I got *going* to an interview, never mind conducting one?

"I'm not sure I'm exactly qualified—"

"Sure you are. All you need to do is ask a few questions on my behalf. I'll compensate you."

It annoyed me that he wanted to throw money at me again.

"I don't need you to pay me. Consider it a favor. From a friend. So, is he going to work in the same department as me?" The camping gear fell alongside the hiking products, but I wasn't as familiar with cooking gear and backpacking tents. Another, more knowledgeable person by my side would be nice.

"No...no, it's for a managerial position."

"What? Asher, don't you think—"

"I'll text you a list of questions. I mostly need a sense of his personality, his work ethic. I trust you with that."

"Asher, if he's going to be my boss, I don't—"

"Lizzie, please. I have no one else."

I have no one else.

Something about the words strummed notes of compassion and empathy across my heart. But of course, he didn't mean he had no one else in *life*. He meant he couldn't get anyone else to interview this guy. He'd probably tried a bunch of people before settling on me as a last resort.

I sighed. "You'll send me the questions?"

"Yes. I'll text them right now. Thank you, Lizzie…this means a lot." His voice sounded tense again, as if he were on drugs or having trouble concentrating…or in pain. "Interview him outside. The store's locked, and you don't need to be alone in the building with him."

"What if he wants to see the place?"

"We'll handle that on a possible second interview. Okay, I got to go. You good?"

Peachy.

"Yeah. Sure."

"Thanks, Lizzie. I owe you one."

You bet your extreme sport-loving backside, you do.

"I'll let you know how it goes."

❧ 13 ❧

Waves of nausea rode over Asher until he thought he might drown. In and out of sleep, fatigue pulled at him, fever raging.

He'd been sick the whole night, pouring the contents of his stomach into a nearby wastebasket. He needed to drag himself up to get a drink, drag himself to the bathroom to empty his bladder.

He'd tried to push himself into his chair two times during the night, but had ended up on the floor, his head by the basket of vomit, the stench unbearable. The thought of dragging himself up into his wheelchair, wheeling to the bathroom, and inserting the catheter to empty his bladder was more than he could manage.

But the last thing he needed was a kidney infection on top of the virus.

He struggled up to one elbow, concentrated every ounce of his efforts on lifting his torso off the floor. *Come on, Hill.* He'd climbed Everest. Won triathlons. This was nothing compared to all of that. What in the blazes was wrong with him?

He reached for his phone, but it had slid across the floor when he'd fallen from the bed, now out of reach.

He was pathetic.

He thought of Ricky, then. Tried to pretend his brother was in the room watching him, that he'd prove himself strong in his younger brother's eyes. But all he saw in those green orbs he'd once known so well was disappointment. With a pinch of regret, Asher remembered a call from his brother a month ago. It had been awkward and stilted, magnifying how they would never regain the relationship they'd had before the accident.

Elise had blamed the failure of their relationship on Asher—could she have been sincere? Was the failure of his relationship with his brother also on his shoulders?

The disturbing thoughts pulled at the tattered edges of his consciousness. He let out a primal scream as he pushed himself up, heat swallowing his body. Too soon, he was falling. Falling fast. A hard knock on the back of his head.

Then, nothing.

❧

I WATCHED THE INTERVIEWEE DRIVE AWAY IN HIS TRUCK FROM the seat of my car. I opened the notepad on my phone and voice recorded a few notes I wanted to remember to reiterate to Asher. I'd sweat through the entire interview, but the man—Ryan—was gracious. I'd told him at the start that I was only filling in for Asher at his request, and that I had never conducted an interview.

And while he should have been the nervous one, he put me at ease with his friendly, forthcoming nature. He had a wife and two children—not one of Asher's questions—and loved taking his sons fishing in his spare time. He'd been a manager at a nearby superstore for the last seven years but was looking for hours that might allow him to spend more time with his family.

If it were up to me, I would have hired him on the spot.

I scrolled to my contacts and found Asher's name, pressed the call button.

The hollow ringing in my ear lingered for an interminably long time until, finally his voice mail picked up.

"Hey, it's Lizzie. I think the interview went well. Call me, okay?"

Then I texted him, in case he was the type of person to ignore voice mails.

I looked at the empty parking lot of the store. The crew was starting tomorrow. Shouldn't Asher be here?

I put my car in drive and headed home. Mom probably needed help catching up with laundry after the amount of towels we'd used earlier. After that, I'd work on my song. If I finished it before Josie offered her help, it would truly be mine.

I checked my phone one more time at a red light. No text. If I didn't hear back from Asher, I'd call him again tonight. He seemed very committed to the opening of the new store. I'm sure he'd want to know how the interview went.

🙧

I PULLED ON AN OVERSIZED NIGHTSHIRT WITH A PICTURE OF A kitten on it along with some shorts before curling up on my bed. I looked at my phone for what must have been the hundredth time since I'd left the store earlier that afternoon.

Asher's voice from earlier in the day haunted me.

I'm kind of tied up right now.

I have no one else.

I picked up the phone and called again, not leaving another voice mail when Asher's suave, recorded voice came on the line. I tapped into my messages.

Hey, are you okay? I thought I would have heard from you by now about the interview.

I pushed send before I could overthink what I'd written, then, after rereading the message, cringed and wished I could take it back. It sounded insecure. Was it my imagination, or perhaps my paranoia? But how well did I know this man? He struck me as the type to disappear off the grid for months at a time if it suited him.

I put the phone down and grabbed my notebook and guitar. But my fingers wouldn't cooperate. Flitting across the strings, they shook. My voice wobbled.

Asher wouldn't disappear off the grid, now. I may not know him well, but I knew he saw his projects through. The opening of the store was of ultimate importance to him. So why hadn't he followed up on the interview?

I have no one else.

I sat up, suddenly decided.

I did a quick Google search on my phone, found Asher's address without too much hassle. Unless there was another Asher Hill in Camden. Possible. But no doubt I could easily identify his home by the ramp that would be present.

I pulled on a sweatshirt to ward off the chill of the spring night and grabbed my car keys. I walked past Amie's open door.

"Hey, where you going?" she called.

I ducked into her room. Her arms wrapped around a circular frame. Wire was clenched between her teeth as she began to construct one of her beautiful leaf lamps.

"I'm going for a drive. I'll be back soon. I have my cell."

Her brow furrowed, and she spit out the wire. "That's not like you. Everything okay?"

All I needed was for my younger sister to pull out the overprotective act now. "I'm fine. I'll be back by ten."

"You need some company?"

I shook my head. "I kind of want to be alone."

It was on my lips to tell her the truth, but I didn't need her telling Bronson or Mom that I was going out in the darkening night to search out the home of a guy I barely knew.

Asher was surely fine.

His phone had probably died.

He was fine. It really wasn't my job to care so much, but I was working for him now, so at least I could justify it that way.

Besides....

I have no one else.

I trotted down the stairs and flew out into the night.

❧ 14 ❧

The address I'd Googled was a surprisingly simple, one-story ranch. With a ramp in front.

Score.

I contemplated the dark home. New, clean-cut and simple, no landscaping yet. Apparently, Asher was more concerned about his store than his home. I leaned forward, peering at the lonely house and the closed garage door, no welcome in sight. Asher said he'd possibly go south. Clearly, he hadn't intended anything permanent when it came to his house.

I sucked in a breath and pushed open my car door, gripping my phone in one hand, my keys in the other. I gripped the biggest one—my car key—in case I needed to use it as a weapon against a wild hungry animal, a flying bat, or a man hiding in the woods. I approached the front door, using the simple ramp. An overhead light turned on, and I jumped.

Crickets chirped.

I knocked on the extra wide front door.

Nothing.

Then again. I craned my neck to peer in the shade-drawn

window, but couldn't make out the glow of a light, a television, a cell phone, anything. I repeated my knock.

"Asher!" I glanced next door at the neighbor's lit, welcoming home. "It's Lizzie. Are you home?"

Still no answer.

Was I crazy? Why had I come here? The guy was a grown man. Sure, he was handicapped, but me rushing over here proved I believed him incapable.

But no. That wasn't it.

I have no one else.

I remembered our dog, Scabbers. When old age gained on him, I'd lain with him and stroked his scraggly fur over and over again. Cleaned up his messes and held him tight while he took his last breath.

I thought of my friend Rose, who had gone through chemo at the same time I'd had my thyroid removed. How many times had I visited her, prayed for her, wept with her?

I didn't think of myself as a great person, but I did sense that if God had given me one gift, it was compassion. It wasn't wrong of me to check on Asher. He'd asked for a favor. If he hadn't called in the first place, I wouldn't be worried about him now.

Sudden dread filled me, an unexplained urgency. Was it my imagination, or something more?

"Asher, please open!" I pounded on the door, then, a bit frustrated, I tried the handle.

It slid open.

I let out a surprised gasp before pushing the door farther. I knocked lightly again on the outside. "Asher?"

I ran my hand alongside the wall, searching for a switch. Nothing but fresh paint. Then, thinking like Asher, I moved my hand much lower on the wall. There.

Overhead lights splashed on, illuminating a small foyer with a neat row of shoes. I swallowed down the horrible sensation that I invaded his privacy, and moved toward the left, flipping on every switch as I went.

"Asher?"

Still, no answer. He mustn't be here. Though I might as well make sure now that I was inside his home.

He'd probably gone away for a day or two. I'd text him tomorrow and honestly explain that I had broken into his house and checked out his living arrangements.

He'd be thrilled.

I spotted the garage door and went for it, opening it slowly, almost expecting Asher to pop out from behind it. Darkness encompassed the garage. I flipped on the light. Asher's familiar truck sat nestled in the first bay.

"Asher?"

Nothing. I shut off the light and closed the garage door. He could have gone on a trip—maybe he didn't want to leave his truck at the airport.

I bit my bottom lip as I wandered away from the garage and toward the right, into the next room, which revealed a tasteful, spacious tiled kitchen with wood cabinets. A low counter, a large working island in the center, no top cabinets. Everything had been built with Asher's disability in mind. Perhaps he intended to stay around for a while after all. I walked across the hardwood dining room—void of rugs—and continued on toward the far hall.

"Asher? If you can hear me, or if you have video surveillance, I'm just checking on you because you didn't sound so great earlier today." I kept talking, my voice the only thing soothing my frantic nerves, taut as a guitar string. "I like your house. But I'm wondering how you ever have anyone over for dinner...there's no dining room chairs. I'd think someone like you who pays attention to such detail would notice—"

Was that a sound?

I crept down the hall, past a large, spacious bathroom and into the next room across the hall. The door was open. I ran my hand along the wall, searching for a light. The scent of sweat and something putrid met me as I moved deeper into the room. I found the light and switched it on, half afraid of what it might reveal.

"Asher!"

I flew to the form beside the bed, sweaty and pale, his handsome face drawn and fragile-looking. I fell to my knees, smoothed my hand over his clammy forehead, much as Mom used to do when I was sick as a girl.

"Jesus, please let him be alive. Please, please, please." I shook him slightly and his eyelids fluttered open. "Thank God."

"What...?"

"Don't worry, I'm here. It's going to be okay." I punched 9-1-1 on my phone. "I'm calling an ambulance."

He moaned. "No. Ambulance."

"Yes, ambulance." My tone brooked no possibility for argument. I spoke to a dispatcher, gave her Asher's address. She promised an ambulance within ten minutes.

"Lizzie?" Asher's voice cracked and I realized he must need water. How long had he been on the floor like this?

"Yes, it's me. I'm going to get you some water." I ran to the kitchen, searching for a cup in the waist high cabinets, finally finding one. I remembered the many times we treated Isaac's low blood sugar with juice. I opened Asher's refrigerator, found the sparse shelves neat, but juiceless. Water would have to do. I filled the cup in the faucet, ran back to his room.

"Turn that blasted light off, would you?"

I obeyed, glad he felt well enough to reveal his sunny disposition.

"There's a lamp...in the corner."

I turned the flashlight of my phone on to find the indicated lamp. It bathed the room in a soft glow instead of the harsh overhead lights.

"Can you sit up?"

"If I could, do you think I'd be down here in the first place?"

Apparently, I'd been worried for nothing. He appeared right as rain.

He blew out a long breath. "Sorry." He clenched his teeth, his pain apparent as he bent his torso over his stomach. "The one thing I hate worse than being sick is being sick in front of a pretty girl."

My mind tripped over the words *pretty girl*. I knelt beside him. "You need water." I eased my arm beneath his sweat-dampened shoulders and tried to lift his solid torso. He managed to prop himself on one elbow. I raised the glass to his lips and he drank greedily, flopping back on the floor as soon as the cup was emptied.

"Thanks."

I grabbed a tissue from his nearby nightstand and ran it along his chin where the water dripped. Surprisingly enough, he didn't resist.

"The ambulance is on its way."

His mouth pressed into a firm line. "Probably for the best."

I ran my gaze discreetly over his body, my eyes drawn to his legs in shorts. They didn't seem to match the rest of him. White, skin-and-bones, almost birdlike. Pity tugged at my heart.

"Don't look at them," he said, his eyes closed.

"I wasn't—"

"Yeah, you are. Besides, aren't you religious? I thought religious girls didn't lie."

"I—" I had no words. How could he put me in my place with so little effort when I was the one trying to help him?

His head moved from side-to-side, and I placed my hand on his forehead again. His pulse pounded through to my fingertips. "You're burning up. Your heart rate's out of control."

"I sure hope you don't catch this thing."

"I'm not worried about that."

"Martin, I'm afraid I have another favor to ask you. And it's not a pleasant one."

"Okay."

"I need emptying. Bad."

My mind stalled on his words. Emptying? Oh! Thank goodness for the dim lighting.

"Would you go in the bathroom? I have supplies on the windowsill. Wipes, hand sanitizer, a catheter. Sorry."

I popped up on wobbly legs. "Yes, of course. Whatever you need."

I walked to the bathroom. A plastic toilet chair with handles sat over the toilet. The sink, like the kitchen counters, was low. I found the catheter box and plucked one wrapped package out. I grabbed the wipes and hand sanitizer, came back into the room.

If he asked me to assist him, I think I might have to die right there on the spot.

"Is this what you need?"

"Yes."

I laid them on the floor, then stood waiting for further instructions.

He glanced up at me. "Come on, Martin. Do you really want a peep show right now?"

"Sorry, sorry, sorry!" I scrambled out of the room and shut the door. "Let me know when you're...finished."

I paced up and down the hall, my heart pounding out a staccato rhythm in my head. In the distance, sirens sounded.

After a few minutes, he called out. "All set."

I opened the door cautiously. "Feel better?"

He scrunched up one half of his face. "Yeah, sure."

I winced. Right. He probably hadn't *felt* that he had to go to the bathroom in the first place.

I picked up the wastebasket beside the bed, now filled with vomit and a urine bag. "I'll just take care of—"

"Don't!"

I placed it back down. "I'm only trying to help. If you leave it here while you're in the hospital, this place might never be habitable again."

He shook his head. "I'll call my maid. Or my nurse once I'm settled. Please, don't touch it."

I settled on the floor beside him.

"Will you get my phone?" he asked. "I think it's on the floor. Near the lamp."

I scooped it up.

"Do I have any messages? Code's 0921."

I punched in the code, saw only my text messages and voice mail.

I have no one else.

"Just me," I said in a light voice.

"Good."

I stood and peered out his bedroom window. "The ambulance is here. I better go meet them."

He grunted and I left the room, wondering if he was grateful I'd found him at all.

❧ 15 ❧

Asher peeled open his eyes, his mind registering the lifeless, sterile walls and curtained-off room of an ER. The all-too-familiar hum and beep of medical equipment.

But there'd been a beautiful song, hadn't there? That's why he'd pushed himself to wake. He wanted to see who possessed that angel voice.

He groaned as reality took over, bunched his fists as he remembered the events that had gotten him here.

Lizzie.

Oh, man. Shoot me now.

As he regained consciousness, wave upon wave of memory washed over him. Lizzie in his room. Staring at his scarecrow legs. Bringing him his bladder supplies. Insisting on emptying his waste.

If he never saw her again, it wouldn't be soon enough.

"Hey. You're awake."

He turned to see the object of his thoughts sitting in a gray plastic chair, her face drawn, but pretty. Her ponytail hung lopsided and uneven, one half of her straight brown hair sticking

out on the side. She wore a large t-shirt with a printed kitten on it
—something that looked incredibly young for her, and yet
somehow appropriate.

"Martin, what the blazes are you still doing here? Go home."

Her face pinched. Man, he'd hurt her.

"I—I wanted to make sure you were okay."

"I am. Please go home. What time is it, anyway? Your family
must be worried."

"It's eleven in the morning. I called them. In fact, Mom
already stopped by to bring you some of her banana cake. You
liked it so much last week, she thought it might be just the thing
once you feel up to eating."

His insides lurched, almost like a car slamming on its brakes.
She'd been here all night with him? Her mom had dropped off
banana cake?

He looked at her sweet face, almost angelic, and then at that
stupid cat shirt.

"What's with the shirt?" he asked.

She looked down, crossed her arms over her chest. "It's my
pajamas. When I came over...well, I didn't exactly plan or think."
She shrugged. "I like kittens. Who doesn't?"

"I've always been more of a dog person myself."

"Anyone ever tell you you're super charming when you're
sick?"

He rubbed a hand over his face, let out a small snort. "Yeah,
actually. Sorry about that. They tell you the prognosis?"

"They won't tell me anything. Violates your privacy. Doctor
should be in soon."

"You should go home and get some sleep."

"I will, after the doctor comes."

"I really can't believe you stayed here through the night. You
didn't have to do that."

She leaned forward in her chair. "I wanted to."

"Thank you," he said quietly. "For everything. I can compensate you for your time as soon—"

"Asher Hill, if you offer to compensate me one more time for something not related to working at your store, I'm going to—to —pop a hole in one of your wheelchair tires."

He let out his first real laugh in days. Not so much at her words, but at her mortified face when she realized she'd said them.

"I'm sorry." She covered her face with her hands. "I—I shouldn't have said that."

"Yeah, you should have. That was funny stuff, Martin."

"Lizzie," she corrected.

He swallowed. "Fine. Lizzie." He liked calling her by her last name. It was a barrier of sorts. A safety net.

A woman in a white coat with dark skin and maroon reading glasses stepped around the curtain. "Asher Hill?"

"That's me."

She stepped toward him and held out her hand. "I'm Dr. Patel. How are you feeling?"

"A lot better now."

She smiled. "That's good news."

Lizzie stood from where she'd sat in the corner, sweatshirt clutched to her middle, covering that ridiculous t-shirt. "I'll wait outside..."

"You can stay." He didn't know what he was saying. He did, and he didn't.

He didn't want to be alone.

Lizzie pressed her lips together so tight they almost disappeared inside her mouth. She nodded and sat back in the chair.

He turned his attention to the doctor.

"The bad news is that you have a virus and a kidney infection. The good news is you arrived here just in time. Any longer and you could have gone into septic shock. We've started you on high-dose antibiotics. We'll keep you overnight for observation."

"Doc, I got a lot to do. Can't you send me home with some

pills? I'll have my nurse come by and check on me."

She raised an eyebrow from where she punched something in on her tablet. "And where was your nurse last night, Mr. Hill?"

He cleared his throat. "Well, I've been doing pretty well, so I kind of...laid him off."

Dr. Patel made a sound of acknowledgment in her throat. "I suggest you rehire him, Mr. Hill. Today. Even if you're managing well, it's good to have someone around you can call. Do you live by yourself?"

"I'm perfectly capable of living on my own."

"I'm not doubting that you are. But during your recovery it's a good idea to have your nurse stay overnight. At least for a few days or so."

"Whatever you say, Doc."

"Why don't we plan on you staying overnight. If you can get a nurse at your house by tomorrow, I'll write your discharge papers first thing in the morning."

Not exactly what he'd been going for, but considering his vulnerable state, he couldn't disagree.

The doctor left and Lizzie smiled at him. "That sounds good."

"Sure. Hey, listen, why don't I give you the keys to the store? You think you can run over and let the crew in? If they bothered to hang around, that is. Oh, how'd the interview go?"

"Good. I think he'll be great. I asked your questions and made some notes. When you're out of here, we can go over them."

He nodded, about to suggest they do so now. But his eyes grew heavy. Besides, she needed to get out of this place.

"Go home, Mar—Lizzie. I'll talk to you tomorrow."

She tapped her feet on the linoleum. "Are you sure? I don't mind staying. What about letting the crew in?"

He shook his head. "Go. You need rest. I'll call someone else. Thank you for everything."

That earned him a small smile, one he wouldn't mind seeing more often.

"Will you call me if you need—"

"I'll call you. Get out of here. Get some sleep because tomorrow we're diving into work."

"Okay." She clutched her sweatshirt to her middle, laid one hand on his leg that lay beneath the white hospital covers. He couldn't feel it, of course. But that one natural moment, seeing her hand on him, made something warm inside him. "See ya." She turned to walk out, then twirled on her heel. "Oh, I almost forgot. I called your Mom last night. You gave me the code to your phone, so I thought someone should—"

"What?" The warmth in his chest turned to hot fury as he came fully awake. She had no right. He'd worked so hard to get away from it all, to gain back his independence.

She backed up until she ran into the partitioned curtain. "I know it was a bit presumptuous, but I thought someone should know. You weren't waking up and they didn't tell me what was wrong with you. What if...well, if I were in the hospital, I'd want my mom to know."

He closed his eyes, shook his head. "If you couldn't tell, we're not the same people. At all."

"I was only trying to help."

"Yeah, well next time, stay out of it, okay? In fact, you shouldn't have come to my house at all." He knew what he was doing. He was mad, and he was pushing her away. Where he wanted everyone. His mom, his family, Ricky, Lucas, Elise, Lizzie. Everyone. They could all go to—

"What is wrong with you?" Her bottom lip trembled with emotion, and she took a step toward him. He remembered that small hand on his lifeless leg, regretted his words already. "If I hadn't come, you'd be dead, Asher. Dead. Don't you care?"

He looked at her, didn't say anything. In that moment, he glimpsed himself in her eyes, and he hated what he saw. At the same time, he couldn't summon up the energy to fix what he knew he should. It was safer this way. She shouldn't have seen him like she did. On the floor of his bedroom, helpless beside his own vomit. His legs. His urine bag. Man, oh man, why did she show up at his house, anyway?

His silence compelled her to continue. "You know what? You don't care, do you? I don't think you care about anyone except yourself. Yourself and your stupid store. Well, have it. It's yours. I quit."

She whirled on her heel and by the time he could make himself call out her name, she was long gone. He let his head fall back on the pillow. When a middle-aged nurse shuffled in, he didn't acknowledge her presence.

"Well, if those weren't the ugliest tears I've ever seen...."

He bit the inside of his cheek. "The girl that just left here was crying?"

"Mmm hmmm."

He cursed. He'd made her cry? Oh, man. He deserved the guillotine.

"That was a sweet one, too. Didn't sleep a wink last night, held your hand when you were crying out for your mom, soothed you like you were a little baby. Sang the most beautiful songs to you."

He raised his eyebrows. "You're pulling my leg, I hope." No way had he been crying for his mom.

"No, sir. There's no room for jokes in an ER."

He cursed, mumbled something about the drugs they'd given him, claiming they messed with his brain.

The nurse shuffled over in her Crocs, checked his IV. "Well, I have good news, Mr. Hill. You have another visitor. Your mom's here."

"Please tell me you're joking."

"You remember what I told you about jokes in the ER, don't you?"

He groaned. Of course, his mom flew out. She'd look for any excuse to come and stick her nose in his life, and unfortunately for him, Lizzie's call had been the perfect ticket to do just that.

❧ 16 ❧

I finished crying my tears by the time I left the hospital parking lot, and I swore that was the last of them. Asher Hill would not get one more drop of emotion out of me.

I calmed my last quivering breaths while sitting in my car, convinced myself the tears were more from lack of sleep than bruised emotions. But really, what a lowlife. To treat me so cruelly when I was only trying to help. I heard Josie's voice in my head, knew what wisdom she might dole out in a time like this.

You deserve better than that, Lizzie. Don't settle for less.

Then I imagined Amie's.

But I couldn't repeat the words she would call Asher, even in my head.

It didn't matter. They were right.

When I went home, I'd write up a formal email resigning from my position at Paramount. Then I'd put Asher Hill out of my head, and out of whatever small corner of my heart he'd weaseled himself into—forever.

"Honey!"

In a swirl of Estee Lauder perfume and the Talbots spring line, Mikayla Hill swooped down upon Asher. Her tan, toned arms stayed by her side as she bent to kiss his temple.

"I came as soon as I could. How are you feeling?"

"I'm better. Mom, you really didn't have to come all the way out here. I wish you hadn't."

She straightened her spine. "Your friend told me you were asking for me. What was I supposed to do, ignore that? Now, tell me what the doctors said. They *have* seen you, haven't they? If not, I'll give them a piece of my ever-loving mind."

"Mom!"

She stopped in her tracks on the way to the door.

"We're not doing this right now, okay? I can handle things. The doctor's seen me. It's a stomach bug and a kidney infection. I should be home by tomorrow."

"Good. Then you can show me around this town. I only drove through on my way from the airport, but it's absolutely charming. Not the backcountry hoedown I expected."

"I can't entertain. I have a store opening in less than three weeks, and I'm already behind schedule as is."

"Then I'll help you. We can work together. I don't want you making yourself sick, honey. Nothing's worth your health."

Huh. He tried to picture his mother conducting an interview, or washing windows, or setting up a mod. Not in a million years.

"Really, Mom. I'm good."

She gave him a tight smile before sitting down in the seat Lizzie had vacated not ten minutes earlier. "Then tell me about this Lizzie. She sounded like a sweet delight. Are you dating?"

"No," he ground out. "She works for me."

Worked, rather. Did she really quit on him? Could he blame her?

"Aww, pity. She sounded like a keeper. Elise and Lucas are planning to honeymoon in Alaska, of all places. Can you believe that?"

"I don't care, Mom."

"Really, Asher, your social skills have taken a massive hit since your accident. Why, I'll bet if you weren't so miserable every waking hour, this Lizzie girl *would* be dating you."

"*Mom.*"

"You can't expect life to always go your way. You know what Grandpa used to say, when life hands you lemons, you have to—"

"You know what? I actually do need some help. Do you think you could drive over to the store and see if any of the team is there? They were supposed to start today, but I've been preoccupied, as you can see. Keys are in the pockets of my pants over there."

"Uh, yeah. Sure, honey. Whatever you need."

He gave her the address and when she left, he savored the peace, the rhythmic beep of the hospital machines almost comforting.

He should be able to rest, soon. As soon as he figured out a way to make things up to Lizzie.

❧ 17 ❧

I closed my eyes as the worship music moved over me, stirring my soul with warmth. My voice melded with it, without effort, opening up a portal to a holy place—a place full of love and peace, a place where fear no longer existed as I sank into the arms of my Creator.

Church had always been one place I didn't mind singing. When I stood in front of our small congregation, it didn't feel like a performance. It didn't feel like I was being judged for every right or wrong note I hit. It only felt like lifting my voice up to the heavens to give glory to God.

The perfect one who never lashed out at me in anger or treated me cruelly.

I sang out the Zack Williams' song from a hidden place inside of me, asking my Creator to cast out my fears. As the congregation joined, our praises and proclamation of what God could do giving testimony to one another, I sensed that, in the grand scheme of things, Asher Hill didn't matter one iota.

No, but that wasn't true. God cared about Asher. And I had tried to. But I couldn't change the hard man any more than I could change the color of the sky. I refused to subject myself to more of his abuse.

We finished the song, Pastor Greg spoke the benediction, and the congregation mulled around, greeting one another or emptying out the doors.

My friend, Ashley, came over and hugged me. "I love singing with you. It's like singing with an angel."

I pushed aside her compliment. "I only sound good because of your sweet alto."

"Let's get together soon, okay? It's been too long."

"I'm planning to do Bald Rock Mountain tomorrow. Want to come?" Looks like I wouldn't be busy with Asher's store this week, after all.

She wrinkled her pert nose. "Sorry, Liz. You know hiking isn't my jam. If you ever want to get your nails done or go for coffee though, I'm game."

I grinned, not having the money or the inclination to get a manicure. "We'll do coffee soon."

We said goodbye and Ashley skipped down the steps of the stage.

"Hey, Lizzie."

I turned to see Mike, one of the guitarists. I smiled up at his six-foot, lanky frame, the dancing blue eyes behind thick black glasses.

"Hey, Mike. Great playing today."

"Thanks. You—you're always amazing."

I stared at my feet, a blush rising to my cheeks. "Thanks."

"I'll go with you," he blurted out. "I mean, if you want company."

I shook my head. "Go with me...?"

"On your hike. I've done Mount Battie a ton of times, but I haven't done Bald Rock before."

My thoughts stuttered. Was this what I thought it was? Mike

HEIDI CHIAVAROLI

and I were friends. We practiced and sang together nearly every week, had shared the playpen in the church nursery as toddlers. But I never thought of him in a romantic way. I wasn't sure I could.

Yet here was a guy—a really decent, talented, sweet guy—who wanted to spend time with me doing one of my favorite things. We shared the same faith, had practically grown up together in our small church. Why had I never given him much thought?

All this time I'd been daydreaming about a fantasy drive-thru dreamboat who liked to play guitar and hike when an actual guy—an upright citizen who didn't throw grown-man hissy fits and didn't make fun of kitten t-shirts—had been right in front of me.

"You know what? I'd love some company on the hike."

***

THE MUGGY AIR WRAPPED AROUND ME LIKE A WET BLANKET, and I struggled to breath in the middle of a particularly steep incline.

"Sorry, Mike. I need a quick break again."

"No worries." He slid off his own backpack and dug a water bottle out from its depths. "The humidity's a killer today." Sweat poured down his face. He took off his fogged-up glasses and wiped them on his t-shirt.

I swigged down my water, recapped it. "Sorry about the breaks. I didn't realize how many I usually take."

He shrugged. "I don't mind. It's the journey, not the destination, right?"

See? Totally sweet. I tried to force romantic notions into my head. Could it be possible? If I dug really deep?

After another couple of minutes, we continued on our way.

"You're almost out of school, right?"

I nodded. "Wednesday's my last day."

"I'll bet you're already planning next year's lessons."

"Actually, they cut the budget. I won't be going back next year." I kept my tone light.

"Aww, Lizzie, I'm sorry."

I stepped onto a rock, pulled myself up with my right leg. "It's okay. I was bummed at first, but I'm trusting another door to open." Even if it wasn't in teaching. Or retail.

I thought of my songs, tucked so far inside I couldn't seem to pull them out. Would anything ever become of them?

"It will." Mike climbed up a particularly large boulder, then held his hand out to help me.

My stomach fluttered, and I allowed his gentle pull to assist me in my ascent, anticipating the hummingbird's wings in my stomach to quicken.

But Mike's sweaty, large hand in my own small one didn't accomplish the feat. Without wanting to, I remembered the first time I met Asher, then the deal we'd made by handshake. How both had tilted my world more than this chivalrous gesture.

What was wrong with me? Did I want to subject myself to pain? Didn't I want a nice man to spend time with? Well, here he was.

I needed to try harder, that was all. Put some effort behind this. "I'm not sure I know what you do for a living. What about you?"

"I was just hired on as a lawyer for the International Justice Mission. It's a global organization that protects people in poverty from violence. Combatting trafficking and slavery, violence against women and children, and police abuse of power. My job is keeping the criminals accountable, stopping the cycle, and deterring others from hurting the vulnerable."

He said it so simply, as if it were nothing to be Spiderman and change into spidey gear in the back of an alley in order to save a powerless child.

"Oh, wow." *Wow.* Really, could this guy be any more perfect?

"I'll be heading to D.C. next month, but there's a chance I'll

be able to work remotely once settled. I'd hate to leave Camden."
He looked at me. Did I imagine the meaning behind his glance?

"I hadn't realized the worship team would be losing you," I
said.

He shrugged. "We'll see where it all leads."

I asked him more questions about his job, genuinely interested. I thought of my dad, then. He and Mike would be nonstop
talking over Mike's work. Dad would probably go out of his way
to support the young lawyer.

When we reached the top, the Gulf of Maine stretched before
us in majestic splendor. The breeze chased away the humidity on
our faces, and I breathed deep.

"Good hike," Mike said. "Thanks for letting me tag along."

I glimpsed him out of the corner of my eye. He studied the
view before us, *appreciating* it. How long had I been looking for a
hiking friend?

"I'm glad you did."

"So we can do it again, sometime?" His piercing blue eyes met
mine, and I nodded.

True, sparks weren't flying. But neither did Mike have the
capacity to throw me into turmoil—whether that be pleasant or
chaotic. It was a good thing. It was.

If I were to have a man in my life, this was the kind of man I
needed. Steady. Full of faith. One who fought for the needy.
Listened to me as if I mattered.

Why then, was a certain handsome, bearded face the only one
coming to my mind?

❧ 18 ❧

Three days.

Three days since Lizzie had first sat in the ER with him. The image of her, drawn and tired in that ridiculous kitten t-shirt, had embedded itself in his mind and wouldn't let go. Through his time in the hospital. Through his transfer home as he rehired his nurse, Zack.

He needed to see her, to set things right between them. And yet his mom had swarmed down on his home like a thick fog on a summer morning. He couldn't think straight with her hovering. Cleaning. Looking over Zack's shoulder, a million questions on her tongue. Making Asher food he wasn't hungry for. Force-feeding him shakes and smoothies.

Finally, he'd had enough.

"Mom, I appreciate your concern, but you have to leave or I'm going to throw myself off a bridge. Really. I need some space."

She'd laughed, a light, nervous sound. "I'm only trying to help."

"I know you are, and I do appreciate it. Really. But I'm twenty-nine years old. The hospital released me. I have Zack. I think it's time for you to go home."

"Well, what about the store? You said I could help with it."

"Do you want to go stock shelves?"

Her mouth pulled downwards.

"I didn't think so."

She tapped her finger on her lips. "I'll leave this afternoon. On one condition."

"What's that?" he'd asked through clenched teeth.

"You come for the wedding. Or at least a visit if I can't get you to agree to that."

He should have figured. But her softening stance on the wedding moved him an inch toward agreeing. If she wanted him at the wedding to save face, to prove he'd moved on from Elise and could still be friends with Lucas, she would have dug in her heels. And if he couldn't stand tall—let's face it, he never would again—then at least she would.

But if she was open to him visiting without the stipulation of Elise and Lucas's wedding, then maybe she didn't just care about her reputation. Maybe she really did care about rebuilding their family.

She sniffed, her voice quivering. "It's Ricky, Asher. I haven't said anything because your father said I shouldn't, but...he's not doing well. His job's decent, if he can keep it, but he's been aimless lately. Drinking, going out with friends he met at some club. I think he has a gambling problem."

"What? Why didn't you tell me earlier?"

"Your father and I didn't want you to worry. Despite what you think, we do want you to rebuild your life as best you can. Close by or away from us. We thought we could handle whatever's going on with your brother, but..."

His heart broke at what he sensed was to come. "But?"

"He got a DUI three days before I flew out here. He's lost his license, has to attend classes and rehab. I don't see how he'll keep his job. He's falling apart, Asher."

The words served to sucker-punch him in the gut. But...

"What do you want me to do, Mom? How is me swooping in going to change anything? Don't you see, him looking at me like I'm half a man will only make things worse."

He used to be his younger brother's hero. But at times, it seemed Asher's prognosis and disability bothered Ricky in a different way than it did him. Ever since that September day, whenever Ricky looked at him, all Asher sensed emanating from his brother was complete and utter disappointment.

"I'll give him a call."

"It's not enough."

He sensed the truth of her words. Ricky needed something drastic. But what?

"I'll come," Asher said.

His mom deflated into a puddle of gratitude. She clasped his hands. "Thank you."

"Not the wedding. But I'll come home."

"Thank you." She kissed his cheek, and he didn't pull away. Poor woman. His mother hadn't been perfect, but she'd tried. And she'd done a pretty bang-up job of raising two boys, for the most part. She cared. And now she was strapped with not one, but two sons she constantly worried about.

"I suppose I'll go hold up my end of the deal and pack my bag, then."

He gave her a small smile. But before she exited the living room, he called out to her. When she turned, he met her gaze, hoping she sensed what he couldn't manage to put into words. "Thanks."

AFTER HIS MOM WAS SAFELY ON HER WAY TO THE AIRPORT, HE turned his focus to the two things nagging him the last three days—the store opening, and his abominable behavior toward Lizzie.

The longing to make up for it consumed him, trumping everything else. She didn't deserve how he'd treated her.

Yes, he needed her help with the store. But more than that, he needed her to know he hadn't meant to hurt her.

He'd texted Lizzie, asking if they could talk. She hadn't responded. Could he blame her?

Now, driving to her family's bed and breakfast with a small pet carrier on the passenger seat of his truck, he glared at the little creature inhabiting the plastic crate—the only peace offering that might pave the way for a heartfelt apology. Again, he doubted himself. What in the blazes was he trying to accomplish?

He pulled into the bed and breakfast, beside an older Toyota Camry, and winced at the bad timing. The inn probably welcomed guests this time of day.

Fighting the urge to turn around in the large drive, he spotted Lizzie getting out of the Camry, a hiking backpack slung over her shoulder. She leaned into the car and said something to the driver, a guy who made her smile as she turned away.

That smile bent Asher in half. *That's* how you treat a sweet girl like Lizzie. Not as he'd done at the hospital. Not like some scumbag lowlife who thought the world should be served to him on a silver platter. He *was* selfish. He'd had to admit that much.

The Camry drove away, and Lizzie looked after it, seemed to sigh deeply. Asher pushed aside the twist of jealousy cramping his chest.

He unrolled his window. "Who's that?"

She jumped, startled, then twisted around. When she saw him, her smile melted quicker than an ice sculpture in a Los Angeles heat wave.

He'd done that. If he could use his legs, he would have kicked his sorry backside the whole five miles home.

He shouldn't have come. He'd only make things worse for both of them. As much as he wanted her help with the store, what he'd miss most were those deep, inquisitive eyes. The way her ponytail tended to slump on one side. The way she blushed when he said something a little off color, or when she was angry.

Like now.

"I have nothing to say to you." She whirled on her heel toward the bed and breakfast.

He opened his door, though where he thought he was going, he hadn't a clue—by the time he wrangled his chair out and rolled to the door of the inn, she could have made it in and out of the shower. Nix that idea.

"Lizzie, please. Wait. I was horrible. There's no excuse. And I know it's not the first time. But I can't live with myself if I don't at least try to make things right between us."

She whirled again. "You're right. You were horrible. I don't know why I let it get me so upset, though. You're not worth it, Asher Hill. You go around thinking you've got all the answers when really you are a small, childish, lonely man who's afraid to let anyone get close to you because it might make you vulnerable. You're a coward, that's what you are."

She stood back, her arms crossed under her chest.

"You done?"

Her bottom lip quivered, and he could practically see reality swooping down upon her as she realized the bold things she'd said to him. But she shook her head. "One more thing." She stepped closer to his truck but didn't speak.

"Yes?"

"I don't think you can play guitar. I think you like carrying it around in your truck, like some sort of trophy or bumper sticker in your back window. I'll bet you use it to hide your wheelchair, which you make a way bigger deal about than half the people who cross your path."

His insides pinched at that one.

From the other side of his truck, the door of the bookshop opened. He glanced over to see a tall woman with long, wavy hair. "Everything okay, Lizzie?"

Lizzie nodded. "Asher was just leaving."

The woman at the bookshop shrugged and went back inside.

"I came to tell you how out of line I was, Lizzie. Everything you accused me of...you're right. I am selfish. I am insecure. And I'm sorry."

Her arms loosened a bit from where she held them crossed at her chest. A letting down of the guard?

"You forgot to admit you can't play guitar."

A smile twitched the corners of his mouth. "I can't play guitar *well*. But I can play." He swallowed. "Does this mean you'll forgive me? Please?"

She closed her eyes, mumbled something about seventy-times-seven before opening them. "I guess I have no choice."

"Thank you." Their gazes met and hooked. His heart pinged with a longing one has for someone they haven't seen in ages. Yet, how was that possible when he barely knew her? He turned to the crate on the passenger seat, opened the door, and reached his hand in.

"I brought you something to try and make it up to you." He revealed the sweet calico kitten cuddled in his arms. "And if you don't want her, I guess I have a new pet."

Lizzie put a hand to her mouth. A single strand of hair lay plastered to her temple with sweat. The crazy urge to lift his hand and smooth that glossy lock back came over him, but he didn't give in.

She shook her head. "She's adorable. Oh my goodness. Can I hold her?"

He transferred the kitten to her arms. "She's got her shots and a clean bill of health. She had some food before I left the house, so she's pretty content."

The kitten nuzzled Lizzie's neck, rubbing its nose against her chin. Lizzie giggled, stroking the small face with one finger. "Oh, she's darling."

"You said you like kittens."

"I'll have to check with Mom..."

"Okay, go ahead. I'll wait."

"Don't you want to come in? I think it's hummingbird cake today."

"Wow. I really am forgiven."

She sighed, looked down at the bundle curling itself into her arms. "I suppose you are. Hate to admit it, but you know how to get to a girl's heart." Her gaze flew to his, the awkward moment fleeing fast.

"So you'll come back to work for me?"

Her mouth fell open slightly. "Is that what this is about? The kitten...the apology...you need me to work at your store?"

"Lizzie—no. You have to believe me. I've been nothing but miserable about the way I treated you in that emergency room. If you don't want to come back to work for me, I understand. But I can't live with myself if you're still angry at me."

She rolled her eyes. "So surprising that once again it's back to you."

He dragged in a deep breath, refused to let his frustration get the better of him this time. "I'm trying here. I really am. I hate that I upset you so much. I came over to ask your forgiveness, and yeah, I'd still like you to work for me. But that's not why I'm saying 'I'm sorry.'"

She looked down at the kitten. "What do you think, Bets?"

"Bets?"

"Well, I can't call her Beethoven since she's a girl, so I think I'll call her Betty. Bets for short."

"Okay..."

She glared at him before turning her attention back to the kitten. "What will it be, *Bets*? Do you think we should give Mr. Cranky Pants here another chance?" She made her voice high and ridiculously squeaky as she leaned closer to the cat. "Ahh, okay, then. Yes, yes, I think you're right." Lizzie pinned him with those searing eyes. "Bets says I should come back to work for you only if you say, 'Purrrrty please.'"

"What? No, that's ridiculous."

"Say it."

"Can we talk this out like normal—"

She held the kitten up to him, it's impossibly gray eyes soft and entreating above snow-white whiskers. "Say it."

He exhaled. "Fine. Pretty please."

"*Purrrrty* please."

He shook his head, one corner of his mouth inching up even as he commanded it down. "*Purrrty* please."

Lizzie tucked the kitten back in her arms, where it snuggled deep, already at home. "Okay, I will. But only because you asked so nicely."

He closed his eyes. "I'm not sure I'm the only one here who's impossibly difficult."

She gave him a wordless smile.

"The invitation for that cake still open? I want to know if your mom's going to go for this or if Bets—whom I would definitely rename—is coming home with me."

"You're welcome to come in. But Mom's not going to turn Bets away. She has a soft spot for strays." Her eyes met his, and he avoided them, twisted around to get his wheelchair.

A few minutes later, they approached the house together.

He cleared his throat. "You did some hiking today?"

Did he imagine that blush creeping up her neck?

"Yup."

"Who was that? Who dropped you off?"

"A friend from church."

A friend from church. Ugh.

A guy who was perfect for Lizzie, no doubt. He should be happy for her. Jealousy would get him nowhere. And, if he truly was interested in working on his selfishness, this would be a perfect place to start.

"Good for you," he said, forcing enthusiasm into his voice.

She bestowed a sweet smile on him, genuine to the core. Man, oh man, he better be careful around smiles like that.

"Thanks, Asher."

There. He'd succeeded at being unselfish—at thinking of someone else's best before his own.

Too bad it hurt so incredibly much.

❧ 19 ❧

"I don't know, Lizzie. What does this guy want, bringing you kittens and everything? He's your boss, isn't he? Something seems off." Bronson forked a meatball in his mouth with the delicacy of an ogre before gulping down a tall glass of frothy milk.

"Eww. I have to eat too, you know. Get some manners, will you?" Amie scrunched up her nose as she looked at our brother in disgust. She took a dainty bite of salad.

"My manners are fine." He jerked his head at the kitten in my lap. "And it's actually staying? What about Cragen?"

Aunt Pris waved her hand in the air. Her lap dog had taken to Bets surprisingly well. "I told Hannah to let the girl keep her kitten. She's always wanted one."

I looked up at Aunt Pris in surprise.

She gave me one of her rare smiles. "I pay attention more than you think I do."

I savored the warmth of Bets in my lap, remembered Asher offering her to me. I'd agreed to work for him again, for he'd certainly been singing a different tune today. And while I couldn't ignore my volatile emotions when around him, I needed to keep my guard up. Like one of his extreme sports he'd loved so much, the man simply wasn't safe.

"I have it under control, Bron. I don't really want to talk about it."

"Well, then tell us about your date today." Amie tapped her fork lightly against her plate. "How'd it go?"

"Wait. What? You went on a date with him?" Bronson asked.

Amie shook her head, her large raindrop earrings shaking back and forth. "Not with Paramount guy. With Mike, from church."

Bronson sat up straighter. "Really? That's great. I mean, that's the kind of guy you should be dating."

I blew my hair out of my face. "It wasn't a date. It was a hike."

Since when did how I spend my time become such a source of fascination for my brother? But I knew—ever since Asher Hill had come along.

"Well, I vote for Mike, if we're keeping count."

"Bronson." Mom's mouth pulled downward. "I think you need to give Lizzie some space."

I shot her a grateful smile.

"I agree," Amie added. "But if we're keeping tallies, I'd go with Mike, too. I know I was impressed with Mr. Paramount, but he's sure put you through the wringer, Liz. And you haven't even been dating."

"We are *not* keeping tallies. And right now, I'm not dating anyone. Can we please drop it?"

"That sounds wise." Mom turned to Bronson. "The orchards are looking great this year, honey. You're doing a fine job."

Bronson wiped his mouth with his napkin. "Thanks, but there's still tons left to do. I actually have an idea I've been mulling over."

He looked so much like Dad when he prepared to expound on one of his notions. How many ideas had Dad brought to us over the dinner table in a similar way? I stole a glance at Mom, a wistful look on her face.

"Tell us then, honey."

The same way she responded to Dad. It seemed my father's legacy continued.

Bronson's leg started jiggling under the table, a telltale sign he was nervous or excited, or both. "It's too late for this year, but I've been pondering the idea of a summer camp, here at Orchard House."

Aunt Pris blinked. "You young ones continue to insist testing the amount of chaos I can tolerate, don't you?"

"It wouldn't be in the house, Aunt Pris. It'd involve the orchards. If I can get things into full swing this fall, kids could learn about the production of the apples, how the orchards grow. We could offer some hands-on classes. Something for underprivileged teens helping them be creative thinkers. We could set up something indoors in the barn. If we thought they were a good fit and they wanted to stay on, we could hire them for orchard help."

Wow. It *was* a Dad idea. Something big and involved. Something only tenacity and dreaming could get done. And it benefitted those on the outskirts of society. I held my breath, waiting for Mom to speak first.

"It's a lovely idea, honey. It sounds like an enormous amount of work, though. You think you're up for that?" Her gaze flicked to Aunt Pris. "And of course, Aunt Pris would have to be on board with it."

"If those little hooligans are helping with the orchard, I can't say I can see a downside. When I was a girl, you should have seen the bushels of apples we brought in. Ask Esther. But yes, it was a lot of work. With a lot of help, too."

"My goal for this summer and fall would be to get it in tip-top shape. Hire more guys from Dad's mission if it's in the budget. I've been reading up on how to make a profit. We could offer hayrides and apple picking in the fall. We could sell tickets at the bookshop. Maybe add in some candy apples, baked goods—"

Amie held up her hand. "Whoa, there, Tiger. We went from a

summer camp to a full-blown apple picking venture in thirty seconds flat. And Mom has enough to do without whipping up apple pies to sell."

Bronson had the decency to look sheepish. "You're right. But if we could get this place making multiple streams of income—the B&B, the bookshop, and the orchard—it'll be able to withstand the ups and downs of any normal business."

Mom reached a hand out to Bronson's tanned forearm. "Honey, I love the idea and your enthusiasm." She turned to Aunt Pris. "What do you think about this?"

"I think our driveway isn't big enough to turn into a parking lot."

"People could park on the grass on the side of the orchard," Bronson said.

"It'll be a mud pit when it rains." She sighed, raised her eyebrows. "You've really thought this through, haven't you, young man?"

He shrugged. "I have one year left of college. I want to teach, but that still leaves me with time for this endeavor. I want to get this place running again, Aunt Pris. Like it was when you were a girl. And if we can help a few disadvantaged kids while we're at it, I say the more the better."

"Well, I know one thing." Aunt Pris exchanged a knowing look with Mom. "The apple doesn't fall far from the tree with this one."

Mom bestowed a smile on our brother. "You certainly have been reminding me a lot of your father lately."

Bronson squinted at Aunt Pris. "Is that a go-ahead?"

"It's a let's-take-one-step-at-a-time-and-see. Starting simple is wise, I'd say. Let's see what the harvest looks like in August and go from there."

He got up and gave her a peck on the cheek. "Thanks, Aunt Pris. You won't regret it."

"I'm entirely sure I will, but that doesn't change my answer."

I bit back a laugh, looked at the four people surrounding the table. I would be back at Paramount tomorrow, setting up mods. I'd see Asher again. Probably experience the myriad of chaotic feelings he managed to elicit. But, in the end, it would all be okay, because in the end, I always had my family waiting for me back home.

🏵 20 🏵

I straightened and stretched my back. I grabbed the last of the cardboard boxes and ripped the tape off, folding it so it would fit neatly in the backroom baler. The scent of new clothes and camping gear met my nostrils. I surveyed the area. Something like pride filled me.

It was actually coming along. The backpacks sat neatly along an aisle, each in their uniform row. Everything easy to see, easy to peruse. I'd also managed to set up the clothing, the propane grills, the tents, the coolers, air mattresses, and sleeping bags.

The store lay quiet, most of the crew having already gone home for the night. Two stragglers approached me—Joel and Titan. They'd helped me move some of the heavier equipment the day before.

I smiled tentatively. "The store's looking good."

My role as team lead left me more than uncomfortable. Every time I stepped into it, I would pretend I was Josie or Maggie— anyone besides my trembling self.

"Almost ready," Titan agreed. He went to college in Boston but was home for the summer. He opened his mouth as if to say something.

I cocked my head to the side. "Everything okay?"

"We were wondering what the chances are of Mr. Hill letting us try out the rock wall before opening? I'm itching to get some practice in before my big climb at the end of June."

"Where are you climbing?"

"Acadia."

"Nice." I dreamed of hiking Acadia someday myself. "I don't see what asking would hurt. I think he's in his office now."

Titan looked from Joel to me. "You think you could ask him for us? We have a better chance of him saying yes if it comes through you."

I tried not to read into that more than I should. Instead, I waved them away. "I need to talk to him about a few things before I leave anyway. I'll mention it and let you know tomorrow, okay?"

They grinned and thanked me, grabbing their water bottles before heading out. When the store lay empty, I surveyed our work once again. Another day of setting up and we'd be in great shape. Ryan would begin tomorrow, ensuring last-minute details came to life.

When Asher and I finally sat down to talk about the interview I'd conducted in his absence, Asher had been hesitant to hire Ryan at first. The man didn't want to work more than three nights a week because of his family—something bold for a prospective manager in retail to demand.

But whether it was my cajoling, Asher's hidden soft side, or the fact that he was still trying to make up for his rudeness in the hospital, Ryan was now Asher's new store manager.

An excited hum started in my belly. A deep satisfaction at being part of something. Much like the bed and breakfast, Paramount was beginning to grow on me.

I grabbed up the cardboard and took it to the baler in the back. Then, I headed toward the front of the store. The sun began its descent, though it wouldn't be dark for another few hours. Nothing better than long summer days.

I passed the vacant registers, the checkout lights dimmed, and walked down the hall to the right. I knocked on the open door of Asher's office. "Hello?"

"Come in."

His familiar voice made my insides perform an enthusiastic solo across tight strings. No matter my attempt to suppress it, this man needled his way into my spirit. I was getting to know him—the real him. Not some drive-thru fantasy, but the genuine man beneath it all. And he perplexed and challenged and drew me in an altogether uncomfortable way.

My thoughts turned to Mike. We'd gone hiking again this past weekend, and I had a great time. Really. He'd asked me out for dinner the following week, but I told him I couldn't because of the store opening, which Asher had asked his employees to attend.

I hadn't thought to invite Mike, and I wasn't sure why. Bronson was right. Mike was the kind of guy I should be with. Why then, was I twiddling my thumbs?

I turned the corner to Asher's office and found him studying the screen of his laptop, a baseball hat on backwards, a concentrated look on his face. My gaze flew to the corner of his desk where his stack of pictures took up residence. With some satisfaction, I noted that the picture of him and his old girlfriend wasn't in sight.

"The crew's gone for the day. We made good progress."

He looked up from his laptop. Did I imagine his gaze running over me, the genuinely happy look on his face?

"You have. I snuck out there about fifteen minutes ago to check. It's looking phenomenal."

The compliment stirred something sweet in my heart. I was *good* at something. I may not be able to keep my job at the school. I may not be able to finish a song. I might not be ambitious like Josie, or creative like Amie, but I had done something of worth.

I thought about the idea I'd had yesterday. There likely

wouldn't be a better time to broach the topic. I pulled in a breath before I chickened out. "Actually, I was thinking about the store set-up."

He sat back in his chair. "Go ahead."

"It would be amazing to bring some nature into the store..." The hesitation in my voice hung heavy, but I rushed on. "Kind of like you've already done with the rock wall. Some sort of landscaping in the camping and hiking department. You could set up a tent, have trees, some sort of small wooded trail. Maybe a water fountain or stream near the water sports. I think it'd really add to the place."

I dared to meet his gaze. He stared at me, but I couldn't read the expression on his face.

I dropped my eyes to the floor. "Probably a stupid idea. Too much money. Forget I said anything."

Why had I opened my mouth?

"It's not stupid. It's brilliant."

I blinked. "What—really?"

"Yeah. When we started out, someone suggested a similar idea, but we tabled it because of the cost. Now, though...it might be a great way to set us apart from other chain stores."

"I guess it's kind of too late for this store..."

"No, I don't think it is. We can start small. Can you come up with a plan for your department and run it by me tomorrow?"

"M—me?"

"Yeah, Martin. You. It's your idea, and it's a good one. Run with it."

"Um, okay. I'll try."

He withdrew a wrapped square box the size of his hands from beneath his desk.

"Here. A little something to thank you, alongside your paycheck, of course."

I tried not to balk at the sight of the gift. "Really, Asher, I think a kitten is plenty gift enough for at least a year."

"How's the little gal doing?"

"She's a perfect companion. And she's living up to her name and helping me play some songs."

He raised his eyebrows at me. "I'd love to hear them sometime."

I shook my head, almost frantic at the thought. "I don't really sing for anyone besides my family. And at church. You're welcome to come hear me sing there anytime."

He tilted his head to the side and opened his mouth. I held my breath, hope stirring.

"I'd take you up on that, but I'd probably burst into flames the moment I crossed the threshold."

My insides dropped, like one of the shot puts at Josie's old track meets. Did he really feel he wasn't good enough to come to church? Or was it an excuse not to accept my invitation?

"Everyone's welcome," I squeaked.

He handed me the box, sidestepping my comment. I took it reluctantly. "I've never been comfortable opening gifts."

I remembered our growing up birthdays and slim Christmas mornings, that horrible moment when it was my turn to open a present and so many sets of eyes landed on me.

"It's just a little something for your hikes."

With horror, I thought of the pee pants. He wouldn't...oh, but I wouldn't put it past him. Insides trembling, I ripped the paper and breathed a sigh of relief at a picture of binoculars on the front of the box.

I'd set the display up yesterday, had admired them, but balked at the price tag.

"I can't wait to use them! Thank you."

He winked, causing my fingertips to tingle. "You're welcome."

I cleared my throat. "If you were thinking of gift ideas for the rest of the crew, I think I have one."

One corner of his mouth lifted in a half smile, highlighting a slight dimple beneath his freshly-clipped beard. "I wasn't, but what've you got?"

"They want a shot at the rock wall."

"Consider it done."

I grinned. "Great. When?"

"Next Wednesday night sound good?"

"I'll let them know."

"You're going to join them, aren't you?"

I laughed. "No way. I wouldn't know where to begin. Never mind venturing into something like that in front of a bunch of college students."

He wheeled around his desk. "Come on, then. I'll give you a lesson now."

"Oh, no, I don't think—"

But he was already out of his office, wheeling into the store and toward the back corner where the climbing wall and equipment stood.

"Asher!" I ran after him. "I don't think this is a good idea."

He kept wheeling, those impossibly strong arms making him glide fast across the laminate flooring. "Why not?"

"I—I don't know what I'm doing. I could slip and fall. I could break my neck."

"You're right." He slowed to the half wall where a line of harnesses and helmets stood, a variety of sizes.

I breathed deep. "Thank you."

"You don't know what you're doing. Yet. And I happen to be one of the best climbing instructors around. Do you trust me?"

"Well, yes. But that doesn't change the fact that I'm scared."

"You'll never know what you're missing if you don't stare fear in the face and take a risk or two once in a while."

Take a risk for once.

Amie's words came to me. Those she'd spoken when she'd begged me to take the radio station call. I had. If I'd pressed that red hang-up button, I never would have met Asher. Was that good or a bad? I supposed I wouldn't be standing here now, contemplating breaking my neck on this ridiculous rock wall, at least.

"I..." I licked my lips. My gaze fell to his wheelchair, then moved to his face.

Something in his demeanor darkened. "That's not how it happened."

"I—I'm sorry."

"What are you apologizing for, Martin?"

"Lizzie," I whispered.

"Lizzie."

Goosebumps broke out over my skin. "How did it happen?"

He sighed, looked at his legs. "I hate talking about it. You accused me of being a coward the other day? Well, this is one place I don't like dwelling on."

I shook my head. "Forget it, then. It's okay—"

"I was crossing the street outside my office in L.A. It was raining."

His words broke off, the sudden silence almost sacred in this big store. I waited, not knowing whether to speak or stay quiet.

He continued. "I swear I looked, but I was on the phone with my lawyer. I don't know, I wasn't paying attention. A car came out of nowhere and hit me."

I wanted to say I was sorry again, but my tongue swelled within my mouth.

He grimaced. "Most people think as you did—that I got hurt doing something dangerous. Something like climbing or bungee jumping or water skiing. But no. I was crossing the street to get my girlfriend some flowers."

"Oh, Asher."

"Don't pity me. Please. It doesn't help anything. There's no going back. Cruel twist of fate. One of God's jokes."

I wanted to assure him God didn't use human misfortune to amuse Himself, but sensed it wouldn't soften him in that moment.

"I wish it didn't happen to you."

"Yeah, that makes both of us." He grabbed a harness. "So, what do you say? Now that you know I didn't end up in this wheelchair from rock climbing—in fact, I'm happy to report we've had zero incidences of anyone in Paramount stores becoming a paraplegic from using one of our rock walls—are you ready to give it a shot?"

I was still scared. But I sensed it had been scary for him to open up about his accident, too. I could at least meet him halfway.

Suddenly, more than anything, I wanted to bring a smile to his face.

"I only have to go as high as I'm comfortable, right?"

"Right."

"And if that's three feet off the ground, you're okay with that?"

"I'll be disappointed, but I'm okay with it." He pointed to the section closest to him, straight up, with the slightest curve inward. "This is the easy wall. No crazy outward ledges and stuff."

"Okay, let's do this before I change my mind."

"Grab some shoes over there." I sought out my size and slipped my sneakers off, donning the Velcro climbing shoes. He held out the harness. "Step in and buckle up."

I did, pulling the gear over my shorts and buckling it first around each leg and then as tight as I could on the waist. As I did so, he did the same, shimmying a harness up over his own legs and body with some effort.

"Good?"

I nodded.

"Now grab that rope for me." He gestured to a blue rope hanging from the wall. I obeyed and handed it to him.

He wheeled up alongside me and checked my buckles, working the rope through a hook attached to my harness, knotting it expertly with strong movements. I swallowed as his fingers danced over the rope, so close to my stomach, his capped head and broad shoulders so near I could touch them. He smelled of spice and leather. If there was ever any doubt that his wheelchair would get in the way of attraction, it was dispelled in that moment. My legs weakened, betraying me.

Why, God? Why must I feel this way for a man who would only end up breaking my heart?

When he was done tying the rope, he rolled back a few feet. "Now, grab that other end."

I bent to pick up the other end of the blue rope. Both ran to the top of the wall.

He slipped that end through his own harness and slid it through a metal pulley.

"This is a grigri. It helps me secure you as you climb. I keep it tight and gather any extra rope as you ascend. If you ever slip, you're not going to fall because I got you." His liquid chocolate eyes fixed on me, making my heart speed up. "You can trust me. Nothing in this world is going to make me let you go, okay?"

I nodded, unable to speak. He didn't mean those words in any sort of romantic way, so why was I twisting them into something amorous?

"Okay, so start climbing. Use the red holds. They're the easiest."

I approached the wall, a small lump in my throat as I shook the foolish thoughts from my head.

I grabbed the first hold and pulled myself up. One notch at a time. I managed the first couple without too much of a problem, got up five feet sooner than I originally thought.

"You're a natural," Asher called.

His voice sounded much farther away than it had been only moments earlier when he promised to never let me go. I tried not to think of him looking up at my backside.

The wall made a slight jut to the right, and I hesitated. The rope grew tense, a gentle reminder that Asher held me secure, as he'd promised.

"There you go, easy does it. One hand, one foot at a time. You got this, Lizzie."

His encouraging voice pushed me onward and upward. Arm muscles straining, fingers burning. At first, I hadn't wanted to disappoint him, and then, as I neared the top—never once looking down—it was my own will that pushed me.

I was *actually* doing this. I was high—really high. And my body was strong, pulling me up this foreboding piece of wall, moving it higher and higher. In a way, it was like conquering a tall mountain.

My muscles burned with tension, but I continued, hungry now for the top.

When I reached it, I clutched tight to the holds. "I did it!" I said, still refusing to look down.

"You did great! Now ring the bell."

I looked up at the metal bell just above me. With one last oomph, I rang it, its triumphant melody playing out across the empty store. I let out a victory shout, and below me, Asher laughed.

Now that I'd accomplished the goal, all I could think about was getting my feet back on that floor. I glanced down, measuring what my first step downward might entail.

Far below me, I glimpsed Asher's red shirt. I gasped, pressing my forehead to the wall, my fingers clutching the sweat-dampened holds tight. *Dear Lord, help.* I was high. At least fifty feet up, but it felt so much higher from this view. Like a House of Mirrors, everything appeared different up here. My breaths came fast and jagged. Black fuzzy dots clouded my vision, and I clamped my eyes shut.

"Lizzie, you okay? All you have to do is let go with your hands and fall back. I have you."

Clinging tight, I forced my left foot off the hold and bent my right leg, tapping the air with my shoe, trying to find a foothold. It found nothing, and I panicked, bringing it back to its original spot. "I can't, Asher. Please. Please, help me."

"I have you. Hear me? You're not going anywhere. I'm going to get you down. Ready?"

I swallowed. His calm voice somehow made me braver. "Okay."

"You feel that tension on the rope there? That's me. I'm going to lower you down nice and slow. Be mindful of the wall so you don't smack against it. Are you ready? Let go nice and slow, Lizzie. I got you."

I tested out the surety of the rope by loosening my grip on the holds. It proved tight. Slowly, I leaned into it.

"There you go."

Eyes still clenched closed, I gripped the rope with my left hand and kept my right hand outspread to guide along the wall, my legs braced to bounce against the wall, should I hit it. Little by little, I descended until finally, blessedly, my foot hit solid ground. I collapsed onto the floor, had to stop myself from kissing it.

"You did it. You did great."

"I think 'great' would entail not having a panic attack at the top."

"I should have had you practice before you got so high. You seemed like a natural—I figured I should let you go for it."

I grabbed at the knot at my harness, my fingers pulling at it uselessly.

He reached a hand out. "Here."

I rose to my knees, still tugging at it. "I'm sure I can—"

But he grabbed hold of the rope, dragging me an inch closer. I couldn't stop myself from looking up into those chocolate eyes. Couldn't help but thrill that right now, in this moment, I was their sole object. He smiled. "You were amazing."

"I *was* amazing until I looked down."

We shared a laugh. He finished unknotting the rope and let it fall to the floor.

I didn't move away. "Thank you for talking me through it."

He reached out a finger, pushed a strand of hair from my face.

The gesture, so very gentle, made something jolt within me, like a single flawless note. It melted my limbs until I wasn't sure I'd be able to stand on my legs if I tried.

"I could tell you were scared."

My body hummed, alert for every move and word coming from this man. My gaze dropped to his mouth, and then flew back to his eyes after realizing what he must have seen. Part of me wanted to run. Part of me knew I should run. And yet another part of me never wanted this moment to end. "What about staring fear in the face and taking chances?"

"I guess losing your trust was one chance I wasn't willing to take."

❧ 2 1 ❧

Asher didn't realize the truth of his words until he'd spoken them aloud. When Lizzie was up there at the top of the wall, pleading for him to help her, he'd wanted nothing more than to fly up and take her in his arms. Soothe her fears away, not allow her one more second of anxiety.

But the closest he'd been able to do was bear her slight weight, bring her carefully down with the rope.

Now, his thumb caressed her smooth cheek. His breathing came a bit heavy. The urge to pull her close, sit her on his lap, and kiss her washed over him. She shifted slightly closer to him, and the hook of her harness clanked against the footrest of his wheelchair, reminding him why a kiss was asking for too much. Far too much.

He'd vowed not to be selfish, and it started here, with self-denial. He was not the best thing for Lizzie. She had so much going for her, so much potential. She'd climb again. She needed a guy who could climb alongside her, not just one who could hold her rope.

He blinked and pulled away. "There you go. All unknotted. You can leave the harness and shoes right over there."

Her mouth fell open, but she recovered quick. "Yeah, sure. Thanks."

"So, you ready to climb on Wednesday?"

"I don't know..." She unbuckled the harness and wiggled it off over her shorts.

"Sure you are. That was amazing. You were amazing. Don't you see?"

She hung up the harness. "See what?"

"You can do anything. You have your whole life ahead of you. You're young, beautiful, talented, smart. Lizzie, why are you hanging around in this small town waiting for life to pass you by? Don't you think you're meant for more?"

A soft smile shadowed her face. "You sound like Josie."

"One of your sisters."

"Yeah, the one who runs the bookshop. She always wanted to go out and do great, big things. Until she realized..."

"Realized what?"

"That everything that mattered most was already right in front of her."

Could he have mistaken the double-meaning behind her words? But of course. This shy, slip of a girl wouldn't be bold enough to say something so provocative to his face. It was his imagination. She didn't want him. Not on this side of his accident, anyway.

But that didn't mean he couldn't help her.

"If I ask you something, will you answer me honestly?"

She blinked. "I think so."

"What do you want from life?"

"That's a big question."

He shrugged. "It's an important one."

"Okay, I'll tell you, then." She leaned against the half-wall where she'd hung her harness. "I want to give people peace. I want to know the freshness of mountain air. I want to play in the flowers, give glory to my Creator by loving and creating. I never want to be far from my family because to me, family's what makes life worthwhile." She pressed her lips together before continuing. "I want to bring beauty into the world with my songs."

Her authenticity drew him like a bee to clover. The way she spoke—with such simple purity—made him long for something deeper and truer in his own life. He'd believed time had cut him off when it'd cast him in a wheelchair, but the way Lizzie spoke, such a thing as walking was secondary to a greater...something.

He allowed her words to swirl around him, tried to pull them apart. But just when he came to the edge of understanding, it slid from his fingers like sand through an hourglass.

"What about you?" Her face shone red, and he wondered if it was due to the words she'd spoken or his entranced stare.

He grasped for an answer more worthy than his true one, but came up short. In the end, he decided on honesty. "I think I've always thought the most important thing in life was building."

"Building?" Those fine eyebrows crept closer to her eyes.

He shrugged. "Yeah, you know, build this company. Build a name for myself. Build a long list of sports accomplishments. Build a Paramount store in each state. Build an empire."

She studied him for a moment. "I think you've done more than that."

He didn't answer. Was he lacking in her eyes now that he'd admitted his pathetic life?

"I read about the business online," she said.

He looked up. He could only imagine the pictures she'd seen of him on the cover of *Sports Illustrated*. A simple Google search brought up dozens of pictures of the great Asher Hill performing one daring sports feat or another. Strong. Healthy. *On top of the world.*

Did she wish she had met him then? Man, he wished he'd met her when he'd been whole. The old Asher. The old Asher would have lowered her down from that wall and taken her in his arms, kissed her breathless against the wall.

And probably would have scared the living daylights out of her.

"A portion of your proceeds go to charity."

He shrugged. Maybe she hadn't read about him, but his business. "I've always believed in giving back. Besides, it doesn't hurt with promotion."

"Why do you say stuff like that?"

"Because it's true."

"I don't think it is. I think you want to talk tough so people don't get close to you."

"Think whatever you want, Martin. My motivations are my own." The hum of the store electricity sounded in the silence. He swallowed. "What about you? Hiding away in a small town, hiding your music from everyone except your family? How can you ever bring beauty to the world if you won't share it?"

"You're right."

"I don't understand—what? I am?"

"Yeah, you are. I'm a coward. I've always been a coward. I don't have what it takes to make it out there with the competition and pressure. Maybe that's why I tell myself I'd rather live a simple life, one that doesn't involve taking risks and getting hurt."

He hadn't expected that. "You're wrong. You do have what it takes. You just need to prove it to yourself first."

A small smile flickered over her face before she pushed off the wall. "It's getting late. I should go."

"I heard you sing."

She stilled. "What?"

"At the hospital. At least I think I did. It was—you were beautiful."

She wouldn't look at him. "Asher, you were probably drugged up on painkillers. I'm sure it wasn't as great as you think you remember."

"Prove it, then. Sing to me now."

"No." She took a step toward the exit.

"Why not?"

"I—it would be weird. It's one thing to sing in front of my family or my students or at church or an occasional concert, but just you?"

"What if I show you my guitar skills?"

That earned him a smile. Had he ever appreciated a woman's smile as much as he did hers? Elise had flashed them like she was Miss America on a parade float, dishing out handfuls of candy. But he hadn't realized the sincerity they'd lacked, until now.

She tapped her chin. "What about we make a deal? I'll sing for you if you show me your guitar skills...and we go for a hike."

"Woman, I think you're forgetting something." He tapped the rims of his wheelchair. "This bad boy doesn't do wooded trails."

"There's a paved path up to Mount Battie. The view's beautiful. You should see it."

He didn't overthink the proposition. Could only concentrate on spending more time with her, however unwise and foolish it might be. He stuck out his hand. "Good old-fashioned handshake to seal the deal?"

She walked forward, stuck her hand in his. They shook for longer than necessary, tension playing between them, neither of them willing to let go.

"You know, Martin. You're really starting to grow on me. When I first heard you on the radio, I never would have thought—"

"About that." She slid her hand from his, leaving it suddenly empty and hollow. "I don't think you've met my sister Amie yet, but when you do, that entire radio station call is going to make a whole lot more sense."

❧ 22 ❧

I scrolled through my laptop, my gaze blurry from lack of sleep. I'd lain in my bed for hours after sketching out a crude drawing for my indoor landscape idea for the store. I'd found a great company that specialized in lifelike artificial trees, and I planned to talk to a representative tomorrow morning. My insides hummed to life at the thought of creating natural beauty within Asher's store.

They also hummed thinking of my time *with* Asher in the store. His strength while lowering me from that wall, his fingers moving nimbly at my waist to untie my rope, his thumb on my cheek.

He'd been about to kiss me. Why hadn't he?

I thought of the blonde on the back of the jet ski picture on his desk. Toned, tanned arms, a generous chest pressed against his back, perfect white teeth to go with that confident smile.

No doubt, I simply didn't measure up. Like his wheelchair could never measure up to legs used to conquer mountains and ski daring slopes, I would never measure up to someone like his old girlfriend.

You were beautiful.

He spoke of my music, of course, but the words had made my heart lift like a crescendo on the page of one of my music books. They didn't let me sleep, until finally, I'd propped my laptop on my desk and did a search on everything paraplegic.

I started with possible cures for spinal cord injuries, then went down a myriad of stray rabbit holes until I landed on a paraplegic man's YouTube channel. I watched video after video. His story of being paralyzed in a motorcycle accident. How he got in and out of his wheelchair, how he drove, how he swam, the accommodations in his home. I watched him propose to his girlfriend. And then more. He explained the way he traveled, went to the bathroom, got dressed, had sex, even how he and his wife had a child with the help of IVF.

By the time I was finished, I was completely encouraged, not only for myself, but for Asher. I had to admit, before I'd met him, I only pitied those with severe spinal cord injuries. It seemed they missed out on so much. In many ways, I thought they were half living. But as I read and watched and learned, I realized I'd been dead wrong.

Living wasn't defined by walking. Many who'd been handicapped insisted they'd become better people *after* their injuries.

I thought of Asher. No doubt he would have never given me a second glance while he was posing for pictures for *Sports Illustrated*. No doubt he had changed. Was it for the better? What would he say about it all? The man who insisted he'd erupt into flames if he came to church.

I sighed and closed my laptop, rolling over to click off my lamp and slide beneath the covers.

I needed to pull on the reins of whatever this was between me and Asher. And yet, how could he ever see the beauty and hope of God if no one ever bothered to get close enough to show him? I'd broken through a barrier, and now I was drawn in—could barely breathe around its power.

I remembered Asher urging me to climb the wall today, urging me to do something with my music. I liked that he didn't think of me as weak and frail, like my family so often did. He thought I was strong, capable. He saw my fear and called me out from it.

I wondered if, in some ways, he saw me better than anyone else.

I fell asleep, thinking about our planned hike the following Sunday afternoon. Mike and I would go Saturday, but Mike was the farthest face from my dreams.

And yet, I couldn't help but wonder if in getting close to Asher, I would be the one who would end up burned.

❧ 23 ❧

Asher thrust his gloved hands against the push rim of his chair, using his arm strength to propel himself up the steep incline of the mountain. A car drove past them, and he wondered if this was actually what Lizzie had in mind when she suggested the hike.

"I could have driven us up in my truck, you know."

She gave him a sideways smile. "What fun would that be? Besides, I thought you liked a challenge."

"I do. Just not sure this is exactly your ideal kind of hike."

She tilted her face to the sun. "It's a perfect kind of hike. We picked a beautiful day."

"I had a conference call with the team back in L.A. yesterday. They loved your indoor landscaping idea."

"They did?"

"Don't sound surprised. I can hardly wait to see it come to life. We ordered everything. It'll be close, but we might be able to get it done for opening day if the supplies come in time."

"That's great. I'd be happy to help any way I can."

"It's your project, Martin. I'm not taking over now. But if it turns out half as good as I think it will, I'm going to promote you as my interior designer. I'm thinking we should go big for the water sports section. Maybe a small waterfall."

Her mouth hung open. "Yeah...yeah, that would work."

They hiked in silence for another minute. The paved road turned steeper, and he pushed hard against his wheel rims, his arms burning in a satisfying way.

"Gone on any other hikes lately?" he asked through heavy breaths.

"I went yesterday."

"With the church guy." He didn't sound jealous, did he?

"His name's Mike." She blushed. Or was that exertion from the steep incline?

"Mike." He tried out the name. To his dismay, he couldn't find anything particularly offensive about it. "So tell me what you like about *Mike*."

"He's a friend, Asher."

"A friend you spend long periods of time alone with."

She shrugged. "I'm doing the same with you now, aren't I?"

And they were clearly just friends. "Good point."

They continued in silence. A bird flew overhead, the wind rustled the leaves, and the constant uphill strain really did give a good workout.

"I think we need to go kayaking next." He maneuvered around a dip in the pavement.

"You kayak?"

"One of my favorite sports since the accident. It's quiet, gives me time to think. It's kind of like my church, I guess."

"You pray out there?"

He laughed. "I'm not sure if you want to call what I do praying."

"Well, what would you call it?"

"Self-therapy?"

She smiled, kept walking. The slight swish of the lightweight fabric of her pants the only sound between them. "Are you angry at God for what happened?"

"Nah. Things happen, I get that. When you don't pay attention crossing the road, when someone drives like a moron, things are going to happen. I don't blame God. I kind of think, if there is a God, He's indifferent to my problems."

"Oh."

The one word spoke so much—surprise? Disappointment?

"What?"

"It seems sad to think of God like that."

"Just is, I guess. I'm a practical guy, you know? It's not like God's ever swooped down and showed Himself to me. Doesn't really make one difference or another to me."

She didn't speak for a moment. The lull in the conversation made her next words all the more potent. "Always the tough guy, right?"

"Fine then, Martin. Tell me all your thoughts on God."

"I don't know if I can, you're scaling this mountain pretty fast. Not sure we'll have time."

He liked the way she teased him often now. She was comfortable with him. It made something warm swirl in his chest.

"Give me the short version, then," he quipped.

Her hand went to that scar at the base of her neck, before it dropped back by her side, swinging with her strides. "I had cancer when I was fifteen. Thyroid cancer."

The information sent a jolt through his body. Fear, then a strange sort of camaraderie. She'd known what it felt like to have your body fail you. "Wow. That must have been terrifying."

"They got rid of it with surgery, so it could have been a whole lot scarier, but I was terrified. Before then, well, of course I believed in God. It was the way I was raised—my father was practically a pastor at our church. He was always preaching to us, instilling in us the importance of Heavenly things. But it wasn't until I was diagnosed with cancer that God became real to me. I mean, I *knew* Him." She glanced at him. "I know what you're thinking—that I created Him out of necessity during a trying time."

He *had* been thinking that.

"But I didn't. It was this crazy sense and stirring of peace when nothing else could calm." She grew quiet. "It was the Holy Spirit. I knew because..."

"Because..."

"It was right after my youth group at church prayed for me. We were reading about Jesus sending the Holy Spirit to His followers, and that's what we prayed for. Then they prayed for my health. I felt that peace for months, before and after my surgery. It held me in that time. I didn't make it up. In fact, I wish I *could* manufacture it, so I could get it back in such a powerful way whenever I wish." She pressed her lips together. "He visited me like a friend in that time—close and filling me with comfort. He rescued me."

He didn't know what to say. To voice his doubts seemed cruel. She seemed so certain.

"God sent that peace to me because I asked Him. It's as real as you and me, only it's kind of like the wind...I can't see it, but I can feel it."

He shook his head, blinked. "It would have been nice if He visited me like that after my accident."

"Maybe He knew you weren't ready."

Asher snorted. "Okay, enough of this. I like you better when you're not so deep."

"And I like you better when you're not so rude. You did ask me."

His arms burned. "Mind if we take a water break?"

They pulled off to the side in a patch of shade where they swigged their waters.

Lizzie raised her YETI to her lips. He watched her swallow,

his eyes on that thin scar at the base of her neck. Somehow, it was beautiful to him.

She lowered the water and capped it. "I could push you, you know. If you get tired."

He cringed. "Do me a favor, Martin."

"Yeah?"

"Never ask to push me again. If I need help, believe me—I'll ask."

"Okay. Sorry." She sat on a rock to retie her shoe. "You know it's not always easy on this side, either."

"This side of what?"

"Your wheelchair. I don't want to be awkward about it, but I want to be useful. It's hard to know what to say or do. You don't make it easy."

He swallowed. "Yeah, I know. I don't mean to give people a hard time. Sometimes they can be stupid about it, you know? Not you. You've never made it weird. So far." He shot her a grin.

"How do people make it weird? So I know what not to do in the future."

He grinned, tucked his water bottle in a pocket in the back of his chair. "Me pushing myself in my wheelchair is my independence. And I fought hard for it. When someone asks to push me, it's like they're saying I can't do it."

"That's not what I meant—"

"I know. But I'm telling you how it comes off."

She bit her lip. "I think I can understand that. My family still makes a big deal over me sometimes. Like if I'm tired or my color's off, they scramble around as if they expect me to keel over and die. I want them to think I'm strong, but I'm paranoid they're always looking at me as if I'm frail."

She did understand, better than he thought, too. He'd never much talked about these things—his therapists had labeled him uncooperative—but sitting here by the woods in the shade with Lizzie, it felt good to explain. Good to be understood.

He continued. "Sometimes my family acts like I'm too fragile to handle normal human interactions, because I can't walk. It's one of the reasons I moved out here. To get away from them protecting me. Smothering me."

"And you've always been independent, haven't you? Ready to fly off on your next adventure?"

He stared at her, and for a moment she scared him. He hadn't been this close to someone—this understood—in a long time, maybe ever, and it made him feel vulnerable. Something that certainly didn't complement his hard fought-for independence.

"So what else?" she asked. "What are some other things people do that annoy you?"

"Going out in public used to be super hard. People waiting for me yards away from a door so they could open it for me, parents grabbing their children out of my way as if I was going to run them over. What message is that sending to children? Stay away from the handicapped man. Be scared of him." He raked a frustrated hand through his hair. "I was going to the office one time, in the early days of getting used to my chair. The streets of Los Angeles are crowded, of course, so I knew it'd be a challenge. But this one kid—six years old or so, ran up to me as if I was the most intriguing thing in the world. His mom chased after him. I still remember the panic on her face.

"The kid asked why I was in a wheelchair, and before I could answer, his mother stepped in. Gave some nonsense answer about my legs being tired and I needed to rest. That stuff really gets to me because it's like we're training our kids to have a pathetic, fake view of what it means to have a disability."

Lizzie nodded. "Wow. You're right. I never thought of it like that."

Her sympathy gave him courage to keep speaking. "I've gotten used to it over time, but it grated on me in the beginning. My best friend wouldn't even deal with my injury, at first. Refused to visit me in the hospital. I get it, believe me. I know it's uncomfortable, but I was the one who woke up and found I couldn't walk, you know?"

"That's...horrible. I can't imagine going through cancer and having my best friend abandon me."

"Yeah, it sucked. More so when he decided to marry my girlfriend."

"Oh my goodness." A pained expression crossed her face.

He waved his hand in the air, pushed himself forward. "Sorry. Time to leave this pity party. Tell me something about you instead."

"My stories aren't half as interesting as yours."

"I doubt that. Tell me about when you were a kid. What'd you like to do?"

She put her hands behind her on the rock. "Me and my sisters used to put on a ton of plays. I acted a little, but Maggie and Josie were the stars. Sometimes, if there was a fight scene, we could get Bronson to join us. I mostly liked to play my guitar during the scene changes." She laughed out loud. "I used my Barbie 'Jam With Me Electric Guitar.' It was the only thing on my birthday list when I was seven. Mom wasn't happy at all. She was so against anything Barbie—thought it demeaned what true womanhood stood for. She never compromised on her convictions, so I was so surprised when I actually received it for a gift that year."

"I'd love to hear you play it sometime."

The corners of her mouth pulled downward. "I left it in the driveway one day. It got crushed by the car. I wanted to fix it, but Dad said it was no use. I found it in the church dumpster one Sunday."

Asher gritted his teeth, suddenly angry at Mr. Martin, a guy he'd never known, for putting that frown on Lizzie's face. "Why didn't you get it out and fix it? Or buy another one?"

She shrugged. "It was pretty busted. We didn't have extra money to replace toys we'd been careless with. Besides, I never went against what my parents thought best."

He whistled long and low. "Never?"

"Not that I can remember. You?"

"All the time. Can't tell you how many times I snuck out during high school. To be honest, my parents didn't deserve the grief I gave them. They were great, paying for skiing lessons, surfing lessons. Whatever I was into at the moment, they gave it to me."

"And that didn't make you spoiled?"

He studied her. "You know what, Martin? I think it probably did."

Asher's biceps and chest muscles burned as he crested the top of the small parking lot. He wouldn't admit it to Lizzie for the world, but this was *hard*. He hadn't pushed himself to such physical limits since well before the accident.

And it felt amazing.

Beyond the sparkling sea, curves of green trees sheltered Camden Harbor and its many boats. Past the inlet, Curtis Island sat like a small scoop of pistachio ice cream.

He'd seen a lot of mountain views in the course of his adventures, but for some reason this one appealed to him differently. Not terribly high up, it almost looked as if he could reach out a finger and swirl it in the pools of the Gulf of Maine.

Lizzie stood beside him, breathed a long sigh of satisfaction. He looked at her, then back to the view.

"Wow."

She grinned, revealing straight white teeth. "Right?"

They went past a large, circular stone structure, almost gazebo-like in appearance. He nodded towards it. "What's that?"

"It was built to honor the men and women of Camden who served during the first World War."

He nodded, took in the top of the mountain, vacant save for a few stragglers on the far side.

The wind tickled his skin and he thought of what Lizzie said about sensing God. Knowing He was there.

He looked at her, thin ponytail slapping her shoulder in the breeze. How had he ever thought her plain? In that moment, he glimpsed a beauty he couldn't begin to describe. Something soul-deep, something mysterious, something drawing him with a throbbing kind of foreign attraction. He thought of Elise. Her model perfect body and alluring face could not compare to Lizzie in this moment.

The thought snagged deep within him, creating an aching hollow in his chest where he assumed his heart had been. Were there different kinds of love? Here he was, nearly thirty years old, and in many ways half a man, but experiencing love for the first time. Not infatuation or lust...but something altogether deeper.

And then, she started singing.

"The way the sun covers the trees, the way the ocean swallows the beach."

The beauty of that voice consumed him. His skin prickled, his senses hummed. Her voice came alive, almost as if it went through him, filled him, cast him under a spell.

He held his breath, never wanting it to end, never wanting the sacredness of the moment to reach its conclusion. Verse after achingly beautiful verse melded into a simple chorus that caused an elation to rise within him. A glimpse of what it meant to live. And he couldn't get enough of it.

"The way the moon absorbs the dark, is the way you grabbed my heart."

She looked out toward the sea when she sang, didn't meet his gaze. But she must have sensed how he couldn't take his eyes off of her. How she pulled him in with that voice, those evocative lyrics, the purity of her fluid movements which, beneath the song became confident and sure. Sensual and exotic.

It opened up possibilities, stretched him in a way he hadn't thought possible, made him think the impossible *was* possible.

Perhaps there was a good God. How else could he explain the arrival of Lizzie into his life—an angel he'd almost overlooked.

"It's the way you...consume me. Never stop consuming me..."

When the last note in her voice faded, she hung her head, her confidence fast dissipating. "I figured it'd be easier if I just sang it instead of psyching myself up anymore. So there. I held up my end of the deal."

"That...that was the most amazing thing I've ever heard. What the blazes, Lizzie, how have you been hiding something like that?"

Her cheeks turned rosy. Oh, how he enjoyed the way he could make her blush.

"It's nothing. But I'm glad you didn't hate it."

"Hate it? How could anyone hate it? That's your own song?"

She bit her lip, nodded. "Not quite finished, but yeah."

His mind raced to the music agency a floor above the Paramount home office in L.A. He knew the top agent there. Not well, but enough to get Lizzie an audition. The guy—Dane, a friend of his parents—had sent a card when Asher was in the hospital, which is more than Lucas had done. He could still remember the card—a verse on it about God bearing burdens. If he could get Lizzie to sing for Dane, he could help make her dreams come true. She'd see the beautiful enormity of this world. She would see what she could offer it.

But she'd never fly out to L.A. At least not by herself. At least not without a good reason...one that probably wouldn't have anything to do with herself at all.

He made a quick decision, then. Maybe not entirely selfless on his part, but something about it seemed wholly right.

"Can I ask you something, Martin?"

"Lizzie," she whispered.

"Lizzie." It wasn't safe to get close, but he couldn't deny her the name each time she corrected him. Ironic, really—the guy who performed death-defying feats of courage in his former life was scared of one small woman. "Can I ask you a favor? Kind of a big one?"

"Uh-oh. Whenever you ask me for a favor we end up arguing."

"I'm going to ask anyway. I don't need an answer right now, but will you at least give it some thought?"

"I suppose..."

"Will you come to Los Angeles with me?"

Her eyes widened. "What?"

"I told my mom I'd go home and visit. There's this wedding..."

"You want me to go to a wedding with you?"

"Well, yeah..." True, he hadn't decided he was going until now, but that was beside the point. "It'd be nice to have some travel company. I'd love to show you the city. The flagship Paramount store is in L.A. We could talk interior landscaping. I'd really like your input." He was reaching now. Grasping for reasons why she should come along, why he needed her.

He almost laughed out loud. Mr. Independent, finally admitting he needed help.

But it wasn't only for him. Although it might bolster his pride if he showed up to the wedding with a pretty, talented girl on his arms. A girl that was quickly consuming his thoughts, night and day.

"Who's getting married?"

She hadn't said no. He'd take that as a good sign.

"You know that girl on the jet ski...the picture in my office?"

"Your ex-girlfriend's wedding?" Realization lit her features. "And your best friend? The one who didn't visit you in the hospital?"

"Yes."

She let out a breath. "I'm surprised you're going."

"I wasn't sure about it until...now." Until her song made the thought of new beginnings seem attainable. New life, beauty in the imperfect. "I think it might be good. For me, for Lucas and Elise. For my family. And I need to check in on the home office. I could really use a friend. A friend that...understands. Please, Lizzie?"

"Oh, Asher."

Was that pity in her voice? He prayed to God it wasn't. But if pity's what it took to get to L.A. and sing for Dane, then he'd pull out that card without hesitation.

"When are you going?"

You. Not *we*.

"Mid-July. Two weeks after the store opens."

"You said I could think about it."

He pressed his lips together before answering. "I did."

"Then that's what I'll do."

❦ 24 ❦

"And you actually told him you'd consider it?"

I slid a plastic tray of pink impatiens closer to me, hyperaware of Amie's words and judgment. My sister sat in one of the wicker chairs on the Orchard House veranda, legs tucked beneath her, drawing pad in her lap.

But her sketching fell by the wayside after I confessed Asher's recent request.

I answered with care, attempting to make my voice confident and assertive as I snuggled a few impatiens into a pot beside me. "Yes, I did. I don't think it's out of line. He needs a friend."

"You barely know him, Lizzie. It seems a bit drastic."

"What seems drastic?" Maggie opened the screen door and slumped onto a chair beside Amie, her hands on her round belly. "The boys should be off the bus any minute," she explained, her face pinching as she shifted in her seat. "I'm *done* with maternity pants. So, what's drastic?"

"Asher wants Lizzie to take a trip to Los Angeles with him."

Maggie sat up. "What? And you're actually considering it?"

Amie flung a hand up in the air. "That's what I said!"

Bets came up beside me and ran the length of her body

against my knee. I welcomed the distraction, pretended to be preoccupied with the kitten as I shed my gardening gloves and picked her up, allowing her to nuzzle my neck. I inhaled the late spring afternoon—the slight salt of the sea air carried on the wind mixed with the scent of Mom's baking cookies, and the annuals surrounding me. To the side and back of the bed and breakfast, greening orchards spread for acres—Bronson's pride and joy, the trees much healthier than last year.

"Bronson's been working hard," I said, trying for the change of subject.

My silence sobered my oldest sister. "Lizzie. What's up with this guy?"

I heard her unspoken question. *What's up with you?*

Could I blame her? I barely ventured outside Camden, never mind to the other side of the country. I was as surprised as my sisters that I entertained Asher's proposition.

"He's my friend." My voice sounded lame, even to my own ears.

Maggie pointed down the driveway. "There's Josie and Amos. Maybe she'll be able to talk some sense into this conversation."

I rolled my eyes. Josie slowed to a walk and pushed a sleeping Amos up the rest of the driveway in the jogging stroller. She spotted us and waved, weaving carefully through hostas, blooming phlox, and heirloom irises on the path to the porch. She set the brake on the stroller and collapsed onto the floorboards of the veranda.

"Boy, did that run feel good. I finally sent my story off to my agent, so I figured I'd reward myself."

Maggie and I exchanged a smile. Ever since Josie had landed an agent, we joked that she loved to include the fact in any sentence she could.

Amie shook her head. "*Run* and *reward* should never be in the same sentence. Ever."

I squeezed Josie's arm. "Congratulations. How do you feel about the story?"

She grinned, her eyes lighting up. "Good. But we'll see if we get any interest from publishing houses." She grabbed my hand. "Hey, now we can work on your song!"

Amie shook her head. "Lizzie's too busy to work on her music. She's planning a trip to Los Angeles. *With Asher.*"

Josie lolled her head to one side, squinted up at me. "Whoa, whoa, whoa. Back the truck up."

"I'm *thinking* about it."

"What? And when were you going to tell me?" Josie looked genuinely hurt, and a pinch of guilt started inside me. I always told her everything. We were one another's secret keepers. But she'd been so busy looking for house lots, finishing her book, running the bookshop, and taking care of Amos. And I'd always been around to cheer her on. But lately, I'd been so busy with Paramount, landscaping Orchard House, finishing up my music classes at the school, and hikes with Mike and yesterday with Asher, that it seemed I hadn't a moment to seek Josie out for a good heart-to-heart.

Or perhaps I hadn't wanted to seek her out. Hadn't wanted to open up, for fear my sister would knock the idea down like Amos knocked over the tower of blocks I sometimes built him.

"He only asked me yesterday." I hated my defensive tone, hated that my sisters ganged up on me.

"What exactly is going on between you two?" Amie tapped her chin.

"Right. And what about Mike?" Maggie wiggled again in her seat.

The screen door popped open. Mom stood with a tray of chocolate chip cookies. "Putting some out for the guests. Tripp and August are coming by to put a final coat of paint on the ceiling. Thought I'd leave these out for them. You girls want any?"

Josie dove for the plate, taking a large, soft cookie and shoving it into her mouth. "Mom, did you know about Asher inviting Lizzie to Los Angeles?"

I groaned, lay my head back against the rail of the veranda.

Mom slid out onto the porch. "No..."

"And she's actually considering it!" Amie said.

I held up my hands. "You guys are making way too big a deal of this. He doesn't like to travel alone. He's going to his best friend's wedding and asked me to go with him. I think he feels... comfortable with me."

"Obviously," Josie said through a mouthful of cookie.

I opened my mouth to tell them that Asher needed my support. That his old girlfriend was the one marrying his best friend. That he heard me sing and thought I had real talent. That I was counting the hours until I saw him again.

But no. I could never tell my family any of that. They would study and decipher my words like one of Aunt Pris's crossword puzzles. Break it down until I wanted to melt into the floorboards of the veranda.

Mom studied me. "Honey, Asher seems like a very sweet guy. But how well do you know him? This seems like a big step."

Tripp's Colton Contractors truck pulled up the driveway. Time to wrap up this awkward conversation. "It's not a step, Mom. It's nothing. It's a friend helping a friend."

But did I believe that? Hadn't I just admitted to myself that I felt strongly for Asher?

As much as I tried to wrangle my feelings, they were only that —feelings. In the end, they weren't dependable. They were fleeting, obsessive, even. What would happen if I chased after them? We'd likely end up as two people disillusioned by an attraction, and disappointed by differing values.

I thought of our conversation on the hike. I had poured my heart out to Asher about my faith and he had shot me down.

I like you better when you're not so deep.

But laughing over a wheelchair joke or sharing a rock climbing adventure gone wrong wasn't all I ever wanted to talk about. I thought a lot, about big things. Things that were important to me. Things like faith. If Asher couldn't share them with me, what did we really have but a few shared hobbies, a few laughs, and what was likely a fleeting attraction?

Then again, I wasn't signing up to marry the guy. I wasn't even dating him. I only wanted to help him get through what would no doubt be a super hard wedding.

"Mom's right. We hardly know him!" Josie said.

Tripp, August, and Bronson came around the front of the house. I contemplated escaping to my room.

"We having a pow wow?" Bronson, dirty from working in the orchards, wiped a hand on his jeans before reaching for the plate of cookies.

"We most certainly are," Amie said. "Lizzie wants to go to Los Angeles with Asher."

"Asher who?" Tripp grabbed a cookie.

"The radio guy?" Bronson paused, cookie half-raised to his mouth. "No way."

"I think we need to get to know him better, Lizzie. I saw him the day he gave you Bets. You were almost in tears." Now Josie looked with pity on me. "Oh, I know! Invite him to help us move Maggie and Josh on Saturday. We're ordering pizza after. We can all hang out."

"Grill him, you mean," Bronson interjected. "Run a background check, do a personality test, ask about his intentions."

"Wow, you guys are rough." August reached for a cookie. "Just because half the Martin girls fell for the men next door doesn't mean Lizzie shouldn't venture out." He squeezed my shoulder. "Good for you, Liz."

"Wait." Amie peered up at August from where he stood next to her. "*Half* the Martin girls did not fall for the men next door."

August winked at Amie. "Admit it, babe. You're crazy about me."

"Ew, you call me *babe* again, and it's the last time you'll ever call me. Got it?"

August grinned, blond hair falling in front of one eye. "Sure thing, *honey*."

"Why's he want you to go to California, anyway?" Bronson asked. "Some Paramount convention?"

"It's for a wedding," Maggie said.

"A wedding!" Bronson shook his head. "You know what happens at weddings, don't you? People get caught up in the romance. They drink too much. They do things they regret later."

"And how do you know so much about it?" Josie teased.

"I know. And I know that I don't trust this Asher fellow the length I can throw him—in his wheelchair."

"That was rude, Bronson," Maggie said. "What's he ever done to get on your bad side?"

"He was an idiot to Liz on the radio. And, I Googled him, dug deep. Before his accident, he was a regular playboy. Now that he can't walk, he's going to try and settle down with a sweet, unsuspecting girl like our Lizzie? I don't think so. And what about Mike?"

Maggie sat up. "Yeah, Mike's a nice guy. And you have so much more in common—including your faith."

"I think we should at least invite this Asher to moving day. We can't speculate without spending some time with him." Josie said.

"Oh yeah, great introduction. 'Hey, we're Lizzie's family. Nice to meet you. Now grab that box.'" Amie rolled her eyes.

"Enough!" I shouted the word above my rowdy family

The group fell silent. I swallowed, grappling for words. "I know you all love me and are acting out of concern, but I am almost twenty-four years old—plenty old enough to make my own decisions about who I date, or don't date, and plenty old enough to decide if I want to go on a trip or not."

Tripp slapped August's stomach with the back of his hand and gestured toward the door. They slid into the house.

"I'll invite him for pizza after we move Maggie and Josh on Saturday. But the store opens on Friday, so he's still going to be busy. Whether he accepts or not, when it comes to me going to Los Angeles, I'm making my own decision."

I strode into the house with Bets on my heels, leaving my stunned family on the porch behind me.

Somewhere along the way, I associated them, and my little world and my little town with safety. I never questioned that my life would be a simple, peaceful one. There was no need to leave, no need to take unnecessary risks. All I needed to fulfill my purpose was right in front of me.

And I never questioned any of my logic—not until Asher Hill came along.

❦ 25 ❦

I stood off to the side of the fountain in front of Paramount and watched Asher, microphone in hand, making a short speech to the generous crowd in the parking lot.

Navy blue and white balloons—the color of the Paramount stores—blew in the breeze from their lamppost anchors. The pristine landscape stood crisp against the building. Hydrangeas full and green with small blossoms sat at the base of the tiered wall. Colorful annuals and ornamental grass surrounded the gurgling fountain. The scent of fresh mulch baking in the sun lingered in the air.

Asher sat in his wheelchair in jeans and a gray polo shirt that highlighted those toned arms. A recent tan—whether from our hike or his kayaking—gave his skin a healthy glow. My stomach jumped as I watched him in his element, opening his store in front of the crowd.

"I'd like to invite the entire team up here to cut the ribbon with me." He gestured to the men and women—most of them on the younger side, whom Ryan had hired to run the store. And to me. When I hung back, he crooked a finger at me, and though I wanted to shrink into my seat, I pushed my legs forward. Asher introduced his new manager to the crowd, then the various team leads, including me. "Lizzie Martin, ladies and gentleman! She's not only responsible for our camping and hiking department, but for the beautiful natural display inside."

My cheeks warmed. The display *was* beautiful. The artificial birch and pine trees I'd found created an ethereal paradise for a nature lover. I'd set up a tent to display beneath the trees, padded by realistic ground covering. I'd add a few finishing touches—a squirrel or a bird—as soon as I could find the quality I sought.

Asher continued. "Lizzie will also be leading some group hikes courtesy of the store, so be certain to check in with her or sign up on our website."

Applause rose up among the crowd and I ducked around the ribbon, trying to hide behind the many Paramount employees. Asher craned his neck, though, waving me forward. I stood behind him. He shook his head. "We have photo ops right now. I want you on the right of me, Ryan on my left."

Though I wasn't thrilled, I obeyed and pasted on a smile while cameras flashed and clicked, Asher posing with scissors hovering over the fluttering ribbon. Finally, he snapped the scissors down, and the two sides of the ribbon fell to the ground. A huge round of applause filled the air.

"Thank you for your support, Camden!" Music came from a DJ tent off to the side. "I invite you to grab a drink and some appetizers out here, then head inside and spend some money on your next adventure."

The crowd laughed before dispersing.

I spotted Josie, Tripp, and Bronson and went over and hugged them. "You guys are so sweet to come."

"Are you kidding? This is huge!" Josie nodded toward the store. "I can't wait to see inside. Asher's obviously pleased with what you've done. You've worked hard enough."

"Any baseball stuff in there?" Tripp craned his head toward the store, customers crowding through the entrance. "I want to get a glove for Amos."

Josie squinted at him. "He hasn't had his first birthday yet, Tripp."

He slung an arm around her shoulders and squeezed. "Got to start him sometime, right?"

I watched them, a familiar yearning in the pit of my belly. I'd been over-the-moon happy for Josie when she finally admitted the depth of her love for the boy who'd chased after her throughout our growing up years. Seeing them now, married, planning to build a home, living life together and chasing dreams, it stirred hope in my chest that someday, the same thing could happen for me.

"And I want to check out the kayaks. I've been itching to get on the water." Bronson waved his hand at the store. "It's exciting you're a part of this, Lizzie."

"Thanks, Bron." Whatever tension was between us from our conversation on the veranda at the beginning of the week had dissipated.

Something behind me caught his gaze. "And I get to finally meet your friend."

I turned to see Asher, who rolled toward us. My skin grew hot at the sight of him seeking me out—seeking us out. Not to mention the thought of him meeting more of my family.

"Bronson, *please* behave yourself." I spoke out of the side of my mouth.

"Hey." Asher came to a stop beside me. "You must be Lizzie's family." He held his hand out to Tripp first. "I'm Asher. Thanks for coming."

Tripp shook his hand, introduced himself. "Great place you got here."

"Lizzie was a big help. She's got talent."

Asher moved to Josie, who shook his hand also. "Josie. Lizzie's favorite sister."

I rolled my eyes.

"Don't worry, she already told me." Asher gave me a wink.

"And I'm Bronson, her only brother." He stuck his hand in Asher's, pumping hard.

When he finally let it go, Asher shook out his hand. "That's quite the grip you have there. I'll bet you'd do great on our rock-climbing wall inside. Want to give it a go?"

"Do I!" Bronson's gaze flicked back to me. "I mean, that'd be sweet."

Josie and I shared a giggle. We followed Asher and Bronson into the store, where my family's *oohs* and *ahhs* stirred a note of pride within me that I wasn't sure how to interpret. Yes, I had a small part in setting up the store, but this was more. A pride on Asher's behalf, maybe? For in some way, a small part of me was becoming tied up with him.

The thought both terrified and comforted. What would it be like to share someone so fully that their accomplishments and dreams became my own? That it was difficult to tell where one of us began and the other ended? Like Tripp and Josie. Like Maggie and Josh. Sharing the ups and downs of life together. Knowing that, no matter what, you'd never be alone because you'd always have one another.

I stood beside Asher as Bronson, Tripp, and Josie took turns climbing the rock wall, skilled Paramount employees holding their ropes. Ryan approached Asher to ask a question. Some men from the Chamber of Commerce sought him out to introduce themselves and congratulate him on Camden's newest business. A couple of customers wanted their picture taken with him. One boy wanted an autograph.

"Go," I said after a while. "Mingle. Be with your people. I can entertain my family."

"I kind of thought you were my people," he said, a twinkle in his laughing eyes. He was happy. The store had made it. Was that the only reason for his joy? Could I be audacious enough to think I had anything to do with that look in his eyes?

"Lizzie!"

I turned to see Mike, and a moment of panic overtook me. Why? Why was it bad that two of my friends met one another?

He came up to me, gave me a quick hug. "This place is great. Look, I found one of those backpacks you were telling me about with the water pouch."

"That's awesome." I turned to Asher. "Asher, this is Mike. Mike, Asher."

They shook hands. The twinkle in Asher's eyes turned to a hard glint. I wondered then the depth of his feelings for me, if there was more to the invitation to Los Angeles than him only needing a friend during a difficult time.

Asher didn't let go of Mike's hand. I wanted to scream from the amount of testosterone floating around the place.

When he finally let go, he said, "And you're Lizzie's..."

"Friend." He gave me a shy glance. "More than friends, maybe. We're kind of dating."

Asher pasted on a smile. "Dating, huh? Lizzie didn't mention that."

"She didn't?" He looked at me, unsure. "It's not dating exactly. Hiking a lot. But I was kind of hoping—"

"You want to give the rock wall a try there, Mike?" Asher asked.

Mike let out a whoosh of air. "Sounds fun." He turned to me. "You want to try, Lizzie?"

"Oh, she's a pro. I helped her out on it the other day." The corner of Asher's mouth twitched.

I looked down at my sundress. "I—I'm actually not dressed for it. But go ahead. Bronson's right over there."

Mike took off. I watched his tall form approach the half wall of climbing equipment. A pretty young Paramount employee with long red hair approached him.

"What was that about?"

Asher looked at me, complete innocence painted on his face. He wasn't fooling anyone. "What?"

"You know."

"Afraid I don't."

"He's a good guy." I didn't want to hurt Mike. I didn't want to hurt anyone.

We stood in silence for a moment, watching the climbers before he spoke again. "Have you sung for him?"

"We sing together in church almost every week."

"No. Have you ever sang, just for him?"

I swallowed. "No."

He smiled. "Good. Don't. Because then he'll really fall in love with you."

⚜

BECAUSE THEN HE'LL REALLY FALL IN LOVE WITH YOU?

What was he thinking? Why didn't he carve out his heart and serve it on a platter to the woman beside him? What was wrong with him? This was *his* night. The opening of *his* store. The culmination of months of hard work. He didn't need to make a royal idiot of himself.

He scrambled for a change of subject. "You give my invitation any more thought?"

She bit her lip, her color returning to normal after his last remark. "About L.A.?"

"I can't recall any others..."

"Didn't you ask me to go kayaking with you?"

He pointed a finger at her. "You're right. I did. So what's it going to be?"

"Yes."

"On the kayaking or on California?"

She smiled, swaying slightly. His gaze dropped to her lithe

figure beneath the yellow and white sundress she wore. "Yes on the kayaking. Still thinking on California."

"I'll take it. But I'll need to know by the end of next week. I have to RSVP for the wedding." Who was he kidding? He didn't want to give either Elise or Lucas the pleasure of preparing for his arrival. Much better to show up and shock them, let them be the ones on the receiving end of surprising news.

"My family wants to meet you." She put her hands behind her back and swayed again. The simple movement drove him to distraction.

He forced his eyes to her face. "Haven't I met them all?" He counted on his fingers. "Your mom and Bronson, Josie and Tripp... how many more are there?"

"Well, there's my other two sisters, Amie and Maggie. Maggie has a family—her husband Josh and twin boys, Davey and Isaac. Aunt Pris, of course. And then there's Finn, the birth father of Josie's son. August is Tripp's brother and Amie's kind of boyfriend. Oh, Esther is practically part of the family, too. She's Aunt Pris's close friend."

He raised an eyebrow. "Is that all?"

"I think so."

"And you need me to meet every one of them before you make a decision about L.A.?"

"Not exactly...but my family's pretty close. It's more of a consideration. They can't fathom I'm thinking about saying *yes* to your invitation. They're not sure if you're trustworthy. I think meeting you would put them at ease."

"Is that what's up with your brother? He's not *at ease*?"

She grinned. "Distracting him with the rock wall was a smooth move."

"When do I get to meet them?"

"Pizza tomorrow night? We're moving my oldest sister's family into her new house. We should be done by six."

"You want me to come after all the hard work's done?"

She shrugged. "Josie wanted you to help, but Amie thought it was a poor way to invite you to meet the family."

He shook his head. "I'm flattered they've put so much thought into this."

Lizzie placed a light hand on his arm. It stirred warmth inside him. He hoped that Mike guy saw it.

"You should have been there. I thought they were performing an intervention or something."

He laughed. "Okay, I better make an appearance, then. What time tomorrow? I'll bring my truck. We can load it up."

"Eight." She took out her phone, started tapping away. "I'll text you her address."

A lady in her forties approached Lizzie—probably someone wanting to sign up for one of her hikes.

"Great," he said, turning over what he'd agreed to in his head.

Nothing like meeting the family on moving day. If he'd been in his old state—strong as a horse, able to lift and move furniture and boxes without breaking a sweat—it would have been an ideal time to introduce himself. Now, he imagined what the day would entail. Him, waiting outside the house for someone to hand him a small box or lamp—something he could wheel to his truck or the moving van. He'd watch guys like Tripp and Bronson with their robust working legs move the bulk of things while he sat around twiddling his thumbs with Lizzie's sisters.

He sighed deep, studied Mike climbing up the wall alongside Bronson. Tall and lanky, he'd make it easily. His calf muscles stretched as he reached for one red hold and...oops, slipped.

Asher tried not to take pleasure in seeing the guy fail. It was childish, really. And hadn't he vowed to put selfishness aside, to seek not his best interest, but that of Lizzie's?

He turned the thoughts over in his head, convincing himself that inviting Lizzie to L.A. *was* in her best interest. She didn't know it yet, but he'd already called Dane and set up an appointment a few days after the wedding. Having her company was the only thing making the thought of attending Lucas and Elise's wedding bearable. But it wasn't solely a selfish move.

And he'd take part in moving day tomorrow. No matter how humiliating or degrading. He'd do it all, because Lizzie was worth it.

❧ 26 ❧

Asher tucked his legs into his truck and shut the door. The moving van, Tripp and Josh's trucks, Maggie's SUV, and Mrs. Martin's car had already left the old house, but he'd taken a bit longer to get his wheelchair in the truck.

"Thanks for helping." Lizzie sat in his passenger seat, a high ponytail in her hair, a loose pink tank top on. He'd watched her discreetly the entire morning. Her thin, strong frame. Those toned arms. The strap of a sports' bra that kept appearing at her shoulder. He tried to behave himself, but it wasn't exactly the work of moving that caused him to break out in a sweat.

"I'm not sure how much help I was," he said.

"Are you kidding? We couldn't have moved the fridge without those extra set of dollies you brought. And another truck was a huge score. Maggie and Josh are grateful."

"So, two down. How many more people do I need to butter up before you agree to California? Ten? Twelve?"

She grinned and stared out the window as they neared a stop sign on Route 1. She must have sensed his gaze though because she looked at him. "What? Do I have spinach in my teeth? I had an omelet this morning."

He brought his eyes back to the road. "No. No spinach. I just like having you here, in my truck. I like driving you around."

"I can see why my family wants me to be careful around you." She wagged a finger at him.

"You can, huh?"

"Yeah. You're a smooth talker. I'll bet what Bronson read about you online is true, too."

A growl started in his throat. He had enough local gossip to go with his name and his store to fill up a Barnes & Noble bookshelf. "Better tell me what he said."

"That you were a playboy before your accident. A ladies' man. Something like that." She said it like it didn't matter, but he wasn't fooled. And why shouldn't it? She was pure as the white-driven snow. He, on the other hand...not so much.

He thought of lanky Mike. Probably the farthest thing from a playboy any man could get. A true gentleman. Why then, did Asher insist on fighting for this space in Lizzie's life?

He dragged in a breath. He'd paused too long already. Better stick with the truth.

Sudden exhaustion pulled at his frayed edges. Just thinking about the way he used to live exhausted him. Embarrassed him.

"There was a time, during college and before Elise, that I was a bit of a...what did you call it? Ladies' man, if you want to put it politely."

He didn't miss her slight cringe.

"But Elise changed that?"

He drummed his fingers on the steering wheel. "Elise distracted me. She took me seriously, made me feel less aimless. Does that make sense?"

"I think so."

"Elise kept me...interested. Things were never boring with her. I didn't want to chase after other women."

"You loved her."

"No. No, I don't think I did."

"It sounds like you did."

"Infatuation and love are not the same thing."

The truck glided along Route 1, massive houses and sparkling sea to their left.

"What about you? Have you ever been in love?" He gave her a quick glance, knowing he'd miss one of her blushes if he didn't look quick.

He wasn't disappointed.

"No. I don't think so."

"You don't think so?"

She glanced at him, but their eyes caught, a millisecond of infinitesimal time that seemed to speak more than any words could say.

She broke their connection. "As I said, I don't think so." Her tone told him to back off. "The store did well yesterday."

If she wanted to change the subject, he'd let her. "Thanks for being there. Oh, that reminds me. Tomorrow, kayaking trip?"

"I have church in the morning. Later in the day?"

"Sure."

"And that reminds *me*. You never held up your end of the bargain."

"Excuse me?" He couldn't keep a smile from his face, as he much preferred this to serious questions about his past.

"I sang for you. You hiked the mountain, but I'm still waiting on my little guitar show."

"I was hoping you'd forget."

"Not a chance." She pointed to where he should take his next turn.

"Okay. Tonight. After pizza."

"Deal."

THERE WAS ONLY SO MUCH YOU COULD DO IN A WHEELCHAIR ON moving day without feeling you were more hindrance than help. And if you felt like that, chances are everyone else felt that way, too.

Asher wheeled over the loose gravel to grab another box from the bed of his truck. He balanced the square labeled *Nativity* on his lap and wheeled toward the back door of the house. His wheelchair kicked up rocks as he went, and he waited at the door for someone to come and relieve him of the box, since Maggie and Josh's door wasn't wide enough for him to roll through.

He'd never admit it to Lizzie, but this was the worst sort of punishment. Not being able to help, not being able to do what everyone else could. Walk inside a simple door. Watching Tripp and Josh and August and Bronson lift refrigerators and bureaus and tables and beds. On the outside, looking in—nothing new, but something he'd never get used to.

His therapist had once suggested connecting with a group of people with disabilities. Friendships could form. Bonds could be made. One didn't have to succumb to loneliness.

But Asher had never ventured to take that step. Part of him didn't want to align himself further with the disabled population. Part of him didn't want to bother. Better to be alone than in some pitiful support group.

Now though, he doubted the wisdom in that. Today, he could understand how an alignment with others might help him feel a bit less alone, a bit more understood.

Josh came around the corner of the kitchen, took the box from Asher. "Thanks, man. Really appreciate your help."

Asher gestured to the house. "Lizzie said you did a total renovation. It looks great."

Josh looked back inside the house, his stance tall. "It was my dream. Maggie was patient with me."

"Lucky guy."

"You bet." Something behind Asher caught Josh's gaze. "Boys!"

Asher turned to see Maggie and Josh's twins wrestling and rolling on the ground. They looked up at the sound of their father's voice, one pinned to the ground, the other on top of his brother.

"Hands off each other."

"Isaac started it!" One of them, slightly bigger than the other, called back.

Josh sighed. "I better go talk to them."

Asher held up a hand. "Let me, if it's okay with you. You still have a lot to bring in and I'm not much use out here keeping your gravel company. I have a brother, so I know a thing or two about how this stuff works."

Josh shot him a grateful smile. "Sounds good to me. Thanks, Asher."

Asher turned and wheeled with purpose to the grassy hill where the boys wrestled. They eyed him curiously.

He stuck out his hand to the bigger one. "I don't think we've met yet. I'm Asher, Lizzie's friend."

"My name's Davey." He jerked his thumb in his brother's direction. "This is Isaac."

Asher shook Isaac's hand while the boy's insightful blue eyes studied him.

"Are you Aunt Lizzie's boyfriend?" Davey asked. "Mommy says she thinks you want to be."

Asher cleared his throat to keep from laughing. "She did, did she?"

Davey nodded. "Uncle Tripp was Aunt Josie's boyfriend before they got married. Are you going to marry Aunt Lizzie?"

He nearly choked on that. He sure as Hades hadn't realized what talking to the twins entailed when he volunteered. "No, no. I'm not marrying your Aunt Lizzie."

"Don't you like her?" Isaac asked. "She takes real good care of you when you're sick. When Mommy and Daddy went away and my diabetes was bothering me, Aunt Lizzie took care of me." His eyes, which seemed to take everything in, dropped to Asher's legs. "Are you sick? Aunt Lizzie would take good care of you."

Oh, man. These kids might wreck him.

He sniffed hard, trying to come up with a decent answer. It'd been a long time since he'd been around seven-year-olds. About twenty-two years, anyway, when he was one himself.

"I'm not sick. But I can't walk. I was in an accident and when I woke up, my legs didn't work. Now, my wheelchair is like my legs."

Davey squinted at the wheels. "They sure don't look like legs."

Isaac punched his brother in the arm. "He means they help him walk. Or go places. Right, Mr. Asher?"

He grinned. "Right."

"Does it hurt?" This from Isaac. It was nice to speak to children honestly about his disability without well-meaning parents barging in to try to spare his emotions.

Asher shook his head. "I can't feel anything."

"Can I pinch you?" Davey asked.

Isaac punched his brother's arm. "That's not nice."

Asher shrugged. "It's okay, go ahead."

Davey grabbed a hold of Asher's calf and pinched. He looked up at him. "You feel that?"

"Nothing."

He seemed to put every ounce of effort behind it. "What about now?"

"Nope."

"Wow! I was pinching as hard as I could!"

Asher laughed. "Told you. I can't feel anything." No pain. No pleasure.

He thought of Lizzie sitting in his truck on the way over here, and a strange ache of longing filled him. A longing that would never be realized in his lifetime.

"It doesn't hurt, but I'll bet your feelings are hurt sometimes." This from Isaac.

Asher studied him. "You're a pretty perceptive kid, aren't you?"

"Isaac has diabetes, so he knows about hurt feelings," Davey explained. "He can't eat like everyone else, so sometimes he feels left out."

That earned another push from his brother.

"I guess I do feel left out sometimes." Asher supposed venting his true emotions might be worth it if it meant curtailing another combat session. "Mostly, I miss what I used to be able to do. Walking and bicycling and rock climbing. Stuff like that."

Isaac nodded. "I miss being able to eat as much pizza and cake as I wanted. I miss filling my plate up with food without Mommy having to count the carbs on it."

Asher's heart pinched. "I think we can both understand being a little different than everyone else, huh?"

A small smile pulled at Isaac's mouth. "Yeah. I guess so."

"And it helps to have a brother that understands, like I bet your brother does." Okay, he was pulling this out of thin air, now. But he did tell Josh he'd talk to the boys about the fighting.

"I get Isaac juice when his sugar's low," Davey volunteered. He studied Asher. "Do you have a brother?"

"I do. A younger brother named Ricky."

"I'm the older brother, too," Davey said.

"Only by four minutes!" Isaac argued.

"Does your brother take care of you even though he's the younger brother?" Davey asked.

Asher swallowed. "To tell you the truth, I'm used to watching out for him." Only he hadn't been doing so swell a job the last couple of years. The last several years, really.

"Dad says that's what brothers do—take care of each other."

"Your dad sounds like a smart guy."

"He is. He used to be a teacher, but now he builds stuff." Davey kicked the grass with his foot. "You want to play with us?"

"Depends. What are you playing?"

"Well, we were doing somersaults down the hill and seeing who could do the most, but we had trouble counting."

Asher looked at the smooth, grassy hill opposite them. "I'm afraid somersaults are on the list of things I can't do anymore. Right up there with backflips and handstands."

The boys laughed.

"But I bet I can move down that hill pretty fast in my chair. You guys want rides?"

They cheered, and he lifted Davey onto his knee, instructed him to hold tight while he gave himself a start and propelled his wheelchair down the hill.

The little boy's laughter flipped something within him. As Asher coasted down the hill, the wind flying in his face, a laugh bubbled up in his own throat. Pure and filled with joy, unmonitored. Was it the first time since his accident?

With the rush of wind came a memory from childhood of sledding down a hill with Ricky. His brother had been in front of him, holding tight to the sled pulls, Asher in the back grasping onto Ricky.

"Do you think if we go fast enough, we can fly, Asher?" Ricky asked before they'd shoved off.

Old enough to know such a thing wasn't possible, but young enough to dream that anything *was* possible, Asher had put on a serious face, contemplated the best way to help his brother fly.

He'd got out of the sled to pile snow at the bottom of the hill and smooth it out, creating a slick runway that, if they hit right, would propel them into the air.

Asher'd given the sled a running push and jumped on at the last possible second, like a bobsled runner. The sled had careened down the icy hill. He could still remember Ricky's laughter. They hit the jump and sailed through the air, weightless. When they landed with a hard thud and skidded to a stop, Ricky jumped off the sled, fist in the air. "We did it! Asher, you made us fly."

Helping his brother fly had always been important to him.

Sure, he hadn't been as involved in Ricky's life while Asher was building Paramount, but the kid was older by then. He had their parents. It wasn't like Asher had abandoned him.

And after his accident...well, what could one guy do? He'd found himself stuck to the seat of a wheelchair, unable to walk. Never mind helping someone else find their wings when his own had been so cruelly clipped.

Davey jumped off Asher's knee and ran up to Isaac. "You have to try that! We were going faster than Lightning McQueen!"

Asher smiled, starting back up the hill. Davey continued to gesture, talking a mile-a-minute to his brother. The only thing that would make the boy's joy complete was if Isaac could share in the experience as well. If they could fly together.

Asher thought of Ricky, without a job or a license, living in their parents' home. Making poor decisions. Decisions that, if continued, would lead to more pain. He used to be his brother's hero. The one who enabled him to fly.

Was it still possible to help his brother? To be his hero from the seat of a wheelchair?

He looked at Davey's brown eyes, lit with excitement, as if anything was possible. And Asher chose to believe that maybe, even without the use of his legs, flying was possible.

I fingered the slight dip of the scar at the base of my neck, staring out at the heart-melting sight of Asher giving Isaac a ride in his wheelchair down the back hill of Maggie and Josh's new home. At the top, Davey jumped and cheered.

Once they reached the bottom, Isaac hopped off and high-fived Asher.

Mom came up beside me, hands folded at her stomach.

"I'm going to L.A.," I said. Although I'd made the decision in that moment, I wasn't surprised to hear myself voice it.

"I know." Mom slung an arm around me.

I turned to her. "You do?"

"Yeah. It doesn't make me any less nervous for you, but I'm behind you, honey."

"Do you think it's the wrong decision?" I whispered, suddenly wanting—needing—my mother's approval.

She smoothed my hair back, much as she had done that long ago night in my bedroom when I'd cried myself to sleep after my cancer diagnosis. "I think you know the answer to that better than I do. Asher seems like a good guy, but he also has a lot of baggage. I sense something between you two...I suppose I'm worried you'll both be hurt if you let it go too long without facing your differences—the differences that really matter."

"Mom, his wheelchair's a part of him. How can I—"

"I'm not talking about his wheelchair," Mom said softly. "I'm talking about how you both view the world. How you view God."

I bit the inside of my cheek, a sinking feeling in my stomach. Was it wise to spend more time with Asher when he wanted nothing to do with one of the most important parts of my life? Would my faith wither in Asher's presence?

"You're a smart girl, Lizzie, and a great friend. I know you can handle things. Asher's blessed to have you."

I watched Asher push back up the hill. Davey said something to him before hurtling himself onto his lap. This time, Asher gave them a "running" start, eliciting a scream of delight.

I pushed aside my doubts. I worried for nothing. Asher and I were simply friends. Wouldn't God want me to aid him in his time of need?

Four hours later, we sat around a campfire in the back yard of Orchard House. Two boxes of leftover pizza sat on a nearby table, as well as bottles of water. Lawn and porch chairs scattered around in a circle, the faces of the people I loved most occupying each spot. Beside me, Asher sat in his wheelchair, Isaac and Davey beside him. Apparently, he'd made lifelong friends that afternoon.

Josie, holding a sleeping Amos, shot me a smile from across the fire. She jerked her head at Asher, gave me a discreet thumb's up sign. I closed my eyes and shook my head, suppressing a smile over her theatrics. Deep down, though, I was grateful for her approval.

She wasn't the only one.

Asher and Tripp had gone to pick up the pizza. They'd been

laughing when they'd pulled up in the driveway. Maggie and Amie both admitted they'd been too quick to judge. And Bronson, while he still didn't want me going to Los Angeles, agreed that Asher wasn't the monster his Google search had made him out to be.

Tripp placed an empty pizza box into the fire. "I'm beat." He turned to Josie. "What do you say, Mama?"

"We haven't sung any campfire songs yet," Josie pouted.

Tripp groaned. "Isn't it too late for the old Martin sing-alongs? The last time we sang, I had the Spongebob Squarepants Campfire Song in my head for a week. Give a man a break, will ya?"

"Lizzie could sing a couple for us."

"Oh yes!" Amie peered around August to where Asher sat. "Lizzie has the voice of an angel."

Asher grinned at me. "I know. She sang for me the other day. Most beautiful thing I've ever heard."

I didn't miss the stunned expressions scattered around the campfire.

I shifted in my seat, uncomfortable with both the praise and the questioning looks from my sisters. "Asher plays guitar," I blurted.

"Do you now, Asher?" Mom passed around a plate of brownies.

"Have you two played together?" Amie asked.

Asher shook his head, and it was the closest I'd seen to him looking embarrassed. "I only fool around. I don't really play in front of anyone."

I raised an eyebrow at him. "I'll sing if you play."

He snapped his fingers. "Shucks, I took my guitar out of my truck this morning to make more room for the moving. Maybe next time."

"Lizzie has a guitar," Amie said sweetly.

August flung an arm around Amie. "Come on, Ame, give the guy a break."

Asher lifted a hand off his lap. "Hey, I'll play if you guys don't mind singing along to *Twinkle, Twinkle, Little Star*."

"Amos likes that song, doesn't he, Aunt Josie?" Davey piped up.

Asher spoke out of the corner of his mouth. "Hey, kid, I thought you were on my side."

I stood. "I'll go get my guitar. You did promise to play for me."

⊛

"Not in front of your entire family," Asher muttered, watching Lizzie walk away. The light of the fire played against her retreating figure, and he couldn't make himself look away.

A deep clearing of a throat cut through the air, drawing his attention back to the circle.

"Okay, now that she's gone, we can have a real heart-to-heart." Bronson leaned forward, elbows placed on outspread thighs.

Amie groaned, slumped back in her chair. "Really, Bron? You're going to grill the poor guy in front of the whole family?"

Bronson shrugged. "I just have a couple questions for him. I don't see the harm of including the family." He pinned Asher with his eyes. "You're a family guy, aren't you?"

"As in, I have one? Yeah, sure."

Tripp clapped his hands. "One point, Asher."

"Hey, whose side are you on, anyway?" Bronson asked.

"Lizzie's."

Asher lifted himself slightly, shifted in his seat. "I'm pulling your leg, Bronson. Ask away. I'm an open book."

"Okay...what are your intentions toward my sister?"

Josie looked at the sky, a smile twitching her lips.

Mrs. Martin rubbed her eyes with her hand, as if to hide. She peeked through her fingers, though, clearly interested in his answer.

Lizzie's brother sat, drumming those fingers on the arm of his lawn chair.

"I'm going to be honest," Asher started.

"That's all we ask." Bronson stared at him as if he were a judge on the Supreme Court, waiting to mete out justice in whatever way he saw fit.

"I care for your sister. But we're only friends. I'm not saying I wouldn't like us to become more one day, but I'm also not sure I'm what's best for her."

"Awww," Amie leaned her head against August's shoulder. "Two points for Asher."

Bronson didn't seem deterred. "Why do you want to take her to Los Angeles? That seems like a big trip for a couple of new friends. I'm not sure I like it, quite honestly. I'm not sure you're the kind of guy Lizzie should be dating."

The kind of guy Lizzie should be dating. Because of his wheel-chair, because of his history, or because of his beliefs...or rather, lack thereof? He didn't have the courage to ask. Because any way you diced it, Bronson was right—any of those reasons were reason enough to step away from any romantic thoughts regarding Lizzie.

Asher licked his lips, searched the backyard. No Lizzie. Could telling the truth be the thing to win over Lizzie's suspicious brother? "Can you keep a secret?" Eyes grew wide in the firelight. His gaze met the twins'. "You guys, too?"

The boys nodded. A chorus of 'yes's' sputtered around the fire.

"I have a buddy in the music agency back in L.A. I want Lizzie to sing for him. If he likes her, he could make her dreams come true."

Josie squeezed Tripp's arm. "You're serious?"

"I'm serious."

"What about the wedding, then? Is that something you made up?" Bronson asked.

Asher shook his head. "It's my best friend...well, my former best friend. He's the president of Paramount. We built the company together. He's marrying my ex-girlfriend. I'm trying to be the bigger man and be happy for them. I admit, having Lizzie there would make it easier."

"Oh, Bron," Maggie said. "He passes." She looked around the circle. "Come on, doesn't he pass?"

To his relief, everyone nodded. Everyone but Bronson, anyway.

"You two are just friends?" he asked.

Asher nodded.

Bronson pointed at him. "I want to like you."

"Thank you?"

Bronson didn't lower his finger. "And it really helps that you have that amazing rock climbing wall down at your store."

"Which you can use anytime."

Bronson wavered but didn't lower his finger. Lizzie's sisters tried unsuccessfully to hide their giggles.

"But my priority—*our* priority—is Lizzie. She sees the best in people, sometimes people who don't deserve it. And if you ever do anything to hurt her, if you cross any lines at all, know that I will be all over you like white on rice."

Asher's lips trembled. *Like white on rice?* After this guy warmed up to him, he'd have to help Lizzie's brother up his game when it came to intimidating lines.

"Got it?" Bronson didn't seem to notice that the entire group tittered around him.

"Got it," Asher affirmed. Josie's laughter broke.

"Good." One more jab of that finger before Lizzie's brother finally lowered it. He looked up at Lizzie's approach. "There she is. Now play the best dad-blamed 'Twinkle, Twinkle Little Star' she's ever heard."

The group erupted in laughter, and Asher's heart lightened. He couldn't help it, but he was becoming attached to this family. So much so, that he almost regretted having to go home to his.

🏵 28 🏵

"What'd I miss?" I came back to the campfire to see my siblings laughing with Asher. It warmed my heart to see them together, genuinely enjoying one another's company.

"Bronson gave Asher the third-degree."

I cringed. "Say no more." I sat down, handed Asher the guitar. "My sincere apologies for my brother. I don't want to know anything about it, though."

"It got pretty ugly," Maggie admitted. "But I think he passed."

"We'll hold off on a pass/fail consensus until we hear how slammin' this version of *Twinkle, Twinkle Little Star* is," Bronson said.

"Okay, okay." Asher took the guitar, and I studied him by the light of the campfire. He strummed the first few familiar notes of the child's song but quickly morphed into another song altogether, chords sounding through the air, fingers flying over the strings, persistent, expert. Coaxing fluent sound from my old guitar. I recognized the opening chords of Creedence's "Have You Ever Seen the Rain?"

Time stilled as Asher played, but it absolutely froze when he opened his mouth to sing.

My heart drummed against my chest, beating as if to fly free as Asher sang of the calm before a storm. That voice. Deep, confident, masculine. It maneuvered through the notes without effort, rivaling John Fogerty himself. It pulled emotions from me I didn't know I possessed. Emotions that elicited feelings of womanhood and girlhood all at once. In them, I glimpsed an Asher I hadn't yet known.

He was good. Remarkable, even. And as he played and sang, those deep eyes looking only at me, asking if I'd ever seen the rain on a sunny day, it was like each note, each chord were a magnet, seducing me, weaving in and out of me, pulling from me things I didn't know were possible to experience. My breaths came fast, jagged, and by the time he finished I didn't know if I'd ever catch up with them.

The last chord died out and fierce applause sounded around the campfire.

"Um. Wow." Firelight cast shadows on Amie's face as she looked slack jawed at Asher, almost as if she'd fallen in love with him in the last four minutes, too. I could understand why.

"Man, Lizzie's not the only one with some talent," Josh said. "What else you got?"

Asher shook his head, handed the guitar over to me. "Nope. Lizzie's turn." He met my gaze and I knew that he saw everything. My face burned. How would I ever be able to tell him I planned to go to Los Angeles with him? For how could I now? I'd been fond of him before, but this magnetic pull tearing through me? It was strong, dangerous. I wasn't sure I could fight it.

I thought of Mom's words—her fear that I was getting in too deep with someone who didn't value what I did. I had never intended to become so attached to this man. Now, it shattered my insides to even think about being away from him.

"I—I'm not sure I can follow that." Would my fingers play the chords correctly?

"Of course you can." Asher's smile reflected the campfire. Handsome, brilliant, sucking every last ounce of control from me. I remembered my daydream back when he was Mr. Coffee to me, how I fantasized about us cuddling around a campfire playing guitar. "It's your song. That's something I could never do."

My head spun. How was this happening? And how could falling in love be both so terrible and wonderful at the same time?

"I—I'm feeling a little woozy, actually."

"Come on, Liz. One song, then we'll leave you alone." Amie nodded encouragement.

"If she isn't up to it, Asher could play us another." Josie beamed at Asher, and Tripp elbowed her as if to say, *Remember me?*

Ha. It wasn't love I was experiencing if my sisters were feeling it as well. Infatuation with a voice, perhaps. Fondness for a friend. But not love.

"Why don't I play for you?" Asher took the guitar from my hands.

"You—how do you...?"

"Are you kidding? I haven't been able to get your song out of my head. Even played it a few times myself. Tell me if I have it right."

He started playing, and amazingly enough, the music that had first been written in my heart was being poured out of the guitar by way of his fingers. Perfect. How had he gotten it right after hearing it only once?

It was time for me to sing, but I choked on the words. Couldn't get them out for the emotion and confusion consuming me.

When I missed the first verse, he played the notes again, coming round for me, offering me the spot to jump on. Again, I missed. And he kept playing, glanced at me with a nod and a small smile. An invitation. This time, when he came around again, he caught my gaze with his, began singing my lyrics himself.

"I used to think alone was a good thing..."

I swallowed, wet my lips and closed my eyes. Decided to jump.

"Freedom from heartbreak and hurt, freedom from suffocating. But that was before you consumed me."

Our voices melded together as one, the guitar doing the work of weaving our voices in and out of each other, complimenting the highs and lows, the tremors in mine straightened by the perfection of his.

The pure sound was like magic, making me believe anything was possible. That if I wanted to in this moment, with this song and this man, I could fly.

I let it split me open and take me away, gave myself up to it. The music and words, Asher's voice alongside mine, whisked me away to mountainous heights, carried me upward and over to places I'd never been before. At the same time, the unity of it was like coming home. Like how things were meant to be.

The way the sun covers the trees,
the way the ocean swallows the beach.
The way the moon absorbs the dark,
is the way you grabbed my heart.
It's the way you...consume me."

When the final verses had been sung, when Asher's skilled hands charmed the last of those beautiful notes from my guitar, I clung tight, not wanting it to end. But it died out, leaving silence, save for the sputtering crackle of the campfire.

Slowly, I opened my eyes. I caught Josie's face first, her mouth open as if in shock. Maggie's hand was at her throat, tears in her eyes. Amie grabbed August's arm, eyebrows raised.

Without warning, the circle burst into applause, half a dozen voices with it.

"What in the world—"

"I've never heard anything more terrific."

"You guys must have practiced that before, right?"

"Seriously, you should record it tomorrow."

I shook my head against it, dared glance at Asher, who sat grinning at me.

"We sound pretty good together, don't we, Martin?"

"Pretty good? Pretty good!" Amie stood up. "You cannot keep this a secret. No way. I know what we'll do. I'm going to call the radio station again. Remind them of you two. And then...you can sing the song, like you did. You are going to blow everyone's socks off. You'll have a record deal before you can say...what do you call that song, Lizzie?"

"You cannot call the radio." I shook my head, slowly coming out from beneath whatever spell the music held me under. "You guys are my family. Of course you're going to think we sound good."

Maggie shook her head. "It's more than that, Liz. But I agree. Rushing into anything seems foolhardy. Enjoy the music for now. Why does everyone in this family need to be so crazy ambitious?"

"Because chasing dreams adds spice to life." Josie handed Amos to Tripp.

"I'm not sure that a record label is my dream. I love music, but...I want to make sure I'm listening to God's voice and not my own."

I avoided Asher's stare—too scared I'd know again what I'd felt when I sang with him. Or worse yet, witness his disappointment.

Josh stood. "Well, I'm of a mind that no major life decisions should be made after nine o'clock at night. Boys, time to head out." He turned to the rest of us. "We couldn't have done the move without all of you. We owe you so much more than pizza. Thank you."

The twins dragged themselves off the ground, dead on their feet. They followed Maggie and Josh to the car, but Davey ran back to Asher's side. "I hope we get to ride down the hill again, soon."

"I hope so too, buddy."

"See ya."

"See ya."

The group dispersed, saying goodbyes until finally it was only me and Asher. I walked him to his truck. I liked that he didn't seem uncomfortable with me anymore as he began his routine of transferring from the wheelchair to the driver's seat.

"Thanks so much for helping out today."

"Not sure how much help I was, but it was fun. Your family's pretty cool, Martin."

"I think so."

I wanted to say more. To ask him where he'd learned to play guitar, if he'd played when he was a kid, if it came easy to him. Had he always sung like that? When would I see him again? But my mouth grew dry.

He climbed into the truck seat, disassembled his chair, and put it in the back. He closed the door.

"So I have a problem now," he said.

"What's that?"

"You have the next two days off. I don't think anyone else in your family needs to move. I'm running out of excuses to see you."

His gaze moved over my face, and I wondered, if he were standing, if the car door wasn't between us, if he might try to kiss me.

"If I came to California with you...what would you tell your family?" I asked.

"About us, you mean?"

How awkward. But I needed to know. Was I going as something I couldn't pretend to be? Was I meant to be competition for Elise? If so, I couldn't bear it. "Yes."

"I'd tell them the truth. That you're a good friend."

I relaxed. "Then my answer's 'yes.' I'll go to the wedding with you."

He grabbed my hand, pulled me gently toward him. My heart ricocheted in my chest. "Thank you, Lizzie. You don't know what this means to me." His thumb moved over my hand, and I stepped an inch closer.

I swallowed. "You have an amazing voice."

"Are you falling in love with me, Martin? None of that if we're going to a California wedding together. There'll be no hope for you after you see my dance moves."

I laughed softly, wiggled my hand from his. No need for him to see how close his assessment might be. "I'm sure I'll be able to contain myself."

"I don't know, I wouldn't be so confident if I were you. These wheels can spin some pretty racy shuffles."

I smiled. "I'm looking forward to seeing them. So, let me know if there's anything I need to bring. Oh. And I've never flown on a plane before, so be prepared to talk me through any panic attacks."

"You serious?"

"Yup. Five kids. Little money. Any family vacations were taken in our minivan."

"Oh, man. You're more sheltered than I thought. Okay. I'll walk you through it."

"I am not sheltered. I just haven't had a reason to get on a plane. Please, don't look down on me. I can't bear it."

"I'm not judging. Lizzie, your family's great. I'm kind of scared what you'll think of mine when you meet them."

"I'm sure I'll be completely intimidated."

"And you'll have no reason to be. You're perfect the way you are, okay?"

My breaths were doing that raspy, jagged thing again. I looked away. "I'll see you around?"

"How about dinner tomorrow night?"

"Between friends, you mean?"

He grinned. "Right."

I allowed my eyes to map his face, the handsome lines and edges. We both knew we were lying to one another at this point, didn't we? At the same time, this was foreign territory—to both of us. I had just told myself to slow down, to keep my guard up. But my heart was flying away with myself.

"Okay." I agreed, already battling with doubts.

"Pick you up at six?"

I nodded, then watched his truck pull out of the bed and breakfast driveway. I stood there until the taillights of his truck disappeared. When I climbed upstairs to bed, I sneaked past Amie's room to take a shower.

Once in my room, I donned my pajamas. Bets rubbed her calico body against my ankles. When I slid beneath the cool sheets, I closed my eyes, remembering the events of the day, and especially the night.

Asher's voice wound around me, cocooning me in warmth and hope. I realized then that I hadn't prayed about my decision to go to L.A. It had been pure gut instinct. But what if going to California proved disastrous? What if his family hated me? What if I was homesick beyond belief? What if Asher was really still in love with Elise? What if one of his moods took over and I had nowhere to run?

Worst of all, what if I continued down this slippery slope and couldn't jump off?

❧ 29 ❧

I closed my eyes as the plane barreled forward, faster and faster, throttling at breakneck speed. And then, a gradual weightlessness. A pulling of height.

"Open your eyes, Martin."

I opened the eye closest to Asher. "Please tell me how this big hunk of metal is actually suspended in the sky. And you better make it convincing. Fast."

"The lift force of the plane is greater than the force of gravity. Same with thrust force over drag force. Feel better?"

I wrinkled my nose. "No." I let my eyelids flutter open, saw a few puffy clouds out the window. My breath caught. "We're— we're above the clouds." We climbed higher, through more clouds and then, brilliant sun and a pillow of white below us. "It's beautiful." My nerves settled, replaced with awe. "It's like we've climbed up to heaven."

Asher didn't speak, but when I looked at him sitting in the aisle seat, I caught him staring at me.

"Don't do that," I said.

"What?"

"Look at me like that. Like I'm some strange anomaly or

something."

"But you are, Martin. And I love it."

I leaned back in my spacious, first-class chair. Boarding the plane had been a bit time consuming, but the crew had been extremely helpful with Asher's wheelchair. We'd boarded first, and I'd been grateful for the window seat to be away from the many gazes that walked past us onto the rest of the plane.

"You tell the OG about your trip?"

"OG?"

"Yeah, Other Guy."

"Other guy?"

"The guy at the store opening. Mick or something?"

"Mike?"

He snapped his fingers in the air. He looked so incredibly cute in a backwards baseball hat, a pullover Nike sweatshirt that brought out the green flecks of his eyes. "That's right. Mike."

"If he's the Other Guy, then that would make you..."

"The Main Guy. The hero in this story if we were writing a novel, I guess."

"Right. A novel. About a girl and a guy who are friends."

"Friends. Right. I did say that, didn't I?"

I rolled my eyes but couldn't pretend I didn't enjoy his light-hearted flirting. A part of me knew nothing could ever come of us, but another part—the part that ran away with the idea of a drive-thru dreamboat hiking with me and serenading me with a guitar—thought that anything was possible. That Asher would find God. That we could share a lifetime together. Starting here and now, flying above the clouds.

"You did. And yes, I told Mike."

"Did he throw a hissy fit? I bet he hated the idea."

I blew my hair out of my face. "Mike's a good guy. And he took the news fine. We're friends."

"Like you and I are friends."

"Yes!" I huffed, then shrank back in my seat.

"So if Mike asked you to go to California with him for a wedding, you would have gone."

"I'm ignoring that question. We should make better use of our time. Tell me what I need to know once we land."

He blinked, then shrugged. "My family's nothing like yours. My mom will totally smother us. My father will either ignore us or pretend like we've been there the entire time. And my brother...I don't know what to expect from my brother."

"I didn't realize you had a brother."

"Younger. Kind of a surprise for my parents. He's twenty. We've always been close, but..."

"But?"

"We haven't spoken much since my accident. My mom told me he lost his driver's license and his job. I'm not sure what to expect."

"That must be rough on them."

"It is what it is."

I winced.

"What?"

"I hate it when people say that. Seems like it's a nice way of saying, 'Who cares?'"

"Hey, I care. I care a lot. Ricky's one of the reasons I'm going back home."

"I'll be praying for you, then."

"Please. Don't bother." Asher took off his hat, curving the brim until the two sides touched. His hair lay in uncharacteristic puffs at his temples.

"Why not?"

"Prayer's a waste of time."

Something inside me collapsed at his words. Like a carefully-constructed house of cards I'd built for myself, his words served to blow it all down. I'd believed this could work. But how could I have a relationship—hope to marry someone, even—who thought my beliefs a waste of time?

"I don't think so." My words came out slow. Maybe I shouldn't have come. The future I'd cooked up would never materialize.

He let his head fall back against the headrest, his hat still in his hands. "I was never much of a believer in the mystical. *God*." He said the word *God* as if He were a figment of the imagination, a thing to scoff. My chest ached, but I stayed silent, letting him continue.

"I never prayed much, never went to church. But after my accident, a hospital chaplain came to visit me. He told me a story about Jesus healing a paralyzed man. Telling him to get up and walk." He licked his lips, stared straight ahead at the back of the blue headrest in front of him. "I latched onto that story. Can't count the number of times I dreamt that I was that paralyzed man. I dreamt that my brother and Lucas carried me to Jesus, that he told me to get up and walk. And I did. But only in my dreams.

"When I'd wake up, I was still stuck in that hospital bed. I realized how stupid such dreams were. My best friend couldn't get up the guts to visit me in the hospital, never mind bring me to Jesus. And Ricky had lost his brother, and a hero, the night of my accident.

"I told God I'd give Him whatever He wanted if He let me walk again." He shoved his hat back on his head, clasped his hands on his lap. "You can see what kind of an answer I got."

My heart twisted for him. At the same time, my mind scrambled for excuses to explain God's seeming absence.

I cleared my throat, prepared to tread carefully. "I believe God still works miracles, and I wish He always provided us with one when we want Him to so badly..."

Asher raised his eyebrows. "But..."

"But maybe Jesus healing that paralyzed man was just a glimpse of His kingdom to come. Asher, you *could* be healed one day, when the earth is made new. God...what He offers is better than just working legs or a carefree life. I so wish you could see that."

My words hung in the air. Were they too preachy? Would they push Asher away? Cause him to regret inviting me on this trip?

Perhaps Asher had only needed someone to listen and understand right now. Not someone to swoop in with answers.

"I'm so sorry," I said.

"What are you sorry for?"

"That He didn't heal you. That you lost your hope because of it." I licked my lips. "I wish He had answered your prayer. And selfishly, I kind of don't. Because if He had, I wouldn't be sitting here with you right now."

"Huh." He kept staring at that headrest, as if it were the most interesting thing in the world. "I guess that's one thing to be thankful for, then. I still wish you had known me when I could walk."

"It wouldn't have happened," I said.

"What?"

"Us meeting. If you could have walked."

"Well, I know I wouldn't have come to Camden, but you know, if we crossed one another's paths in another time, another place."

"Still wouldn't have happened."

"Why not?" He finally tore his attention from the headrest.

"Because you wouldn't have had any reason to pay me any mind."

"Sure I would have."

"Asher, it's okay. I'm just saying how it would have been. I'm not offended." I was simply glad I knew him now.

"I still think you're wrong."

"I guess I'll find out soon enough."

"When?"

"When I meet your old world." I smiled sweetly at him. "When I meet Elise."

❦ 30 ❦

Mom never pulled her own luggage. For as long as Asher could remember—whether it was traveling for a Ninja competition or a triathlon—he had known that his mother, Mikayla Hill, did not pull her own luggage. That job belonged to either his dad, his brother, or him.

So when his mom waved to them in the arrival area without either of the other males in his household, Asher resigned himself to the fact that Lizzie would see the true colors of his family sooner rather than later. He cringed imagining Lizzie hauling out the two suitcases to the parking lot while his mother strode on high heels, dressed in a silk blouse, hands empty save for a small clutch bag.

"Asher!" His mom rushed over to him, planting a kiss on his cheek. "How was your flight, honey?"

But before he could answer, she'd turned to Lizzie. "And you must be Lizzie. It's a pleasure to finally meet you. I could have killed this dodo for not introducing us when I came to Maine last month. Here, let me take one of those." His mom grabbed Asher's suitcase and started with it toward the large glass doors.

He blinked. She looked totally awkward. Somehow the suitcase had tilted to one side and she kicked it slightly with one of her high-heeled shoes. It landed safely back on both wheels.

Huh. A first for everything, he supposed.

"Thanks so much," Lizzie said, quieter than she'd been while they'd travelled.

"You both must be exhausted. What time was your flight this morning?"

"Five. It'll be good to get some rest." Hopefully that would be hint enough to put off any extravagant get-togethers on his first night home. Lizzie would be lost. Besides, he only wanted to see his dad and Ricky.

His mother led them to her custom-designed BMW sedan and popped the trunk open. Lizzie helped her lift his suitcase into the back.

"I made your favorite tonight," she said.

"Chicken pot pie?"

She smiled. "With my garlic mashed potatoes. I only hope your father leaves the office early enough. He's been positively avoiding us, especially since Ricky moved back home."

He put the brakes on his wheelchair, slid his guitar into the backseat. Lizzie opened the other side, but his mother shooed her towards the passenger seat. "Ride up front with me, dear. It'll give me a chance to get to know you better."

"Um, okay." Lizzie scurried around the front. His mother better not eat her alive.

Mom backed out of the parking spot. "I'm sure Asher's told you he hasn't had a girlfriend since before...you know. I told him he needs to be patient. It'll take a special kind of girl—"

"Mom." He didn't manage to hold back the bite in his voice.

She flicked her gaze at him in the rearview mirror. "Sorry, honey. I get overexcited, I suppose."

"Lizzie and I are just friends."

"Oh." Her tone deflated.

"I helped Asher set up the new store," Lizzie volunteered.

"Oh, how nice. Are you one of the managers?"

"No, just helping. I've taught music for the last two years and I help my mom run our bed and breakfast."

"A bed and breakfast! How quaint. Perhaps I could get Travis—that's Asher's father—to take a trip out to Maine again. We could stay at your family's place."

Asher inwardly groaned. Nothing like inserting herself into his life. Again.

"We'd love to have you." Lizzie's voice filled with warmth and authenticity.

He relaxed. He was being too hard on his mother. She was trying. Even carried his suitcase, for goodness sake. If Lizzie could take her, then he needed to ease up.

"How's Ricky?" he asked.

His mother's eyes flew upward on a sigh. "Aimless. Sits on the couch most of the day, moping. Your father thinks—" She turned to Lizzie. "I apologize, sweetie. It's poor manners to air our dirty laundry in front of you like this. Please forgive me."

"It's okay," Lizzie said. "Asher did tell me some about his brother."

"I'd like to know, Mom, before I see Ricky. What does Dad think?"

His mom let out another long sigh, and he noticed the slight changes within her. Not quite so prim, not quite so worried about appearances. Or maybe too tired to do the worrying.

"Dad thinks we need to kick him out of the house." Her voice wobbled. Again, something different in his mom. The old Mikayla Hill would never succumb to emotion. Had she so much as cried after discovering her oldest son—her pride and joy—would never walk again?

He didn't think so.

"And you don't agree with him." Asher said.

"I don't see how he'll survive by himself right now. I'm scared he'll wind up dead on the street from some kind of overdose." She ran her hand over her forehead. "I can't believe I'm talking about this in front of your guest. Lizzie, please forgive me."

"You must be worried about him. You know what, I could actually use a bathroom stop. I should have gone before we left the airport. If we stop by a coffee shop, I could grab us something and use the restroom to give you and Asher a chance to talk?"

He could have kissed her for her thoughtfulness. Not that he minded talking about family matters in front of her, but he could tell it bothered his mom something fierce.

She bestowed a grateful smile on Lizzie. "Thanks, sweetie. Are you sure I can't convince you to give that one back there a shot?"

They both laughed, and Asher shook his head. Women.

His mom pulled into the next coffee shop and Lizzie got out, entering through the glass doors of the shop.

"She's a keeper, Ash."

"I don't deserve her." He stared after her out the window.

She turned in the driver's seat to face him. "Don't talk like that. You are one of the kindest, most generous men I know. She'd be lucky to have a guy like you."

He hiked a full breath into his lungs. Inside the shop and through the windows, Lizzie waited outside a bathroom door.

"About Ricky," he started. "He's into drugs?"

"I don't think so, although I never thought he'd be drinking and driving, either. I'm not sure what to expect from him anymore. Your father thinks if we kick him out, he'll hit rock bottom, get some sense knocked into him, and land back on his feet. I'm afraid it'll be more than he can take." She pressed her lips together, drawing attention to an uncharacteristic smudge of lipstick on her upper lip. "You might as well know now...your father hasn't been staying at the house..."

"Mom...what?"

"A couple months now, soon after Ricky moved back home.

We were always arguing anyway. If it wasn't about Ricky, it was about the thermostat or when to run the dishwasher."

"He left?" Hurt and anger bubbled up inside his chest. The man he'd looked up to his entire life, the man who had encouraged him to stick it out and never give up, was leaving? Giving up on his family?

"I'd like to think it's temporary. Sometimes marriages grow stale. You understand, don't you, honey?"

No. No, he didn't understand at all. True, he'd never thought seriously about marriage, but he'd also never considered his parents' marriage in danger. He wondered if his dad was seeing someone else. As much as he might complain about his mom, particularly after the accident, she was a decent person. She didn't deserve this. No one did.

Something foreign and fierce welled up within him, a need to protect and defend his mother. "Is that why he didn't come to meet us? He knows I'm going to lay into him, doesn't he?"

"Asher." His mom rubbed her temples, and he noticed new lines around her eyes and mouth. "Please, don't make things worse. I appreciate your heart, sweetie, but we'll work it out. I'm most worried about Ricky right now."

And then he understood. Understood how his mom could get totally wrapped up in her sons to the exclusion of his father. It had happened after his accident, hadn't it? He'd known the suffocating effects of it, but what if his dad had felt the opposite? What if Ricky's problems had started when Asher left for the east coast? He could picture his mother's focus shifting from him to his brother. Consuming, without fail.

For a brief moment, he imagined his father in his quiet way, sitting in his office to escape his wife's obsession with the adult sons he couldn't help. Had he felt abandoned? Powerless to help his own sons? Not that it gave him a right to leave, but for a fleeting second, Asher saw through his father's eyes.

"Right. Ricky. I'll talk to him, Mom. Of course I will. I want to help, but we've grown apart these last couple years." For some reason, the thought brought to mind that story of Jesus healing the paralyzed man. His brother may not be paralyzed, but he needed help. Needed some sort of healing.

Would Asher be enough to bring it about?

❧ 3 1 ❧

I didn't know what I expected from Asher's childhood home, but it certainly wasn't the massive Mediterranean-style house outside central Malibu. Sleek and modern, Mrs. Hill led me on a tour in which each spacious room offered panoramic ocean views. Interior archways, a curved staircase with scrolled railings that led to a columned mezzanine on the bedroom level. Rooms so large the furniture looked small, though the couches and entertainment centers were anything but tiny. Large patios with a sunken pool and hot tub, pathways that wound among crisp plantings. Very chic. Very Malibu. For every square foot of quaint and cozy that was Orchard House, this California paradise was the complete opposite. I almost laughed out loud at the thought of Mr. and Mrs. Hill staying at my family's bed and breakfast.

But as big and beautiful as the home was, it appeared empty, hollow. A gorgeous shell for something lonely. After she'd finished giving me the tour, Mrs. Hill opened a door to the basement and called down. "Ricky! Your brother's here!"

Asher sat in his wheelchair in the middle of the sharp,

gourmet kitchen, knuckles tight on the hand rims of his wheels, as if ready to flee.

"Can I get you something to drink, Lizzie? Seltzer or wine?" She fluttered around the kitchen, aimless, looking for something to do.

"Water would be great," I said. "Thank you."

The sound of slow footsteps on the stairs, and then a light blond head appeared, hair shaggy, the beginnings of a beard on a young face with hooded eyes. The resemblance to Asher striking. He wore a wrinkled Berkley t-shirt and sweatpants, bare toes poking out from the bottom of the worn cuffs.

Asher's face broke out in a grin. "Little Bro." He held out his hand.

His younger brother didn't take it. "Look who decided to grace us with his presence." His gaze flicked to Mrs. Hill. "You finally gave in to Mom's guilt trip?" His cool eyes moved to me, gave me a once over that left my face hot and no doubt, beet red. "Not doing too bad for yourself, are you, Big Brother?" And then he turned back around and started down the stairs.

"Ricky!" Mrs. Hill acted horrified, though something told me she wasn't surprised.

Asher cursed under his breath, the color of his face no doubt matching my own. "Sorry, Lizzie. This has nothing to do with you—"

"I know." But I didn't. What had I gotten myself into by agreeing to this trip? I had thought I was helping Asher attend a wedding, but it seemed I'd landed smack dab in the middle of major family turmoil. I quickly calculated the amount of money in my bank account, most of it from the work I'd done for Paramount. Could I afford a hotel? I'd been in California only a couple of hours, but it was fast becoming obvious that Asher needed time with his family. Alone.

"He's changed." Asher tapped the door to the basement so it closed just short of latching.

Mrs. Hill handed me a glass of ice water with lemon. "I tried to tell you. Honey, I don't know what to do for him." Her eyes pleaded with her son, as if Asher were the parent and Mrs. Hill the child. My heart hurt for her.

"I'm here for a week. I'll spend some time with him. Don't worry, Mom. We'll figure this out." The way he said it, I believed him.

Mrs. Hill seemed to deflate with relief, her bottom lip trembling. She nodded but turned to open the fridge to hide any emotion.

The door to the garage opened and a tall, broad form in a suit filled the kitchen. A smile broke out on the handsome face, and through it I could imagine what Asher might look like in another thirty years. Silver hair creeping, a rugged, if not aged way about him.

A grin softened the exterior. "Son." He held his hand out, bent over for a hug. Asher held him tight, and I backed away a few steps, giving them space, an intruder on something terribly personal. When he pulled away, the older man cleared his throat. "I'm glad you've come."

"It's good to see you, Dad." Asher gestured me over. "This is Lizzie."

Mr. Hill held out his hand again, smiled, and I saw nothing but genuine welcome in the action. "Glad you could get this guy to finally come visit, Lizzie."

"It's nice to meet you, sir."

He shook my hand with his warm one. "Please. It's Travis. Make yourself at home. Whatever you need, let us know."

I didn't miss Mrs. Hill's slightly perturbed look.

"Thank you."

"Asher, why don't you let Lizzie choose a guest room. Unless you two planned to share a—"

"No, we don't." Asher cut in. "I told you, Mom. We really are just friends."

She shrugged. "That's fine. Lizzie, you might as well stay upstairs then. Better view. I'll show you."

Mr. Hill took my suitcase up the stairs for me. Asher would stay in the bedroom downstairs. Though the thought of sharing a room embarrassed me, as I climbed the stairs—a place Asher could not follow—I couldn't help but feel I was too far away for comfort.

⸙

I LIFTED MY WINE GLASS TO MY LIPS, THE RED MERLOT A compliment to the down-to-earth home cooked meal. Creamy chicken pot pie with plenty of root vegetables, mashed potatoes, biscuits, and a simple salad.

"I'm planning something more extravagant tomorrow night," Mrs. Hill explained, almost apologizing. "But Asher's always been drawn to country meals. I made this in his honor." She beamed at her oldest son.

"It tastes wonderful," I said. We sat outside on the patio beneath a canopy. The pool lay glimmering to our side, seeming to overflow into the ocean beyond. "And this view is gorgeous."

Mrs. Hill smiled sweetly, her gaze flickering briefly to her husband. "Travis worked hard for it."

Was she attempting to convey a second meaning to her husband? Beside me, Asher clenched his fist in his napkin. How ironic that the Malibu view of paradise could contain tension sharper than Vermont cheese. None of the men chose to speak, and I grasped for words to carry the conversation. Perhaps I really should stay somewhere else—allow the Hills to work out whatever was between them. I'd speak to Asher after dinner.

Mrs. Hill spoke. "What are your plans while you're here? You're welcome to the club, of course, Asher. And I'm sure Lucas has plans for the two of you."

Asher cleared his throat. "Lucas doesn't know I'm here."

Mrs. Hill's gaze skidded back and forth, from her husband to Asher. "But the wedding. He must know you're attending..."

Asher wiped his mouth with his napkin. "I didn't RSVP. Thought I'd give them a little surprise."

He'd left that part out. I slumped in my seat, wanted to melt into the pool, or allow the salty air to carry me away.

"Oh, Asher. Really. You can't do that to Maureen. She thinks she has everything planned to a T. Let me at least call her, will you?"

Asher stared at his plate, one hand on the table. "Whatever you think, Mom."

"Thank you." Mrs. Hill straightened, raised a dainty bite to her mouth. "I'm sure Lizzie would love to see the city. Have you ever been to Los Angeles, dear?"

I shook my head.

"Everyone loves to see Hollywood. There's a great tour of the Walk of Fame. They show you Tom Cruise's home, Taylor's Swift's, Leonardo DiCaprio's. A little of everything."

"Lizzie's not really into all that, Mom. I might take her to Griffith Park." He turned to me. "I need to stop by the Paramount home office if you don't mind tagging along."

I let out a breath. "Yes, whatever you need. That sounds great." I paused, then thought to add, "Don't feel like you have to entertain me, though. Spend time with your family. I can amuse myself."

A sarcastic snort came from the other end of the table, where Ricky shoved mashed potatoes into his mouth. A look of annoyance crossed Asher's face, but he contained himself as he addressed his younger brother. "I was hoping to spend some time with the little brother. What do you say, Ricky? You up for some fishing Thursday morning?"

"Depends what time. I'm not much of an early riser these days."

"Even for a deep-sea excursion? I booked us two tickets on a boat Thursday morning. Half day, guaranteed to catch some massive bass."

"I don't fish anymore."

"Ricky..." Mrs. Hill pleaded.

Asher sat back in his chair, drummed his fingers on the table. "Fine, then. I'll take Dad." He turned to his father. "Can you free up Thursday morning?"

Mr. Hill loosened his tie. "I could, but...Ricky, I don't think it's too much to ask to spend some time with your brother."

Ricky pushed away from the table, much like a petulant, spoiled teenager. "Fine. Whatever. See you Thursday. Bright and early." He left the patio, stalked back into the house.

"Lizzie, I'm so sorry." Mrs. Hill raised her wine glass to her lips and drank greedily.

I shook my head. "I'm not bothered by it, really. I grew up with four siblings. Someone was always in a mood, but..." I bit my lip before raising my gaze to Asher. "Should I stay somewhere else? Let you spend time with your family? Connect with your brother? I don't mind, really, I don't." I had a hunch Ricky resented my presence.

"No way." Asher's mouth grew firm. "I wouldn't be here if it weren't for you. If Ricky can't be civil, that's his problem. Not yours."

I swirled my fork in my mashed potatoes, concentrated on the glimmering sea. Paradise. Yeah, right.

❧ 32 ❧

Asher rolled onto the patio. Across the way, Lizzie sat on a single-seat swing hanging from a pergola, legs crossed at the ankles, eyes closed, peace on her face. Having her here meant more than he imagined. But, not surprisingly, his messed-up family was ruining it all.

The last of the sun sank below the horizon. Stars salted the sky. The familiar sounds of waves crashing below soothed the raw parts of him that had become exposed since arriving home. How many nights had he fallen asleep to the roar of the water?

"There you are." He came up beside her.

She opened her eyes, smiled lazily at him, and his heart skipped a beat. "I was praying."

He let out a small laugh. "After that dinner, I'm nearly ready to do the same. You must think we're a bunch of monsters."

"Not at all. I think you're all hurting. And I'm scared I'm in the way."

He scooped up her hand. "You are not in the way. You're my lifeline right now, hear me? Please, don't talk about leaving. I admit, I didn't realize how difficult Ricky was going to be. I apologize on his behalf."

"He feels abandoned."

"I don't understand why. After my accident, he took off. Couldn't get away from me fast enough. If anyone abandoned anyone, it was him abandoning me." He shook his head. "Sorry. Enough whining."

"You're hurt, too. It's okay."

"I don't know him anymore."

"He's a man now."

She was right. Asher needed to approach his younger brother like a grown adult instead of the starry-eyed kid who would have followed him to the ends of the earth and back. Trouble was, Ricky wasn't acting like a man at all.

Not that Asher had acted very adult-like these last two years, either.

"Ricky's not the only Hill male that's screwed up." He breathed deep, the dark making it easier to speak his heart. "You know when we helped your sister move?"

"Of course."

"Your family's special, Lizzie." He dragged in a breath. "But I want you to understand something about me. Not for any special reason other than I want you to understand."

She sat up, leaned toward him. The fading sunlight cast her pretty features in a soft glow and his heart tripped over itself. He'd invited her here knowing it would bring them dangerously close. He'd convinced himself it was an unselfish move, that he would help her in her music, but maybe he'd invited her more for himself, after all.

The thought pierced him.

"Okay," she said. "I want to understand."

"That day, the moving. It was one of the hardest things I've ever done."

She raised an eyebrow, keeping the tone light. "Harder than climbing Everest?"

"In a way, yes."

"How come?" She searched his eyes, as if wanting to pull back the layers of his soul and peer in. No woman had ever cared to do that. Not his mother, not Elise. Both had only wanted what he could supply—love, assurance, security, or physical pleasure.

But Lizzie possessed a depth that drew him like a siren's song. A compassion that saw beneath the ugliness of his soul and glimpsed something better. Something he couldn't see in himself.

How did she do that?

Even now, with her question lingering sweetly in the air, she didn't press. Patiently, she waited for him to unwrap those most vulnerable parts of himself. "Because I hate being helpless. Inadequate. Like less of a man."

"Asher, no one thinks of you like that. I don't think of you like that." She seemed to want to say more but stopped.

He didn't push her. He wasn't searching for assurances or compliments, he was trying to make her understand.

"If that's true—and I'm betting it is when it comes from you—then, thank you. But that's not the way most of society acts. Everything the world values—youth, strength, talent, brains, money, tenacity—I had it."

"And after the accident..."

"I lost my purpose, my worth. Only in the last couple of months have I felt life's worth living." He didn't state the obvious—that his change of heart was because of her. "Problem is, I'm not sure Ricky feels the same way."

"He hasn't seen how you deal with the challenges."

"We haven't been around each other enough."

"Then you need time together."

"Maybe."

She brought her legs up on the chair, hugged her knees to her chest. The length and smoothness of her legs drew him. He longed to reach out and run a finger over her calf and around the curve of her knee. He wanted to pull her onto his lap, hold her close.

"You know, in some ways, I think you're more blessed than the rest of us."

He tried to hide a smirk. "How's that?"

"I wonder if you understand better than us what really matters. People. Relationships."

He sighed. "I'd like to think this accident has made me a better person. But Lizzie, I could lose all my limbs and never be as good as you. And I want to be. I want to deserve you."

The air changed between them, and for a split second he wished to snatch the words back. He'd assured her they were friends, and here he was on their first night, already ruining it.

"You know what I think makes a beautiful relationship?" Her voice barely rose above the sound of the waves as she looked out at the dark sea.

"What?" Was he breathing? He wasn't sure.

"Two people who know what they lack but allow the other to fill in where they fall short. Seeking the heavenly together, learning to love one another more and more with each passing day. Not in a wishy-washy sort of way. But in a genuine, even-in-the-ugly sort of way."

His chest deflated. "It sounds great. I'm just not sure.... Want to know what my mom told me when you were in that coffee shop?"

"If you want to tell me."

"She said my dad moved out. Left her. Do you see what kind of a screwed-up mess I'm coming from?" He waved his hand at the view then at the sprawling home behind them. Frustration welled. "All this is show. None of it's real. And I played along my entire life, seeking to climb higher, be the best. Now, when it's fallen down around me, I wonder why I wanted it so bad in the first place."

She bit her bottom lip. "You are not your parents. And I'm not mine." She paused again. "Can I tell you something?"

"Anything."

He wanted to know everything, every ounce of what was important to her. And everything that wasn't.

She grabbed her toes, seemed to work up the courage to speak. "That night...when you sang around the campfire with my family?"

He nodded.

"I have never known a stronger pull toward anyone. It was terrifying and amazing and it had nothing to do with your ability to walk. You said you sometimes feel like less of a man because of your wheelchair, but...I never appreciated what it meant to be drawn—really drawn—to a man until that night."

๑๒๑

I COULDN'T STOP THE WORDS STREAMING FROM MY MOUTH. What was I doing, pouring my heart out to Asher like that? Was it the glass of wine I'd had at dinner? The dark of the night? The jet lag, or perhaps the view of paradise before me?

"I can't believe I said that." I buried my face in my knees. "Please pretend that didn't happen."

"Lizzie." He said my name with gentle affection, drawing me to those mesmerizing eyes, lit only by the dim light coming from the windows of the house.

"If I wasn't in this wheelchair, I'd stand up, take you in my arms, and kiss you breathless."

My heart beat so fast I thought it might pump the blood clean out of my body.

He pulled me toward him until my feet hit the ground. "Come here. Please?"

Heat coursed through me. He placed his palm against my face, ran his thumb down my cheek. I put a hand on his arm to balance myself, surprised at the knotty mass of hard muscle beneath my fingertips. It stirred desire within me, an unquenchable flame I hadn't known since we sang together around my family's campfire. His mouth dipped closer.

I should pull away. I knew I should pull away. Things weren't supposed to get this far.

"Can I kiss you, Lizzie Martin?" His breath played along my skin, causing a shudder to pulse through me. Anticipation, nerves, pleasure. An invisible magnet pulling me closer.

Reality seemed far away—nothing more than a notion as I moved closer. Unsure, tentative. He met me the rest of the way, gently taking my bottom lip between his in the sweetest kiss I could imagine. His lips lingered, soft and hesitant, before he pulled away. My hand tightened on his arm, wanting more.

"This might ruin our friendship," he said, his voice gruff.

I thought about apologizing—for what, I didn't know. I should push away. But I couldn't bring myself to leave this spot, where I curved into him so perfectly. I swallowed, grasped for words. "You're right. We—we shouldn't—"

"Lizzie," he breathed, "I only want you in whatever capacity you'll have me. All this time, I've thought of myself as half a man when really, I was half a man before. I didn't know what it was to be fully alive. I'm not sure I'm the best thing for you, but God help me, Lizzie, I will try with everything I am to be worthy of you."

"Oh, Asher." I answered him by dipping my head, allowing him to again close the distance and meet my mouth with his. This time, the depth was a smoky fire building to flames. A hum vibrated through my body, making me pleasantly weak. He drew me closer, my chest against his, my soul spilling out into another realm—a realm of pleasure and connection on a different plane than any I'd ever known. His mouth moved over mine like a perfect song written without pause or break. An unbroken melody, whispering of things to come, things yet to be seen.

When we finally parted, I was breathless. I smiled at him, and he kissed me again, slowly and gently this time, asking a thousand questions with the tender gesture.

I answered them the best I could.

When we broke away, I laid my head on his shoulder, the rise and fall of his broad chest beneath my head. The stars shone like jewels across the sky, cascading down on the water.

And then, he started singing. The vibration of the words echoed in my ear, throaty and sensual. When they erupted into the night sky, tears pricked my eyes for the beauty of them. My words. His voice, putting a slightly different spin on them. Like a personal love letter sent for my ears alone.

"The way the moon absorbs the dark,
is the way you grabbed my heart.
It's the way you...consume me."

He nuzzled me closer, put his mouth against my hair. "Never stop consuming me."

Tears gathered at the corners of my eyes, and I couldn't rightly understand why. I couldn't work up the energy to tell him I'd finished the song the night before.

"Lizzie," he whispered, "I'm falling in love with you."

I wiped my tears against his shirt. The warmth of his neck cupped my forehead. It came to me then why I was crying, why a sudden sadness wore through my spirit at his confession of love.

This couldn't happen. I knew it. I'd known it all along, perhaps. And yet the moment I left his arms was the moment it would all end. As long as I stayed here, I at least had this. This one, precious moment in time.

He held me tighter, ran fingers down my face to find the rest of my tears to wipe away.

"We can't do this," I whispered.

I felt his breath hitch beneath me, and I lifted my head.

"Asher, I'll never be an Elise or someone like your mom."

"Thank God."

"I'm simple. I've never wanted much, other than to be loved. Maybe one day loved by a man who shared my faith."

"Shared your..." His fingers stilled. "You're going to turn me away because I don't believe the same thing as you do about God? That seems a bit narrow-minded, don't you think?"

I practically crawled back to my own seat, the magic of the evening fast dissipating. "I'm sorry." Why was I apologizing? "I— He's too big a part of my life for me to ignore. I do care about you. More than I thought possible. But to think you'd be inwardly mocking me whenever I prayed or took out my Bible...it's just too big a factor for me. I'm so sorry."

He grabbed for my hand. "Come on, Lizzie. Give me a chance. We can work this out. I promise you I'll do nothing to hurt your beliefs. I'll even go to church with you, if that's what you want."

Was it enough? I wanted it to be, so very badly. I squeezed his hand, and when he drew me back on his lap, I didn't resist.

"I'll wait as long as I need to for you, Lizzie. You're worth it."

I snuggled closer. We stayed that way for a long time, the waves crashing below us, Asher singing softly, and me quite certain that I'd already let myself fall too deeply in love with him to consider myself in any kind of safe territory. I would get hurt in the end, and likely, he would, too. Why then, couldn't I make myself walk away now, before it was too late?

Mom was right—and wrong at the same time. She was right that I would get hurt, but wrong in thinking I was smart enough to handle things.

For my world had never felt so utterly out of control.

❧ 33 ❧

Asher lifted his face to the sun, the salty air whipping through his short hair as the 3200 Power Catamaran Sportfisher jetted toward the ocean. He focused on its power and with each knot they gained, he tried to slide thoughts of Lizzie into the recesses of his mind.

He'd told her he loved her. Well, pretty much, anyway. *Falling in love.* He'd never told a woman that before. She hadn't returned the words. In some ways, she'd rejected him on a technicality, a differing of opinions. And after a kiss like that.

But she hadn't walked away. She'd stayed. She wanted him—he knew it. If he could just convince her he wouldn't interfere with her beliefs—a mission he intended to accomplish before the end of this trip.

He sniffed hard and squinted at his brother, across from him on the upper deck of the fishing boat. Ricky'd been ready to leave at six that morning, no complaints, hat and sunglasses on, a thin bag slung over one shoulder. He'd gotten into the car without a word as Asher made small talk while hooking up his portable hand controls to Mom's car.

"Bet you never thought I'd be lugging your backside around

again, huh?" Asher tried to joke—both about his handicap and the loss of Ricky's license—but his brother had remained quiet and sullen, staring out the window at the sun's brightening rays.

Now, Asher rolled over to him, set his brake. "Nice day."

Nice day.

Man. What was with him? They'd never been reduced to small talk. Jokes, bantering, a serious conversation once in a while, but this? This was pathetic.

He didn't blame Ricky for not responding.

Better off to shoot straight. "So, what happened?"

His brother stuffed his hands in the pockets of his bathing suit, the long sleeve rugby shirt he wore was one Asher recognized from high school. "You tell me."

"If I knew, I wouldn't be asking." Asher tried to keep his tone patient, but the kid wasn't giving him much to work with.

"You took off. Just like the old man. Two peas in a pod."

Asher bit down on the side of his cheek to get a hold of the anger welling up within him. "I know I haven't been around much, but I'm not talking about me. I'm talking about you. Drinking and driving, Ricky? Losing your job. What's up with you?"

His brother looked at him from behind his sunglasses, and Asher detected accusation. "Mom begged you to come here, right? Talk some sense into me, is that it? But she made a mistake."

Asher cleared his throat. "Why's that?"

"She thought I would give a flying leap what you say."

Ouch.

"You used to care what I thought."

"That was when *you* actually cared. But you haven't, not in a long time."

"Look, the accident screwed me up, I admit that. I should have been—"

228

"No. The accident was a perfect excuse for you to not feel guilty about what you already were—not around."

Asher opened his mouth to explain, defend himself, but found he couldn't. His brother was right. After college, Asher'd been wrapped up in the building of Paramount, in creating success for himself. Spending time with Ricky landed at the bottom of his to-do list too often. He'd told himself his brother didn't need him. He was in high school at that point. Why should Asher be responsible?

The visits had been fewer and farther between until they became virtually nonexistent. The night of his accident, he'd vowed to plan some time with Ricky. He could blame the accident for it not happening, but the reality was his well-intentioned plans never happened. Something always came first—Paramount or Lucas or Elise, a trip to rock climb or ski or surf. Why hadn't he invited his brother along on some of those trips?

Swallowing his pride, he looked out at the ocean. "You're right."

He didn't miss the surprise on Ricky's face.

"I was self-absorbed, set on running the world. I thought about you a lot, but I didn't bother to make you a priority. I was stupid, Ricky. So stupid. Sad thing is, I wonder if I would have realized it if it wasn't for the accident. But by then, it was too late. And I was sure you'd be disgusted and disappointed with me." He sucked in a breath straight to his gut, wondered if any of this impacted his brother. "Things have changed for me recently. I'm starting to see I've been a coward, too afraid to face things—home, Mom and Dad, you. It's hard for me to say that, you know? I was the guy who never feared anything, always willing to take a risk."

Still, nothing from his brother.

"I know I don't deserve another chance, Ricky, but I love you, bro. You're my brother, and I miss spending time with you. I want to be a part of your life, and I want you to be a part of mine."

He gave Asher a sideways glance. "You sure are getting mushy in your old age."

Asher laughed, considered the comment a victory. "Yeah, maybe."

Ricky grabbed the rail of the boat and hung back on it, swinging side to side, still staring at the water. "I'm not the same guy I was when I was fourteen."

"And I'm not the same man I was at twenty-three."

After a minute, Ricky shrugged. "We could hang out while you're here. What'll it hurt? Mom and Dad's basement is getting kind of old."

Asher grinned. "Sounds good. I'd really like you to get to know Lizzie, too. The three of us should do dinner sometime."

"As long as I don't have to push your sorry butt around in the wheelchair."

"Hey, don't make me tackle you. You wouldn't believe how fast I am in this thing."

One corner of Ricky's mouth pulled up in a near grin. Man, this felt good.

"So what happened, Ricky? You dropped out of school—okay, I get you didn't want to study engineering, but drinking and driving? None of that sounds like you."

His brother leaned over the ship's rail. The wind tore through his clothes, pushing them against his body. "I hated school, felt like a caged animal or something. I wanted to be outside, you know? Making my way, earning some dough so I could get out from Mom and Dad's house. They started arguing a lot, in their annoyingly civil and quiet way. I got a job with the electric company. The guys and I would go out after work once in a while. They'd buy me some drinks. I had too many one night, got pulled over.

"Funny thing about a job. The bosses kind of want you there. When I lost my license, Mom drove me to work when she could. I took the train the rest of the time. I missed some days because of the DUI school. I was late a few times. One particularly bad day, I mouthed off to the boss. They let me go."

"And you've been moping in the basement ever since."

"Hey, I said we could hang out. Not that you could run my life. I'm trying, here. Once I get my license back, things will be easier."

"When's that?"

"Four more months, if I'm a good boy."

Asher studied his brother, saw something in Ricky that reminded Asher of himself—pride. It had taken the loss of his legs to quell it in Asher. What would it take with Ricky?

An idea came to him. At first, he shoved it aside to mull over and allow it to take root. He should talk to his parents or get Lizzie's thoughts. At the very least, spend more time with his brother over the next few days, make sure this idea wasn't one he'd regret.

But something pushed him toward the edge. This wasn't about his convenience—it was about his brother's life. Ricky'd veered down the wrong path. If Asher could do something to help, now was the time.

How many missed opportunities had he allowed to slip by already? How many times had he pushed aside the idea of being an integral part of his brother's life? How many times had he told himself there would be more time—another day, another week, another month?

Until there wasn't. Until life surprised him and landed him in a hospital for weeks.

Standing with Ricky in the sunlight on that boat, the remembrance of Lizzie's sweet kisses from two nights ago fresh in his mind, gratitude overcame him. He hadn't died that day. He could have. But he'd been spared.

He hadn't appreciated that fact much over the last two years —had been too busy counting his losses. But now, everywhere he looked, it seemed second chances poked out of the ground like spring flowers. A second chance here, with Ricky. If he could get his act together and convince the woman he loved that he was the man for her, then maybe a second chance at love with Lizzie.

Foreign joy bubbled up within him as a gentle wind fell across his face.

Lizzie words from their hike up Mount Battie came to him. *Kind of like the wind...I can't see it, but I can feel it.*

Is this what she'd been talking about? This stirring of gratitude in his spirit, this unexplainable peace, this certainty that somehow creation or God or someone was prompting him to step out and voice this idea to his brother?

"I have a crazy idea," Asher said.

"You know I've always been up for crazy."

"Why don't you come home with me? Change of scenery might be good. We opened a new store. You could help out there."

Ricky stared at Asher, shook his head. "Big brother swooping in to save the day, huh? A job and everything." He whistled long and low. "Man."

"I'm not trying to be a hero this time, Rick. I want to be part of your life. Not only for a week. Standing on your own two feet, away from Mom and Dad, is what you need right now. You know I won't take any crap, but I will give it to you straight. I believe in you."

Maybe what his brother needed was someone to believe in him.

"I'd have to sign up for a DUI school in Maine."

Asher nodded.

"And I'd need a ride there."

"I have some great bikes at the store. I could give you a deal."

Ricky wrinkled his face. "You're not going to make this easy on me, are you?"

"Nope."

"So you'd give me a job at your store?"

"As long as you can manage to keep it and prove yourself responsible, it's yours."

"Anything else?"

"I want a kayak partner in the annual race at the end of the summer."

Ricky smiled. "That it?"

"Lizzie does have a cute younger sister."

"Okay, okay. I know when I'm beat." He kicked the floor of the boat lightly with his sneakers. "I'd pay you rent."

"You bet your backside you will."

Ricky held out his hand as the boat slowed. "It's a deal. I hope you don't regret it."

"Make sure I don't, little brother. Now, you ready to catch a few big ones?"

❧ 34 ❧

I clipped my second earring, took a step back, and peered in the full-length mirror of the Hills' guest room. The black dress Amie insisted I borrow hugged my curves, flaring out at the bottom. I surveyed the bodice and my neck grew hot. It was perfectly tasteful, and yet it accentuated my chest in a way that would make me blush the entire night.

I panicked.

Scooping up my phone, I Face Timed Amie. "Pick up, pick up. Please, pick up!"

I'd already talked to every member of my family earlier in the day. I calculated the three-hour time difference. Seven o'clock back home. Amie could be doing anything, anywhere. Without her phone.

I was about to hang up and try Maggie when my youngest sister's blond head popped up on the phone.

"Hey, gorgeous!"

"I didn't pack a shawl! I only have my sweater. Do you think I can get away with wearing it?"

"Lizzie," Amie said on a dramatic sigh.

"What?"

"This is a *Malibu* wedding, is it not?"

"Yes."

"The frumpy sweater you've had for the last five years is *not* going to cut it."

"It's not frumpy!"

Amie shoved a chip in her mouth. "Put your phone somewhere and stand back so I can see you."

I scrambled to the vanity, adjusted the phone, and stepped back. "Can you see me?"

"Nice view! Wow, Asher's parents are loaded."

"Amie!" I moved the phone and stepped back again. "Now?"

"Woo-wee, girl! You are smokin'!"

I went closer, angled my top toward the phone. "But look at these!"

"Tell me about it. Where you been hiding them?"

"It's the dress! It's tight on top." I pressed my hands to my face. "That's it. I'm wearing the sweater."

"Lizzie Martin, for the love of all that is tasteful in fashion, do not lay a finger on that sweater."

But I was already digging through my suitcase, throwing aside pajamas and jeans and underwear. I grabbed it up, slid my bare arms into the familiar fabric. "There. Not so bad, right?"

The baggy sweater hung like one of Aunt Pris's old Victorian curtains over the dress.

"Bad. You went from hot to frump in two seconds flat."

"I have nothing else. I can't believe I didn't try on the dress before packing it. I borrowed it last year from you and it fit fine."

"You've filled out since then. In a good way, apparently."

I groaned, slumped on the bed. "What am I going to do?"

"I knew this would happen."

"So why didn't you warn me?"

She cleared her throat. "I *said*, I knew this would happen, so that's why I shoved my black silk shawl in the pocket of your suitcase."

My breath caught. I dug through the pockets until I pulled out a simple but elegant shawl. "Amie, I could kiss you!"

"Save the smooches for Asher, okay? He's not going to be able to keep his hands off you once he sees you in that dress."

I ignored her comment, already regretted texting her about the kiss Asher and I shared the other night. I threw the shawl over my shoulders, draped it casually on either side of my arms. It didn't hide as well as my baggy sweater, but I thought I could get through the night. "I'll have to iron it, but how's this?"

"You look beautiful."

I grinned. "I better go. Asher's waiting downstairs."

"Have fun. And Lizzie?"

"Yeah?"

"Don't be a bore. Lighten up, enjoy yourself. It's a wedding, after all."

"Love you, too."

We hung up. I ironed the shawl, grabbed my clutch, and headed for the stairs, careful not to trip on my heels.

A low wolf whistle sounded when I was halfway down. I looked up to see Asher sharp and crisp in a suit and tie. Hair gelled back, one curl fell endearingly over his forehead. My stomach fluttered, my heart beat like a hummingbird's wings. I descended the rest of the stairs, conscious of his eyes on my every movement. I prayed I wouldn't trip.

"You look gorgeous. Wow, Lizzie." His gaze roamed my body and I self-consciously touched the scar at my neck.

"You clean up pretty good yourself."

"We could skip the wedding and stay in. We'd have the house to ourselves…"

"I don't think that's a good idea. Besides, your mom would throw a fit." Mrs. Hill had left an hour earlier to help Lucas's mother with some last-minute arrangements. I wondered if Mr. Hill would be at the wedding.

"You're probably right. Here, I got you something." He took a

wrapped gift the size of my arm off the bench in the foyer.
"Happy Birthday."

My gaze fluttered to his. "How'd you know?"

"Your mom texted me the day we left. I didn't realize...I'm
sorry you can't be with your family tonight."

"I'm happy to be here. We had a big old Face Time call earlier.
The Happy Birthday song and everything." I twirled the present
in my hand. "Should I open it now?"

"Go for it."

I tore the paper, my breath catching at the retro pink-and-
white box, the words Barbie written in hot pink. "You didn't!" I
ripped open the rest of the paper to reveal a Barbie "Jam With
Me" Electric Guitar. Tears pooled at the corners of my eyes. I
couldn't imagine a more perfect present. Clutching the guitar box
to my chest, I leaned over and kissed his cheek, inhaling the
woodsy, citrus scent of him. "I love it. Asher, thank you so much.
I think this might be the best birthday present anyone's ever
given me."

"I can't wait to hear you play."

I rolled my eyes. "I'll run this up to my room?"

"I'll enjoy watching you."

I slapped him playfully, wondered how I could be so comfortable with him at the same time that he made my pulse throb like
a drum. I anticipated the night before us, spending time together,
eating, maybe dancing?

My thoughts stalled as I reminded myself whose wedding we
were attending. As I reminded myself the reason I'd walked away
from him on his parents' patio the other night. I couldn't
pretend none of it mattered. It mattered all too much. Besides,
Asher would probably see Elise and forget about me altogether.
He'd most likely be filled with regret that he wasn't in Lucas's
shoes.

The jet ski picture crept into my mind's eye. If Asher hadn't
had his accident, this could be *his* perfect Malibu wedding. Could

I really pretend this was only a fun night between two people who enjoyed one another's company?

I came back down the stairs, a cloud of trepidation hanging over me. But it was too late.

Ready or not, Elise. Here we come.

❧ 35 ❧

Asher pulled into the church parking lot and parked the car. He looked at Lizzie, knew without a doubt she would be the most beautiful woman there. He also knew without a doubt that he wouldn't be able to roll into this place without her.

"Thank you. For coming with me tonight."

"Stop thanking me. I wanted to." Glittering earrings hung above her delicate neck. Her hair, curled in ringlets, landed softly at her shoulders. She took his breath away, plain and simple.

She inched out a hand to grasp his. "Are you okay with this? I mean, it's not too late, right?"

"I'm okay. This is something I need to do. It's going to be like stepping into the Twilight Zone, but I'll always wonder if I don't. No matter what's in our past, I want to support Lucas. He's my president. He was my best friend."

She nodded. "Okay, then. You ready?"

They sneaked into the back of the church. No one approached them, but he watched Lucas and his brother and his parents at the front of the church. Lucas said something to his best man, a nervous smile on his face. He looked happy. In another world, Asher would have been the one standing beside his friend on his big day. Making last minute jokes to ease wedding day jitters. Making sure the rings lay safe in his pocket.

A whole other world, indeed.

As the music shifted and everyone stood for the entrance of the bride, Asher peered through suits and dresses to glimpse Elise, but all he could see was a blonde head on top a blur of white. When everyone stood, he saw her from a distance, just as he remembered. Same long blonde hair, same honey skin. A white dress fit for a princess and a Hollywood runway, a figure most women would kill for. And yet nothing stirred within him. Not longing, not even jealousy.

He reached for Lizzie's hand and squeezed. She returned the gesture, and gratitude overcame him again. Never in his life could he imagine being thankful for the accident. And really, he supposed that probably wasn't the right word. But now, with his old life staring him in the face, he saw plain as day that he didn't want to live in his old world.

He didn't want to live in any world that didn't include having Lizzie by his side. If only he could convince her, once and for all, that by his side was where she belonged.

❦

IF THERE WAS SUCH A THING AS FAIRYTALE WEDDINGS ON THE earthly side of *once upon a time*, it was here, in Malibu, at the Casa di Pietra, a beautiful oceanside estate popular for elegant parties. A grand tent and rolling green lawn unfolded to a glistening cerulean sea with a private beach. Couples mingled, sampling appetizers and drinking cocktails. Music and laughter drifted like the call of wind chimes through the air.

Glued to Asher's side, I tugged on my shawl, completely out of my element. His mother introduced me to Lucas's parents and forced a cocktail into my hand. I took dainty sips in between snatches of light conversation. When we finally made our way to seats in a far corner, I practically wilted into my chair.

"You're doing good, Martin."

"You, too."

"Stop pulling at your shawl. Better yet, take it off. Ceremony's over and you look gorgeous."

I tugged at the shawl once again. "Thanks, but there's a chill in the air and I'd rather keep it on."

He winked at me.

A large man in his early thirties with long hair tied neatly back in a ponytail approached us. "Asher, man!"

Asher's face broke out in a grin. "Big Tom!" They shook hands. "How you been, buddy?"

"Good, good. How about you?" His gaze raked over me. "Not terrible, huh?"

"Lizzie, this is Tom. This guy's the best adventure filmmaker on the Pacific coast."

Tom took my hand with his meaty one. "Great to meet you."

"You, too."

"So what have you been up to, man? We miss you on our treks. It's not the same. Don't get me wrong, I love Lucas. But he doesn't have *the edge*."

Asher leaned back in his chair, face relaxing. "The edge." He sighed. "Remember Indian Creek?"

Tom laughed, made a comment about Lucas having an accident in his pants. "And I got all the footage. Including your summit. Sweet stuff, man. Sweet stuff." He was silent for a moment. "I was sorry to hear what happened. It rots."

"I'm getting by. Seeing stuff I never saw before, even."

Tom cocked his head but didn't ask more. After a few more minutes, they said goodbye. Another of Asher's friends came over, someone who worked at the Paramount home office. Then another high school friend, then a friend of his family's. Each one seemed happy to see him. He'd been loved. At the same time, I tried to quell a righteous sort of anger on his behalf. If these people had cared so much for him, where had they been the last two years?

I swallowed down my bitter thoughts as everyone sat and the wedding party entered. Elise's train had been pulled up and her dress showed off her gorgeous figure, her model-worthy skin. She was pretty enough to be an actress, and I tried to remember if Asher had told me what she did for a living. Probably an underwear model or something.

I told myself I wasn't jealous. I tried not to picture her with Asher. As she and Lucas came together on the dance floor, I tried not to imagine the way Asher had once taken her in his arms in a similar way. He'd kissed her like he had me the other night. Touched her. No doubt made love to her.

I breathed deep around the nasty mental images. Asher inched his fingers beneath the tablecloth and grasped my hand in his warm one. I looked at him, tried to decipher his expression, but failed. When he turned to me, he stared into my eyes, caressing my fingers with his own, trailing one up the back of my hand and down along my palm to the inside of my wrist, making me forget about him and Elise altogether.

We ate oysters and sushi and stuffed haddock and roasted potatoes and greens and cake. We made small talk with those at our table, friends Elise and Lucas had met on a trip to Hawaii the year before. As the sun set and guests drifted onto the dance floor, the bridal couple made their way around the tables, finally coming to ours.

Lucas, tall and handsome in a silver tuxedo, hugged Asher. When he pulled away, his blue eyes watered. "Man, thanks for coming. You don't know what this means to me."

Asher blinked fast, cleared his throat. "Glad to be here. Sorry it took so long."

"Asher, I'm sorry. I—we have to catch up. Really. Okay? Can we?"

"Yeah. When you get back from your honeymoon." Asher turned to Elise and held his hand out to her. If possible, she was even more beautiful up close.

She took his hand, bent to kiss his cheek. "Thanks for coming, Asher."

He squeezed her hand once before letting it drop. "I'm happy for you guys. I actually can't believe it, but I am."

Elise's face crumpled and she swiped the bottom of her perfectly-lined eyelids. "You're a sweet guy, Ash. Thank you."

Asher turned toward me, something like pride on his face. "This is Lizzie."

I shook their hands, and any intimidation I held toward them —any threat of Asher's old life—melted as his old world collided with his new one.

As they left the table hand-in-hand, I turned to Asher.

The dark crept in and dim lights illuminated the tent, the sides open to the darkening ocean, creating an intimate setting. "You did it."

"I—I really am happy for them. I've forgiven them."

I squeezed his arm. "She's beautiful."

"Martin, I hope you're not comparing, because it's no contest. Elise is beautiful, sure. But you're beautiful in a way that touches the core of me. It's like, I've gained a sixth sense and no one can touch that place in me except you. Your beauty is outside, inside and straight through. You are real beauty."

He kissed me gently, right in front of everyone. "Happy Birthday."

My gut told me to pull away, but Amie's advice to lighten up seemed so much more appealing. One night. Was it too much to ask? "I hope your mom didn't see that. She might start to get the wrong idea."

"Wait until she sees us on the dance floor."

I giggled, the cocktail I'd had warming my insides. "I'm a horrible dancer."

"Lucky for you, all you have to do is sit on my lap."

I tried to imagine what kind of a scene we'd make. Former boyfriend of the bride taking his new girlfriend—could I call myself that? *Should* I call myself that?—for a spin in his wheelchair on the dance floor. "I don't know…"

He placed his napkin on the table, grabbed my hand as Ed Sheeran's "Perfect" started playing. "Come on, let's give them something to talk about."

I thought to protest, but the fact of the matter was that if he were not in a wheelchair, I wouldn't think twice about a slow dance. Why shouldn't we dance?

Asher found a spot on the wooden floor, pulled me onto his lap as Ed Sheeran sang about finding love that was perfect for him.

Asher took one of my hands with his, moved us around with his other hand steering his wheelchair. I closed my eyes, sinking into the music, the gentle sway of the wheels moving perfectly to the beat.

I didn't care who was watching, all I cared about was that moment, that man. His hand in mine, his voice singing to me, his warm breath against my cheek.

My insides trembled, caught in the moment. When the song ended, moving into the "Cupid Shuffle," I made to get up, but Asher's firm arms kept me to him. "Take a ride with me, Lizzie."

"Okay," I breathed.

Still on his lap, he wheeled us down the sloped path toward the beach and I squealed, grasping his neck as we plunged toward the hill, my shawl flying behind us. We must have been a sight, but I didn't care. Didn't even care if Asher's parents saw us.

With some effort, he propelled us down the beach to the spot where the water met compact sand.

"Now, that's an extreme sport," he said.

"The most extreme sport I've ever participated in."

He moved my hair back from my neck, lowered his lips to the

delicate skin. Goosebumps broke out on my skin, having nothing to do with the temperature and everything to do with the backs of his fingers running down my arms and over my waist. His lips moved up and behind my ear before kissing me sweetly on the top of my head, where I snuggled against his shoulder.

"Two months ago, I wouldn't have been caught dead here. Now, I can honestly say this is one of the best nights I can remember in a long time. You're changing me, Lizzie. Making me want to live again. I don't know how you did it, but you did."

He tilted my chin to meet my lips with his own. The wind danced around us, gentle waves lapped at our feet like a soft applause requesting an encore. Tender, insistent. Asking for more.

I wanted nothing more than to capitulate, but the uneasy feeling that had wedged itself within my chest since that moment on Asher's parents' patio returned. If we didn't have this conversation soon, it would only hurt both of us.

I fingered the collar of his shirt. "Asher, I'm not sure I've been honest with you. Maybe not with myself, either." I swallowed. Did I have to do this now? In this most magical of places?

But I'd already ruined it. He stiffened, and I felt his guard go up. "What do you mean? Honest about what?"

"About...us. I—I like you. A lot. Too much maybe. But we're from different worlds. This casual dating thing...it's not for me. I'm a marrying kind of girl." I placed a hand on his chest. "And that's not me fishing for anything, it's just facts."

I watched his Adam's apple bob by the light of the moon. "Okay."

"Being here with you is amazing, but it also makes me see how we're on entirely different pages about life, about everything that matters." That horrible image of him and Elise together in the most intimate of ways came back to my mind.

"You're talking about your faith again, aren't you? Lizzie, I told you. Whatever it takes. I love you how you are. I wouldn't do anything to change that."

I bit my lip. "I want it to be enough." I closed my eyes. "God, I want it to be enough."

"Why isn't it?" He grasped my hands with his. "Lizzie, I swear I will be an angel. I'll go to church with you. I'll pray with you. Heck, you want to read Bible verses together? I'll do it."

Something inside me bent. Everything was right. Everything but for one thing—it would all be a hoax. A show. Like the time Mom slapped an iron-on patch on the knees of my favorite pair of jeans. It had worked great at first. But after a few hard play sessions and washes, it had begun to curl on the outsides, to tear apart from the whole of the fabric, taking stringy threads with it.

It hadn't really fixed anything, and it eventually ruined both pieces of cloth.

I sank back into Asher's arms, defeated, but not finding the strength to end it all right there and then. He clutched me tight, pressed his face to the top of my head. "We'll figure it out, Lizzie. I promise. *I'm* going to figure this out."

I closed my eyes, listening to the swirl of the sea and Asher's quiet heartbeat. Tears threatened to choke me, but I swallowed them back.

If only it were that easy.

⚜

ASHER TRAILED HIS FINGERS DOWN LIZZIE'S ARM, SAVORING THE warm, slight weight of her against his chest. He meant what he said—one way or another, he *would* figure this out. There was no way he'd let something as trivial as individual beliefs stop them from being together.

The waves lapped at the shore as he played their conversation over in his head. A part of him couldn't believe he'd promised her all that—go to church? Read the Bible? But then again, surprisingly, a part of him didn't regret the offer. True, he might not believe any of it, but what could it hurt? Whatever it was she believed certainly made her pleasant to be around. He could use some help in that regard. Church people were all about love and helping the poor and things like that, right?

Who knows, sticking around such people might even help his reputation. It might help his business.

A prick of something unpleasant started in his ribs. Leave it to him to figure out how sacrificing for Lizzie could benefit *him*. He sighed, and rested his chin on her head. The floral scent of her shampoo stirred a longing within him—a longing for something he couldn't quite touch, and maybe would never be able to.

Was he supposed to let Lizzie go? Free her up to be with Mike?

Emotion climbed his throat and he cleared it, hard. No. Not yet, anyway. They still had the rest of this trip to work things out. Something had to give. There had to be an answer for them.

And Asher planned on doing everything in his power to find it.

❧ 36 ❧

"**B**ut I don't understand why we have to bring your guitar to your office building." I scurried alongside Asher, weaving in and out of lampposts and people and bicyclists, street signs and vendors. Downtown Los Angeles. Asher had promised me a tour of the area, as well as a tour of the Paramount home office. But I couldn't make sense of his harried nature that morning.

We hadn't spoken about our time on the beach during the wedding. It seemed Asher would rather pretend our conversation hadn't happened. But I knew he was thinking on it, for he hadn't attempted to pull me close since then—had kept our relationship strictly platonic, which made me both relieved and hurt all at the same time.

He'd woken in a bit of a mood this morning, grumbling that he'd burnt his toast, that his lazy brother was still sleeping. I assumed it was stress, going to his old workplace, and so near the scene of his accident.

On top of that, he was bent on lugging his guitar on the train and through the city. I'd asked him to let me carry it, but he'd

248

refused, angling it awkwardly between his legs and holding it with one hand while he wheeled with the other.

"You'll see," he said. "But we have to hurry. We're running a little late."

"Late for what?" I asked between labored breaths. "This is your business. Is it a meeting, because I really hate meetings. I hope you're okay if I wait outside."

"You'll do great." He pulled open a large glass door to a sleek office building.

I didn't have time to comprehend that this was where he'd lost the use of his legs forever. It didn't seem right. I'd wanted to study the street in silence, if only for a minute. Give honor to Asher's suffering. But his words distracted me. I shook my head. "Do great? Do great for what?"

Once inside, he pressed the button to the elevator. "Lizzie, I have a confession."

Bitter bile climbed the back of my throat. "No. No confessions."

The elevator door opened and he wheeled in, grabbed my hand to urge me forward. "We have an appointment."

"With someone at your company?"

"With a friend of mine at a music agency on the floor above Paramount."

"A—a music..." My stomach roiled and I leaned against the elevator wall as it lifted us up. He wanted us to sing together for a music agent. "I'm going to be sick."

"Breathe, Martin."

I knelt down, put my head between my legs.

"Lizzie, your voice is amazing. Your song is amazing. All you have to do is go in there and play this guy your song. That's it. One song. Three minutes. I'll be right there. It'll be just the three of us."

"I—I don't know." This wasn't in the plan. How much better to record on my own, send out my music to someone in an office far away. But to stand in front of an expert music executive, someone who knew the business and the talent, and to pretend I thought I had what it took? "I can't."

"Lizzie, please. Do it for me."

He could have said anything else and I wouldn't have listened. But he'd gone through a lot of trouble to get this meeting. How could I bail on him now? He wanted this so badly for me. Maybe for us. And I wanted to make him happy.

Take a risk for once...

And I had, hadn't I? Picking up that phone on the radio call, designing the interior landscaping for Asher's store, coming to L.A. Everything I'd done since meeting Asher had been one big risk and so far, I couldn't honestly say I regretted any of it.

But neither had I consulted with God about these risks. I'd told Asher and myself that I wanted my life to reflect my Creator's. Was this, singing for some top music executive, actually going to accomplish that? Or was my life morphing into a love song not for my God, but for Asher?

A horrible knowing came to me as the elevator jolted before settling us down. The door opened to a neat hallway, a picture of Natalie Cole singing on the wall above a simple stand with brochures advertising various concerts. "You...you brought me here for this, didn't you? Not for the wedding. You didn't really need me at all, did you?" Hadn't I known, deep inside, that I shouldn't have come? That I was chasing all the wrong things, and that in the end it would lead to this...the death of my dreams, the death of who I thought myself to be?

"I need you. With every breath, I need you. But Lizzie, I want to help. I meant everything I said to you this past week. You made me want to live again. I love you. I want to be with you. And I want you to chase your dreams."

My dreams. Asher didn't intend to sing with me, then? The elevator doors stood open. "This is too much."

Asher wheeled halfway out the door. He was probably scared

if he left me alone in the elevator I'd disappear back to the ground floor. He would have been right.

"Don't overthink this. We're just going in to sing."

He led me toward the reception desk, where a young woman with dark-rimmed glasses smiled at us. "Ash. Good to see you. Dane's expecting you. First door on the right." The woman smiled at me, and once again I was reminded of the enormity of Asher's world here. Camera guys and music execs and multi-million-dollar companies. Was he trying to fit me into it all? Did I fit into it all? Did I want to slide myself into a neat compartment I'd never be able to climb out from?

My chest constricted as I followed Asher down a hallway with photographs of various singers and bands. The Beach Boys. Guns N' Roses. Did Asher's friend work with these music greats?

Asher knocked on the open door. A crisp laugh followed by a confident voice welcomed us in. A man in his fifties with red glasses, spiked hair, and a tie with Elvis's picture on it pumped Asher's hand. "Good to see you again, man. I almost fell over in my seat when Rain told me you'd called."

"Well, you know talent, and I think I found you some." Asher turned to me. "Dane, this is Lizzie Martin." He smiled as if I were the sun and the moon. I wondered if he had blinders on. For surely this Dane fellow could see to the core of who I was— or at least what potential fans might see. A plain country girl without a lot of grit. One with a pretty voice that wowed those sitting in church pews in her small-town back home, but not one fit for the big leagues—certainly not for Hollywood and radio stations.

My stomach churned as I took Dane's offered hand. The next few minutes blurred together like a fuzzy, black-and-white television rerun. Asher and Dane making small talk. Asher taking out his guitar, handing it to me, ushering me to a seat across from where Dane stood, leaning against a glossy black desk.

Asher wasn't going to sing, after all.

His guitar was big and clumsy in my hands. Black spots appeared before my eyes.

"Go ahead, Lizzie. Whenever you're ready. Breathe." Asher was beside me, and I felt smothered. Same with this Dane guy. Couldn't they give me some room?

"I used to think alone..." I choked on the words, my fingers stumbled. "Sorry."

Asher laughed lightly, but it was a tense, fake thing. My stomach gurgled.

"Here, why don't I play?" He took the guitar gently from my hands. Strummed a few notes, then started singing, prompting me much as he did around my family's campfire.

Oh, how that night seemed so far away. Like a dream, a slice of heaven. I'd never been more homesick in my life, would have given anything to click my heels three times and be transported back to Maine. Back to Orchard House. Back to my family.

Asher sang the first verse without me. I licked my lips, stared at the floor, opened my mouth...and vomited all over Dane's shoes.

Clamping a hand over my lips, I rushed from the room, past Rain and her desk, and into the elevator, stomach still heaving.

When I finally reached the doors outside, the scents of freshly-baked goods made me queasy again. I slumped in an out-of-the-way spot against the building, sliding down to the cool pavement. I wiped my mouth with my shirt and brought my knees to my chest, my entire insides trembling, shaking. I pressed my face into my knees, covered my head with my arms. Passersby would think I was homeless or suffering a hangover or withdrawal. I didn't care. I didn't care about anything but getting home.

Who had I been kidding that I had what it took to make it big in the world? I didn't want this pressure, no matter if it meant the entire world would never appreciate my music. That was Josie's dream, not mine.

Anger stirred in my belly. Asher should have never brought me here. He said he cared for me. But if that were true, he should have known I'd not do well under such pressure.

I was sick of everyone thinking they knew what was best for me. Amie calling that radio station, Asher urging me to come to Los Angeles, to sing in front of someone like Dane. Why couldn't they believe me when I said I was content with my simple life? Helping Mom at the bed and breakfast, teaching a music class now and again? Playing with my flowers in the garden. Singing in church or for a fundraiser.

Yes, my life had been simple, but it had been filled with purpose. I had let all that was important to me fall by the wayside these last couple of months. I had allowed God to lessen in importance while Asher rose to epic proportions. And Asher didn't understand why that bothered me so much. Oh, how I wished he understood!

I heard the wheels of Asher's chair rolling up beside me. "Lizzie, I'm so sorry."

I wiped my tears with the back of my arm, and then swiped at my mouth. I stood. "Let's forget it, okay? I—I think I'm going to head back home."

"Yeah, sure. Can you just give me a minute? I left my guitar up there."

"No, Asher. You go. You have your coworkers to see. I'll head back by myself. I'm okay. Really."

I didn't think I'd ever lied to him before. I stared at the street before us. A vendor sold flowers on the other side. I imagined Asher crossing the street, a car slamming into him, changing his life. Changing mine.

He hesitated. "No, I don't want to leave you alone. I'll come back tomorrow. Give me one minute so I can get my guitar?"

I didn't answer, but he must have taken it as assent. He disappeared back inside the doors, and when I saw him roll into the elevator, I didn't think—I ran. The streets of L.A. passed by in a

HEIDI CHIAVAROLI

blur as I raced toward the subway, shimmying around the many city folks who knew where they were going and what they were about. The wind dried my tears.

I'd send Asher a text once I was on the train. I'd insist he stay and visit his home office. I didn't want to inconvenience him anymore. I'd use my meager savings to call an Uber, return to Asher's parents' home to pack, and then grab another ride to the airport to get the first flight home. I'd explain in the text. Encourage Asher to finish out the trip with whatever he needed to do—see to Paramount, spend time with his parents, plan Ricky's move, buy Dane some new shoes.

I was only in the way. And I couldn't stand this stuffy, glitzy city another moment. I needed Maine. I needed Camden. I needed Orchard House.

I needed my family.

And as much as I hated to admit it, Asher and I had to go back to being only friends.

❧ 37 ❧

The elevator doors were about to close when a sudden knowing gripped Asher. He stuck a hand out to stop it from taking him back up to Dane's office.

He couldn't leave Lizzie. Not now, when she was so upset. Dane would keep his guitar safe until he could get it tomorrow. Right now, Lizzie needed him.

He pushed back through the double doors, out onto the street. But there was only empty pavement where Lizzie had sat a moment earlier. "Lizzie?"

He turned, caught a flash of her bobbing ponytail and yellow t-shirt weaving through the crowd. She was running. "Lizzie!"

She didn't stop, or she didn't hear him. He pushed his chair forward hard, but as soon as he did, he became compressed in a fresh deluge of people who had crossed from the other side of the street.

He fought them for a moment, yelling "excuse me," but to no avail. Once his line of sight cleared, he scanned the crowds for a glimpse of yellow—but it was all in vain. She was gone. Even if he wheeled himself in the direction he'd last seen her headed, he'd never catch her. She obviously didn't want to be caught. Maybe the best thing he could do right now was give her space. He'd go get his guitar, check in quick at the office, and meet her back at the house. He'd apologize like crazy and pray she forgave him.

Pray. What a funny thing to think of attempting once again. But it wouldn't bring about the results he wanted, just like last time...of course it wouldn't.

He took the elevator back up to Dane's office. Rain gestured him down the hall and for the second time that day, Asher knocked on the open door of the man's office.

"Come in."

Asher wheeled into the simply furnished office. Dane sat behind his desk, tying on a pair of sneakers.

"Man, I'm sorry about your shoes. I'll replace them—just send me the bill."

Dane shook his head, finished tying. "No worries. It happens. Part of the business."

"You're more gracious than I would've been. Thanks." Asher gestured for his guitar. "I just came back for this."

"You know, I never would have pictured you with a girl like that."

Something in Asher's chest caught fire. "Lizzie's a great girl." He looked out Dane's window to the steel and glass of the next building over. "The best kind."

Dane whistled long and low. "Sounds like you really care for her. What do your parents think?"

"They love her. Though I think they know she's too good for me." Asher shook his head. "I don't know—they're probably right. In fact, I know *they're* right." He looked at the various pictures of music celebrities on Dane's office wall. What had he been thinking dragging Lizzie here, as if he knew what was best for her? "She doesn't belong in this business. It'd eat her up alive. She belongs at home, in her small town, singing in her little church, marrying some guy who's never even looked at a woman with more in mind than a handshake."

Dane leaned back in his chair, seeming to listen, wait.

It struck Asher then that he was sharing more with this man he barely knew than he often shared with his psychologists. What was with him?

"She's really gotten to you."

Asher shrugged as if it didn't matter. But it did. All too much. He'd been pushing ahead with their relationship, believing it would happen. But the events of the last fifteen minutes caused him to face reality. "She doesn't want to be with me. And it's not because of the chair. It's because of her faith. Can you believe that?" He shook his head. "Sorry, Dane. I didn't mean to waste your time." He took up the guitar, started back for the door.

"Wait. You said she doesn't want to be with you because of her faith?"

"Well no, she *wants* to be with me." A girl didn't kiss a guy like Lizzie had that night on his parents' patio if she didn't want to be with him. "She just doesn't think she *should* be with me. She thinks I'd ruin her beliefs or something."

"And what beliefs do you have?"

Asher eyed the door, felt suddenly uncomfortable. But he couldn't be rude. Not after Dane made time for Lizzie. Not after she'd hurled all over his shoes.

He shrugged. "I used to think there was a God. I prayed to Him after my accident. But He didn't show up."

"Maybe He showed up in a way you didn't expect."

Asher blinked. This was too much. "What do you mean?"

"I mean, two years ago I couldn't imagine the great Asher Hill caring about the career of a girl who didn't have the power to advance his name or social status or business or career."

Ouch. "That's harsh."

Dane shrugged, his Elvis tie a bit askew at his neck. "Is it not true?"

He blew out a breath. "It's true."

"Maybe God's showing up for you in ways you didn't expect. Maybe all the bad that's happened to you has brought a lot of good. Maybe your experiences don't negate the existence of a Creator—maybe instead, they prove it."

The guy's words pricked something both hurtful and hopeful inside of him. At the same time, they felt out of place. How had they even gotten around to this?

But man, what a thought. That his life and his journey, particularly since his accident, proved the existence of a God.

Dane studied him, serious eyes behind those flashy maroon glasses. "Your parents ever tell you I almost died when I was a little younger than you?"

Asher shook his head. "No..."

"Cocaine overdose. Sex, drugs, and rock n' roll, right? All fun until it wasn't anymore. Until I woke up in a hospital realizing what I'd done. It nearly killed my parents. And I didn't care. I didn't care about anything but the drugs." Dane sighed, as if the story was still painful to remember. "My parents put me in a recovery program. It was rough, but I found my way back to living, and I can't say I did it alone."

Asher stayed silent, but cocked his head to the side.

"God saved me, man. He healed a messed-up part of me."

Asher remembered the story of Jesus healing that paralyzed man on the mat, but of course Dane wasn't talking about physical healing. He was talking about an addiction.

One side of Dane's mouth tilted up. "Should I shut up, or do you want to hear more?"

Asher swallowed, curiosity getting the better of him. Besides, how could he say he wouldn't listen to Dane when Dane had taken time out of his schedule to listen to Lizzie? He'd been excited to show Lizzie the Paramount offices, but she clearly didn't want any part of him right now.

"I have nowhere else I have to be. I suppose I could use a good story about now."

THE ENGINE OF THE PLANE GREW LOUDER AS IT BARRELED down the runway. Asher closed his eyes and leaned back against the headrest, turning over the events of the last week in his head. Kissing Lizzie, the wedding, bringing Ricky home, talking to Dane in his office.

"Don't beat yourself up, big brother. She'll come around." Beside him, in what should have been Lizzie's seat on the way home, Ricky sat, legs splayed so they wouldn't bump into the seat in front of him.

He still couldn't wrap his head around what had happened in Dane's office. Still couldn't wrap his head around the feeling of being a new man. He'd found something he'd never known in that office—the peace and truth that came with laying his disability, his doubts, his fears at the feet of God's Son. His problems were not all up to him to solve. His relationship with Lizzie, his parents' marriage, Ricky's future, even Paramount's success. He couldn't be everyone's hero. And the craziest thing? He never would have known this peace if it wasn't for his paralysis.

Still....

"I just want to talk to her," Asher said.

The plane gained speed and lifted off the ground. The woman in front of him wore enough perfume for three people. His stomach soured.

"She texted you though, right?" Ricky asked.

Asher exhaled long and slow. "Yeah. Said she was super home-sick, told me to thank Mom and Dad for her, that she'd talk to me back in Camden." But he'd called her half a dozen times, left voice messages and texts begging that she call him back. She hadn't. "I really screwed things up."

"You really like her, don't you? More than you ever did Elise."

"I love her." His voice was quiet, as if he were in a church and what they spoke of was holy, sacred. "I can't imagine life without her."

"Then take the plunge, man. She thinks she disappointed you. Bro, you're a good guy, but you're intense, even in that wheelchair. Always chasing after the impossible, the too big. You're a tough act to follow, tougher to keep up with. Take it from someone who knows."

Asher cocked his head. "What do you mean?"

"I mean, part of the reason I didn't want to talk to you for the last several months was because I knew you'd be disappointed. I'd failed you. Sure, I'd failed Mom and Dad, too. But I could handle that. Kids have been disappointing their parents since the beginning of time. But you...you were always larger than life to me. And I failed you. Never mind, dropping out of college, but after the DUI..." Ricky winced.

Asher slapped his brother's arm with the back of his hand. "You never failed me. If anything, you failed yourself. But that doesn't change how I feel about you. You're my brother."

"I'm only saying, it's not an easy thing letting you down."

"I think Lizzie's more angry with me than worried about disappointing me."

Ricky leaned back in his seat, popped in an ear bud. "You'll figure it out. You're a smart guy. And that's one girl you do not want to let go of."

"Thanks, little brother. I think it's going to be good having you around."

"Now, *that* is yet to be seen."

It struck him then that he could pray for Ricky. He could pray for Lizzie. Dane said he'd been forgiven, that humbling himself before God opened up the doors of His Kingdom.

Ricky closed his eyes to listen to his music as the plane soared above the clouds, chasing the sun. Going east, toward Maine.

Toward Lizzie. Toward everything Asher was beginning to think of as his real home.

God...

He stumbled through his first sentence, but then something burst inside of him and he prayed in thought more than words. And he knew. God was listening.

❧ 38 ☙

A fierce banging started in my head. I peeled one eye open. It landed on the prescription bottle for my thyroid medication. That's right. I'd run out while in California, and the pharmacy needed to get approval from my doctor's office for a refill. I needed to get on that today. It was likely why I was so horribly tired and emotional.

When I'd arrived home earlier than anticipated, my family had crowded around me. I'd cried in Mom's arms, unashamed, simply grateful to be back at the best place on earth. I cuddled into their obvious concern but wouldn't open my mouth to tell them the horrifying events that happened in Los Angeles.

The banging again. I rolled onto my side just as my door burst open. I turned to squint at my three sisters.

"Morning!" Josie snapped open the shade and I squeezed my eyes shut, the light sending pain slicing through my head. "It's a gorgeous day. A perfect day for a hike, in fact."

Amie flopped down on my bed, scaring Bets off the covers. "Josie's right. Time to get up. You've moped long enough. Time for an intervention."

"Another one?" I mumbled, sliding my head under the covers.

Maggie tore off my covers. "Yes. Lizzie, it's ten o'clock. You never sleep this late. It's time to tell us what happened in California."

I groaned. "It's too painful."

"But we're your sisters." Josie smoothed my hair back from my face. "You look pale. You need some fresh air."

"I'm fine."

"She doesn't want fresh air? This is more serious than I thought," Amie said.

Now coverless, I curled my pajama-clad legs up to my belly, resting in the fetal position.

"Come on, Lizzie," Maggie gentled her voice. "At least come down for some coffee and breakfast."

The thought of food made my stomach curdle. Made me think of Dane's office, the contents of my stomach on his shoes and on the rug. Asher must have been mortified. I could never face him again.

"My stomach's queasy. Maybe later."

Josie knelt beside me on my bedroom floor. "Fine, then. We talk right here, right now. No more Mrs. Nice Guy. Spill your guts, Lizzie. Whatever happened can't be worse than me getting knocked up by my professor and having to come home with my tail between my legs. Remember that?" Her eyes widened. "Oh no. You didn't sleep with Asher, did you?"

I slung an arm over my eyes. "No."

"Was it something that happened at the wedding? Did he fall all over his ex-girlfriend?" Amie asked.

"No."

"Was it his mother? Was she terribly rude?"

I shook my head. "No."

"Then what, Lizzie? Tell us!"

I sucked in air, thought I smelled my own stale breath. Gross. "Asher took me to the Paramount home office. There's a music agency in the building."

Josie slapped my arm. "That's right! He told us he was going to surprise you with that."

I sat up, instantly regretting it for the wave of dizziness that stole over me. "What? You guys knew about that?"

Amie shifted on my bed. "He told us the night of the campfire when you went in to get your guitar. Bronson was really grilling him and he confessed one of the reasons he wanted to take you to California was to help you chase your dreams. We thought it was super sweet."

Tears pricked the corners of my eyes. I didn't have the strength to hold them back. "You guys should have told me."

"You never would have gone."

"You're right. I wouldn't have. And I never would have had the opportunity to humiliate myself in front of that agent and Asher. I never would have vomited before I finished the first verse. I never would have ruined his shoes and disappointed Asher." I fell back onto my bed, sobs overtaking me.

"Oh, honey," Josie grasped for my hand. They huddled around me, Amie climbing on the other side of me and hugging me, Maggie wrapping all of us in one big sandwich of a hug, her gigantic belly pressing into my side.

"And you guys didn't think it was a big enough deal to tell me. I guess that shows what a baby I am." No one understood. No one at all. "I've been rushing ahead with everything, not even asking God what He thinks about it all. I thought I was falling in love with Asher, but how can we be together? We're from different worlds. He's always going to strive to be the best, to rush ahead and want more. But I don't want to become a big music star. I'm okay with staying at Orchard House forever. We don't believe the same things. We don't value the same things. I don't think we're meant to be after all."

If only the thought didn't completely and thoroughly break my heart.

"Honey, you need to talk to him. If you can't be together

because of the major stuff, you still need to face him. He deserves an explanation, and you owe it to yourself, too." Maggie wiggled off the bed, slid on the floor beside Josie.

Amie squished me tight with her arms. "I agree. You can't run away."

Josie nodded. "Take it from someone who has experience running away—a lot. It doesn't end great. Much better to deal with what's going on between you two, even if it brings you separate ways. Honey, you have to face the music."

"There wasn't any music. There were only chunks of vomit."

"Oh, Lizzie!" Josie leaned her forehead against my arm, laughing softly. "You know what I mean. You can't hide from Asher forever."

Josie was right. I couldn't burrow in my bedroom for all my remaining days. As much as I hated to admit it, I needed to live. To face the music. "I'll talk to him. I will. I just need a couple days to settle."

"At least get some fresh air. Will you promise us that?" Josie opened my window wider and a gust of salty sea air cleansed the room. Strange, but I could swear the Atlantic Ocean smelled different than the Pacific. More like home.

I sat up. "Let me pull on some clothes and brush my teeth. I'll be down in a minute." Perhaps my sisters were right. A little sunshine would improve my energy and my spirits. I needed some time alone in the woods to think and pray, to figure out the mess my life had become.

❄ 39 ❄

I stretched my legs, taking the rocks up Mount Battie in good time. After a cup of coffee and some eggs, Mom and my sisters had pushed me out the door. Even Amie insisted she'd help clean the guest rooms—a first that I could remember—so I could hike.

The smell of damp earth and pine wrapped around me. The hiking pants I'd bought from the store—*Empower Pants*—swished slightly as I climbed up, the trail winding and twisting. I didn't sing today or give my songs any thought. I tried not to think about Asher. Instead, I prayed. Prayed for God's wisdom to come upon me. I prayed for Asher, that he would somehow find the hope of God, that I hadn't hurt him too badly, that he would forgive me for leaving him in California.

As the forest wrapped itself around me, the horrible incident in California seemed farther and farther away. Like a remembered nightmare that faded with the light of day.

A steep dip of rock came up on my right and I sought out the edge, sitting down, breathing in the fresh air, relishing the slight wind on my face. If I'd brought my phone, I might even have called Asher now, but I'd broken one of Mom's cardinal rules and left home without it, not wanting to be bothered. Needing the time alone. I vowed to text Asher when I got home.

I closed my eyes, the sun warming my face, and prayed.

Father, give me wisdom. How do I begin to navigate this? What do you want me to do? What do you want me to go after?

A verse came to me, one often quoted by Dad.

Look to the Lord and His strength; seek His face...

A small measure of peace settled upon me, like a leaf falling gently to the ground. Peeling back layers of confusion, the verse simplified the purpose of my life. *Seek His face.* Whether that was in my relationships or in my music. At home or away.

I'd forgotten my first love, I saw that now. I'd forgotten that God's love is what compelled me to make music in the first place. I hadn't listened to His voice. I hadn't sought what God wanted, hadn't asked for discernment or counsel, or even read the scriptures all that much in the last couple of months.

My heart trembled at the thought of a future without the man I loved, but it trembled all the more at tying myself to someone who scorned my faith.

"I will trust You," I whispered through the hurt. "I will go where You lead. I will look to Your strength and not my own." My strength ended in vomit and rug cleaner. Surely God could trump that.

I stood up, a wave of dizziness and nausea attacking me in a sudden ferocious wave. The ground spun before me, and I groped for something—anything—solid to grasp. My hand met only air.

Below, sharp rocks and treetops blurred.

And then I was falling. Falling fast, the rocky ledge below coming up to meet me as it had done Elenora French all those years ago.

My legs scraped. A searing pain cracked through my head.

And then, nothing.

Asher didn't know if Lizzie leaving her Barbie "Jam With Me" Guitar at his parents' house was an oversight or a message. He chose to think it a simple slip—also the perfect excuse for him to stop in at Orchard House.

Whatever was between them, he refused to allow it to drive them farther apart. His flight had gotten in late last night. This morning, he'd showed Ricky around the house and ordered groceries. This afternoon, he would take his brother downtown and show him the store.

But first, Lizzie.

The sun already climbed high in the sky when Asher pulled into the driveway of the bed and breakfast. Better to wait out the breakfast rush, he supposed. But as he pulled up the drive, Lizzie's car was nowhere in sight.

He slumped in the driver's seat. She still hadn't answered his calls or texts. This morning, his call had gone straight to voice mail.

"She's not here." The voice came from behind. He craned his neck toward the passenger side of the truck. A moment later, Josie hung her arms in the open window. "Hey."

"Hey." He lifted up the Barbie guitar. "She left this in California. I wanted to give it to her."

Josie took the guitar, a soft smile on her lips. "'Jam With Me' Barbie. She was devastated when Dad threw hers in the dumpster."

"Yeah. She told me." He shrugged. "Probably stupid of me to get it for her, I don't know." She'd seemed touched by the gesture. Why then had she left it in California?

"*So* not stupid." Josie flipped her long chestnut ponytail away from her face and studied him with eyes that saw far too much. "She's been in a slump since she got back. You really wrecked her."

"She wrecked me, too," he said softly. "You know where she is? I need to talk to her."

Josie slid her phone from her back pocket, a frown pulling at her mouth. "She went for a hike, but I thought she would have been back by now." Her fingers danced over the phone, and the lines on her face deepened. "My text didn't deliver." She lifted it to her ear. A moment later, she shook her head. "Right to voice mail. She always takes her phone. The service can be spotty, but it's usually dependable in the park."

A tug of worry wormed its way through him. "I called her an hour ago. Same thing, straight to voice mail."

The sound of a screen door settling in its frame made him look up. Mrs. Martin came out, a dishtowel tight in her hands. Her face fell when she saw Asher's truck. "I heard the car—hoped it was Lizzie. She told me she'd be back a half-hour ago." Her gaze flew from Asher to Josie. "Have either of you heard from her?"

He shook his head, his worry growing.

"Amie just found her phone in her room. She always takes it."

What if something happened to Lizzie on the hike? What if she came upon a wild animal or unfriendly stranger? He imagined her alone and hurt or tortured by some madman. He put his truck in reverse. "I'm going to find her."

"Wait." Josie gripped his truck. "What's your cell? We can keep in contact. I'll tell Mom. We'll go look, too. She could be on any one of the trails."

"Right." He spouted off his number.

"How are you going to..." she started.

"I don't know." He couldn't get through the trails in a wheel-chair, but neither could he sit around and do nothing with Lizzie missing.

"Well, at least tell me where you plan to look."

"I can get up Mount Battie in my truck. I'll go from there."

Josie nodded. "I'll try Maiden Cliff. Text me if you find her. I sent you a message."

"Okay. You, too."

He backed up, then tore down the driveway, taking a left onto

Route 1. He'd never known what it was to be so thoroughly scared, so thoroughly helpless.

God, I'm begging you. Help us find Lizzie. Help her be okay. He swallowed. *And if you don't answer this one, help me to continue believing You.*

It was weird, this praying thing. It didn't feel totally genuine, totally effortless. It was work. What if he didn't have all the right words? But now that he possessed this foreign faith, he couldn't ever imagine letting it slide through his fingers.

A calm determination came over Asher, as well as the terrible knowing that Lizzie did in fact need help. He pushed the gas handle harder. "Hold on, Lizzie. We're coming."

✸ 40 ✸

Asher swore as he fumbled his wheelchair out of his truck, grabbing his gloves and a rope, for what he didn't know. When he finally got into the chair and closed the truck door, he wheeled to the spot where Lizzie had sung for him.

He looked out over the hills and rocky outcroppings for a sign of a human in distress but couldn't see any human—never mind one in distress. But Lizzie was close by. Her car had been parked at this trailhead. He'd sent the information to Josie. She and Amie would start their search at the bottom of the trail.

He slammed his hand on the arm of his wheelchair. If he could walk, he'd be down and around these hills in no time, searching every nook and cranny, every crack and crevice. But what now?

He dug out his phone. Nothing from Josie yet.

He closed his eyes, a newfound sense of urgency overtaking him.

The breeze picked up, a sudden gust coming from the direction of the trail.

God sent that peace to me because I asked Him. It's as real as you and me, only it's kind of like the wind...I can't see it, but I can feel it.

Another gust, almost insistent, unwilling to be ignored.

Asher pressed his lips together, started wheeling toward the trail. The first part of the dirt path was steep. Craggy roots and damp, slippery leaves taunted him—a menace for anything with wheels. He donned his gloves and started down, leaning back in his chair, balancing on a wheelie with careful concentration. Managing one root at a time. By the time he'd gotten ten feet, he was sweating and thirsty, but he'd done it. Without falling, too.

He continued that way for another twenty minutes, pausing only briefly to respond to Josie's text that they had started up the mountain, and that Bronson and Mrs. Martin would catch up with them soon. They agreed that if they didn't hear from or find Lizzie in another half hour, they'd call the police.

Fifteen minutes later, Asher hit a smooth slide of rock. He groaned. Was he crazy? Might be safer to get out of the wheelchair and drag himself with the strength of his arms. Demeaning if he happened upon hikers, but probably the only practical way. He set his brakes when something in his peripheral vision caught his eye. A light blue backpack. His chest lurched. He wheeled down the small path toward a rocky ledge.

"Lizzie!" Panic filled every cavity of his being. Frantic, he slid his wheelchair to a stop, peered with trepidation over the ledge. There, about ten feet below lay his heart, her leg bent out of shape, blood marking her forehead. "Lizzie!" He called again, his voice boundless and terror-filled on the cliff. Still, no movement.

He searched out a nearby tree to tie a rope. Finding a sturdy oak, he slid his rope around it, tying a clove hitch knot. He searched Lizzie's bag for a first aid kit and wasn't disappointed. Swinging the bag around his shoulders, he tied the other end of the rope securely around his own waist then lowered himself out of the wheelchair. He reached for his cell phone and dialed Josie.

"I found her. She's near the top of Mount Battie. We're going to need some help. A rescue team to get her out of here. She's hurt and barely conscious."

Please, let her be okay.

He swung his useless legs over the edge and slowly lowered himself down the ridge, pausing often to move his legs from catching on a branch or rock. Muscles straining, inch by inch, he finally lowered himself beside Lizzie. He propped himself against the wall of the ledge to give himself better leverage.

He touched her arm. "Lizzie. Lizzie, please wake up." She stirred. "Oh, thank you, God." Emotion climbed his throat as he tore open a thick piece of gauze and held it to her bleeding head.

He pressed the gauze tighter to her head. "Where you hurting, Martin?" He could pull her up off this ledge, but if she had a neck injury it'd be better to keep her stationary. And with the look of that leg, such a move could prove excruciating.

"Asher?" She blinked, squinted. "What are you doing here?"

"Saving your backside, darling."

"Always trying to be the hero…" But a small smile pulled at her mouth. She propped herself on one elbow, winced with obvious pain. "My neck and back are fine. It's my leg…and my head."

"We need to bandage you up better."

"I'm going to be sick…" She held her stomach and groaned, vomited off to the side.

"Martin, you're making this an all too frequent habit." She started to cry then, and he looped an arm carefully around her. "I'm sorry. I was kidding."

"I know," she wailed. "I don't know what's wrong with me. You're so funny."

He kissed the top of her head. "Come on. You need some water." He dug out her water bottle, dribbling the fluid into her mouth.

"I'm so sorry. Thank you for coming for me."

"I'm glad you're okay. But I'm not the only one you should be thanking."

"Lizzie!" Josie's head poked over the top of the ledge. A moment later, Amie's appeared beside hers.

Lizzie scrunched her nose, still dazed. "Amie? In the woods?" She looked at Asher. "I think I hit my head real hard on the way down."

Asher held her close. "I think you just don't realize how very much you're loved."

I WOKE IN THE CRISP SHEETS OF A HOSPITAL BED, THE ALL-TOO-familiar medical setting unnerving.

I grasped at my throat, certain my end was near. My family was right, after all. I wasn't strong. The cancer had come to take me again.

"Shhh." A cool hand soothed me, and I leaned into it. "You're okay, honey."

"Mom."

"You gave us quite a scare on that mountain, young lady."

Mount Battie. That's right. I'd been climbing, felt dizzy. Asher had been there. Or had he? No, most certainly not, because I remembered Amie right beside him. "Is it the cancer? Did it come back?" I asked, my words slurred.

"No, honey. Your thyroid levels are super low, though. They might need to adjust your meds. You won't be walking without crutches anytime soon, either. Your leg's broken."

My thyroid levels. A sinking failure came over me. The medicine I'd neglected to take when I'd run out in California. I cringed. "I ran out of my medicine in California." Yes. My low energy, my overactive emotions, the nausea and dizziness. I groaned. "I'm so stupid. I was so wrapped up in everything. I made you all worry."

"All that matters is that you're okay."

A knock sounded at the door and Asher wheeled in, looking clean and tan and handsome in a Paramount t-shirt. "Hey, look who's finally awake."

I slowly sat up. "Was I out that long?"

Mom nodded. "A day or so. I finally managed to convince this guy to go home and shower. Same with your brothers and sisters."

"Mom, I'm so sorry. The bed and breakfast—"

"Is managing." She kissed the top of my head. Her gaze flicked to Asher. "We've been taking the chance to get to know one another better, and it's been a pleasure." Mom's eyes sparkled as she looked at Asher. As if she knew something I didn't. "I'll leave you two to visit." She stood, and squeezed Asher's shoulder before leaving, closing the door softly behind her.

"It wasn't a dream, then? I really did fall off the side of a mountain and you really did find me?"

He shrugged. "I kind of have this thing for damsels in distress. And kittens. I've grown awful fond of kittens lately."

"Asher, I—I'm so sorry about California. I have no excuse other than being a major wimp. Will you ever forgive me?"

"Already done. And I'm sorry for dragging you to Dane like that. I knew how much you hated it when Amie called that radio station, and yet I did the same thing. Tried to play God when it came to your life. I'm so, so sorry."

"I know you were trying to help." I squinted up at him. "I can send Dane some new shoes if you know his size..."

He waved a hand through the air. "The guy wasn't fazed. He's got tons of shoes. He said even if you had the voice of an angel, you'd never make it on tour, but he'd be open to listening to a recording if you could do some live gigs first."

I laughed. "That was gracious of him."

"He's a pretty gracious guy."

"I'm sorry to disappoint you."

"Lizzie, I could never be disappointed by you. When I realized you were missing, when I saw you sprawled at the bottom of that ledge, I thought my heart had been torn from my chest." He licked his lips. "I was so scared to lose you. So scared that I'd never get to tell you that I understand."

"You understand?" I scrunched my eyebrows.

"I understand why you thought we couldn't be together."

Something in my chest pinched. "You do?"

He nodded. "Lizzie, all this time I've been trying to be my own hero. Trying to prove myself and push to be first. But that's over. I get it, Martin. I understand why you're so obsessed with God."

Was I imagining these words? Had I hit my head even harder than I realized? "You do?"

"Cause He's already done all the hard work. That's what Dane told me, and I'm choosing to believe it."

"Dane...?"

"I spoke to him after your audition. Lizzie, I admit this following Jesus business is new to me. I don't know a fraction of what I want to, but since God's forgiven me, I'm hoping you can too."

I blinked.

"Martin, I don't care if you never want to sing for thousands of people. I don't care if you only want to stay in Camden for the rest of your life, work at the bed and breakfast, plant flowers, and go get coffee. I don't care what you want to do, but please, please tell me I can be a part of it."

I swiped at my tears, nodded.

He rolled closer. "Is that a yes?"

"Yes."

He lifted my fingers to his lips, kissed them gently. "God helped us find you. You're going to be okay. I have a chance to be with you. I still can't fathom it all, but now I know He answers prayers."

His words spilled a funnel of light into my being. I felt as if I was soaring, flying. I wiggled to the end of the bed as best I could in my cast, using the strength of his arms to pull myself toward him. When I got as close as I was able, I looked straight into those chocolate eyes. "I love you, Asher Hill."

He closed the gap between us, bringing his mouth to mine in a kiss that swept a beautiful melody across my heart. A strain of chaos and uncertainties coming together into a sweeping symphony of love. One that I wanted to play forever.

EPILOGUE

"You guys, wait! This is it!" Amie flapped her arms at the group of us sitting on blankets and chairs for the annual Martin Labor Day barbecue. She turned the volume on the radio louder and I shook my head, laughing. There was no discouraging her.

"And here are our very own *Connection* love birds, Asher Hill and Lizzie Martin singing their own song, 'Consume Me.' We had the privilege of sitting down with the couple last week."

A voice clip cut in—Asher's from an interview we'd done with the same DJ who had 'connected' us back in the spring. "Lizzie showed me what it means to live again. To love again. To be forgiven. For that, I will be forever grateful for this radio show sticking their noses where it doesn't belong."

The DJ, Melanie, laughed, then said a few more words before the chords of our song began to play.

We'd sang the song at the Camden Fourth of July barbecue— news someone had leaked to the station. When they'd asked for an interview with me and Asher, I'd managed it without too much anxiety. And when Melanie asked us if we ever played guitar together, and we admitted we did, she insisted on hearing our song.

It had been an instant local hit, and I'd felt a strange sort of contentment to know my words were blessing others. Best of all, Asher and I were beginning to make a hobby of creating together.

Never stop consuming me...

The song ended and applause and cheers broke out around the yard. Josie hugged me. "I knew you were going to change the world with music."

I grinned. Camden wasn't exactly the world, but for me, it had always been enough. "And you're going to change it with words." We'd celebrated her contract offer last week. *Where Grace Appears* would be coming out next spring.

Maggie bounced her one-month-old daughter, Grace, in her arms. "I'm so proud of my talented sisters."

Bronson sauntered over, chest puffed up, holding a plate of apple pie. The orchard had produced the most delicious apples we'd ever tasted. "Yeah, I knew all along that you two were meant for one another once this guy got his act together." He slapped Asher on the shoulder.

Amie giggled, rolled her eyes. "I believe I get total credit for Asher. Remember, Mr. Coffee?"

Aunt Pris shimmied over to us. "Unless there's a wedding proposal, I think we've had enough preening. When are we eating?"

"Speaking of proposals..." Asher turned to me and my heart stopped. He reached in his pocket. Beside him, Ricky grinned.

He cleared his throat. "I was going to do this later, but I'm not sure your family would forgive me if I didn't include them in on this. Bronson, do I have your permission?"

For once, my brother appeared speechless. He nodded.

Asher smiled, turned back to me. "Lizzie, I never knew what adventure was before you walked into my life. I can't imagine any greater voyage than waking up beside you every day. Marry me, Martin?"

I threw myself at him, curled up on his lap, and kissed him right there in front of my entire family. "There's nothing that would make me happier."

He kissed me again, and my family cheered, a pleasant background to the perfect song God was writing just for us.

NOTE TO READER

Dear Reader,

I hope you're enjoying this series as much as I'm enjoying writing it! This was the story I couldn't wait to tell. I felt a special connection with Lizzie—the way she sometimes draws into herself, the way she struggles with her fears, and the way she loves being in nature.

I've often wondered what would have happened to little Beth March if she had lived in the modern-day world. Quite likely, she would have lived. And so it was fulfilling to write a character that mirrored her. It was fun to give Lizzie a happy ending.

If you enjoyed *Where Love Grows*, I would love to read your review on Goodreads or wherever you purchased this book. Even a sentence is helpful! Reviews give novels street credibility—which is a vital part of me being able to write. Thank you, thank you, thank you!

If you are interested in learning about the phenomenal work of the International Justice Mission, mentioned in this story, their website is www.ijm.org. IJM works to rescue and restore victims of slavery, abuse, and trafficking, and works to bring criminals to justice.

Read on for a glimpse at the next book in the series, a novella that will be releasing VERY soon! I hope you enjoy!

Where Memories Await

Chapter One

The ghosts of my past show themselves on Christmas Eve more than any other night of the year.

I drag in a deep breath and place the tiny sheep figurine from my manger back in its place. It stands out from the rest of the set—slightly bigger, not as intricately carved as the other figures.

That never mattered to me.

My chest aches and I lean back in my bedroom chair and close my eyes, praying for relief from the hauntings.

A knock sounds at my door.

"Come in."

The door creaks open and my niece Josie pokes her mass of chestnut hair around the corner. "Hey, Aunt Pris. Mom's heading to the church early to help with the pageant. She wondered if you were okay going with me and Tripp?"

"I suppose."

She enters my room, coming closer. She looks pretty tonight, has taken time to do her hair and makeup.

"You feeling okay?"

"As well as I can for my eighty-two years." Aches and pains are a normal part of life now, especially in these cold Maine winters. "I'll be out in a few minutes."

But Josie doesn't leave. Always my pesky niece, this one. But she has spunk. Reminds me of myself back in the day. "If you don't feel well enough to come, God will understand. You can join us for carols and food after if you'd like. Lizzie and Asher are playing us their new song."

The thought that she doesn't want me at the service scrapes painfully across my heart. "Girl, I haven't missed a Christmas Eve service in eighty-one years, and I don't intend to begin now. I'm fine. Only keeping company with my memories." I allow my gaze to fall on that sheep, attempting to shove away the ghosts. I inwardly curse when Josie approaches my nightstand and caresses the object of my attention. The girl doesn't miss a trick.

"Tell me why you like sheep so much, Aunt Pris?"

She'd given me two sheep figurines when we opened The Orchard House Bed and Breakfast. One could make the case I was off my rocker for allowing my dead nephew's wife and children to convince me to transform my old Victorian into an inn—complete with a live-in family. But most of the time, though I didn't make it a plain fact, I considered myself blessed beyond measure.

Josie had noticed my fetish with the gentle animal during the extensive renovations Colton Contractors performed.

"Can't an old woman have any secrets?" I shouldn't snap at her. I blame it on my blasted back, sore with every breath tonight.

My tone doesn't deter her, though. She kneels at my feet. She smells like coconut and baby powder, and something in my heart threatens to burst. I am grateful for her and her siblings. For their Mum, Amos's wife. They could have abandoned me, forgotten me. Especially after my nephew died. Especially with my some-times...challenging nature. But they didn't. Instead, they've breathed new life into this old house, gave me company and companionship in this last stretch of my life.

"Don't you want to share your stories, Aunt Pris? I want to hear them—we all do. Would it hurt to open up?" She nudges my arm, a teasing twinkle in her eyes. "It is Christmas Eve, after all. A time for miracles."

Christmas Eve. A time for miracles. Bleh. Too bad I only harbor sad memories.

But the girl is right. My time on earth is short. Even if I lived another twenty years, I knew from experience how fast they could fly. Or how quickly a mind slips. I think of my friend

Esther. Poor dear, I am grateful her days still prove healthy. It's nights that have a way of stealing her mind. Dementia is not kind.

I glance at Josie. Would sharing my story help to make anything different, or would it only serve to open old wounds?

"Don't you have a child and a husband to be with on Christmas Eve, girl?"

She grins. "They're both taking naps." She digs out her phone. How anyone can carry those ringing, beeping contraptions around every hour of the day is beyond me. "We have more than half an hour if you feel like spilling your guts."

"As enticing as spilling out one's guts sounds, I think I shall pass."

"Then at least tell me why you like sheep so much."

So young and audacious. Why do I pretend I don't see my own dear sister in her—a different piece of Hazel was in every one of my great nieces.

My hand takes up a small tremor and I command it still, to no avail. "I don't like them."

She cocks her head to one side and speaks slow. "You don't like sheep, so you cover your bed and curtains and walls with pictures of them?"

I press my lips together. Do I want to travel this path? So many years of keeping it bottled up...then again, do I want to take it to the grave?

"Do you know what penance is?" I ask.

"Yes, of course. It's something you pay to show you're sorry. Kind of like proving you're sorry."

"The sheep are my penance."

Her eyebrows come together, the dim light of my nightstand lamp casting divots of shadow and light on her brow. "Oh, Aunt Pris."

"Don't pity me, girl. You're the one who asked, but I refuse any show of pity. Understood?"

She nods, solemn as ever I've seen her. We remain silent—me

wavering at the bridge before me, her undoubtedly wondering whether to push me to cross.

She doesn't. My heart ceases its wretched pounding.

There is a certain calm in thinking about it, I suppose. Perhaps this would be part of my penance. Dare I hope sharing would finally release me?

"Your grandmother—my sister...she loved sheep."

Josie takes in a small inhalation of breath. No wonder. The child knows nothing of her grandmother, as Amos had known nothing of his mother. I'd been close-lipped about my younger sister for nearly sixty years now. I oft wondered if the family forgot I ever knew Hazel.

"What do you know about sheep, girl?"

"Um...not much. They're kind of stupid, aren't they? And when they fall on their backs, they can't get up by themselves."

My jaw tightens, and I force it loose. "They are not stupid, Josie. But they are emotional. And yes, many times they are help-less." Another moment of quiet.

I stare at the electric candle at my window. Beyond the dark, the apple orchards of my childhood roll up a gradual hill, alive and well thanks to my nephew Bronson. The trees still standing from my youth are at the end of their fruit-bearing years. They've born witness to my entire life.

Something tells me to stop talking, but something stronger urges me forward. "Hazel was not stupid. But her emotions...well, they always seemed to get her into trouble."

Order Where Memories Await

ACKNOWLEDGMENTS

This is my eighth book, and by now I'm noticing the same few names come up over and over as I write my acknowledgment section. I'm so grateful to each beautiful person who makes this writing dream possible. For the writing help, a huge thanks to Donna Anuszczyk, Sandra Ardoin, and Melissa Jagears. I am so incredibly grateful for the insight and unique talents that each of these ladies bring to my stories.

Thank you to those who were brave enough to share about their experiences with spinal cord injuries and in doing so, educate so many of us. Christopher Reeve, Travis Roy, Gary Karp, and Brian Kinney (Paralyzed Living on YouTube).

And to my beautiful family. My husband, Daniel, who threw me the sweetest surprise 40th birthday party on the day I finished editing this book. And to my sons, James and Noah, whose genuine interest in my books (and excitement over my first royalty check!) still warms my heart. Thank you, boys! Lastly, to the Author of life. You write the best stories. Thank you for allowing me the privilege to join in for a scene or two.

ABOUT THE AUTHOR

Heidi Chiavaroli (pronounced shev-uh-roli...sort of like *Chevrolet* and *ravioli* mushed together!) wrote her first story in third grade, titled *I'd Cross the Desert for Milk*. Years later, she revisited writing, using her two small boys' nap times to pursue what she thought at the time was a foolish dream.

Heidi's debut novel, *Freedom's Ring*, was a Carol Award winner and a Christy Award finalist, a *Romantic Times* Top Pick and a *Booklist* Top Ten Romance Debut. Her latest dual timeline novel, *The Orchard House*, is inspired by the lesser-known events in Louisa May Alcott's life and compelled her to create The Orchard House Bed and Breakfast series. Heidi makes her home in Massachusetts with her husband and two sons. Visit her online at heidichiavaroli.com